The Wedding Dress

Four generations of women—
passing along one treasured heirloom
wedding dress—each woman forging her
destiny, making a history of her own

"There is something in Steel's work that readers cling to—that makes them identify with characters."
—*The Washington Post*

"Steel is almost as much a part of the beach as sunscreen."
—*New York Post*

"There is a smooth reading style to her writings which makes it easy to forget the time and to keep flipping the pages." —*The Pittsburgh Press*

"Steel deftly stages heartstring-tugging moments."
—*Publishers Weekly*

"[A] veteran novelist who never coasts is Danielle Steel. . . . She likes her characters and gives them every chance to develop strength and decency; along with her creative storytelling it makes for very satisfying . . . fare." —*Sullivan County Democrat*

"Clever and sweetly dramatic." —*Booklist*

"Steel is a fluent storyteller renowned for taking . . . readers on both an emotional and geographic journey."
—*RT Book Reviews*

"Steel's plots are first-rate." —*Newark Star-Ledger*

"Steel yourself." —*Library Journal*

"Ms. Steel excels at pacing her narrative, which races forward, mirroring the frenetic lives chronicled; men and women swept up in bewildering change, seeking solutions to problems never before faced."
—*Nashville Banner*

"Steel has a knack for writing about real-life issues and invoking an emotional bond with her characters."
—*My Reading Rainbow*

"Steel is a skilled storyteller." —*Booklist*

DANIELLE STEEL

The Wedding Dress

A Novel

Dell
New York

2021 Dell Mass Market Edition

Copyright © 2020 by Danielle Steel
Excerpt from *Finding Ashley* by Danielle Steel
copyright © 2021 by Danielle Steel

Published in the United States by Dell,
an imprint of Random House, a division of
Penguin Random House LLC, New York.

DELL and the HOUSE colophon are registered trademarks of
Penguin Random House LLC.

Originally published in hardcover in the United States by
Delacorte Press, an imprint of Random House, a division of
Penguin Random House LLC, in 2020.

This book contains an excerpt from the forthcoming book
Finding Ashley by Danielle Steel. This excerpt has been set
for this edition only and may not reflect
the final content of the forthcoming edition.

ISBN 978-0-399-17961-7
Ebook ISBN 978-0-399-17960-0

Cover image: © Dimitris Skoulos/Trunk Archive

Printed in the United States of America

randomhousebooks.com

2 4 6 8 9 7 5 3 1

Dell mass market edition: April 2021

To my Beloved children,
Beatie, Trevor, Todd, Nick,
Samantha, Victoria, Vanessa,
Maxx, and Zara,

Be Wise, Be Lucky, Be Kind,
Be Loving, Be Loved, Be Happy,
all my wishes for you
for wonderful lives
and keep the love that we share
close to you always,
just as I cherish you.
with all my heart and love,

Mom/d.s.

The Wedding Dress

Chapter 1

It was a crisp, cold night with a stiff wind off the San Francisco Bay, the night of the Deveraux's ball, a week before Christmas, in December 1928. The elite of the city had been talking about it for months, with great anticipation. Rooms in the imposing Deveraux mansion had been repainted, curtains had been rehung, every chandelier gleamed. The tables in the ballroom had been set with shining silver and crystal. Footmen had been moving furniture for weeks to make room for the six hundred guests.

All the most important members of San Francisco society would be there. Only a handful of people had declined Charles and Louise Deveraux's ball for their daughter. There were fragrant garlands of lilies over every doorway, and hundreds of candles had been lit.

In her mother's dressing room, Eleanor Deveraux

could hardly contain herself. She had waited for this night all her life. It was her coming out ball. She was about to be officially presented to society as a debutante. She giggled excitedly as she looked at her mother, Louise, and her mother's maid, Wilson, held the dress, waiting for Eleanor to step into it.

It was a touching night for Wilson too. She had grown up as a simple girl on a farm in Ireland, and had come to America to seek her fortune, a bit of adventure, and hopefully, find a husband. She had relatives in Boston, went to work for Louise's family there, and had come to San Francisco with her when she'd married Charles Deveraux, twenty-six years before. Wilson had dressed Louise for her own debut twenty-seven years before, and served her ever since. She had held Eleanor the night she was born, and her brother, Arthur, when he had been born seven years earlier. She mourned with the family when he died of pneumonia at the age of five. Eleanor was born two years after his death, and her mother had never been able to conceive again after that. They would have liked to have had another son, but Louise and Charles were deeply in love with their only surviving child.

And now Wilson was dressing her for her long awaited debut. Wilson had lived in America for twenty-eight years by then, and there were tears in her eyes as she watched Eleanor put her arms around her mother and hug her, and then Louise gently helped Eleanor put on the earrings that her own mother had given her for her debut twenty-seven years before. They were Eleanor's first piece of grown-up jewelry. Louise was wearing the parure of emeralds that Charles had given her for their tenth anniversary, and a diamond tiara that had been her grandmother's.

The match with Charles Deveraux had been an excellent one, and the marriage which had produced Eleanor was loving and stable. Louise and Charles had met shortly after her debut in Boston, when she attended a ball in New York with her cousins at Christmastime. Charles was visiting from San Francisco. She was from a distinguished Boston banking family, and she and Charles had met that night. The marriage which was subsequently arranged between Charles and her father had been an excellent one for both of them. Their courtship had taken place during two visits Charles had made to Boston to see her, and their love had taken root during an extensive correspondence and warm exchange of letters for three months after they met. Their engagement was announced in March, and they married in June. They had spent their honeymoon in Europe, and then went to live in Charles's home in San Francisco.

Charles was the heir of one of the two most important banking fortunes in San Francisco. His family had originally come from France during the Gold Rush, to help make order from chaos, and assist the suddenly wealthy miners in protecting and investing their new fortunes. Charles's ancestors had remained in California, and made a vast fortune of their own. The Deveraux mansion on the top of Nob Hill was the largest in San Francisco, and had been built in 1860. After his parents died in the early years of their marriage, Charles and Louise had moved into it. He ran the family bank, and was one of the most respected men in San Francisco. Tall, thin, fair haired, blue eyed, elegant, aristocratic, and distinguished, he loved his wife and daughter, and had waited years for this night too.

Eleanor was strikingly beautiful. She looked a great deal like her mother, with long ebony hair, porcelain white skin, sky blue eyes, and delicate features. Both women had lovely figures, and Eleanor was slightly taller than her mother. Her education had been carefully attended to, with governesses and tutors at home, just as her mother had been brought up in Boston, and as the other girls of their world were raised in San Francisco. Several of her governesses were French and she spoke it fluently. She was talented in the art of watercolors, played the piano beautifully, and had a passion for literature and art history. In a somewhat modern decision, her parents had sent her to Miss Benson's School for Young Ladies for the past four years to complete her education. She had graduated the previous June, with a dozen young women of similar upbringing and age. She had made many friends there, which would ensure that her first season in society would be even more fun for her, attending a round of balls and parties given by her friends' parents.

Most of the girls coming out would be married within the year, or have formed a serious attachment. Charles hoped it wouldn't happen to Eleanor too quickly. He couldn't bear the thought of parting with her, and any suitor would have to prove himself worthy before Charles would give his consent for her to marry. She would be a major catch on the marriage market, since everything he had would be hers one day. It was something he and Louise had discussed discreetly, without ever mentioning it to Eleanor, and it was a circumstance she gave no thought to. All she wanted to do now was wear beautiful gowns and go to exciting parties. She wasn't eager to find a husband, and loved her life with her parents. But the balls they would attend would be a lot of fun, particularly her own. Her parents had been careful not to invite anyone unsavory or that they didn't approve of. They wanted to keep the racier men about town, and any fortune hunters, well away from her. She was a lively girl with a bright mind, but innocent in the ways of the world, and they wanted it to stay that way.

Their preparations for this memorable night had centered around whom to invite, as well as what band they would hire. They had brought one up from Los Angeles for the occasion. All of Eleanor's attention had been focused on what dress she would be wearing. With Charles's blessing, she and her mother had traveled to New York, and sailed to Europe on the French steamship SS *Paris,* which had been launched seven years before. It was Eleanor's first trip abroad. They had spent a month at the Ritz hotel in Paris, where they visited several designers, but Louise was determined to have a dress made for Eleanor by the House of Worth.

Jean-Charles, the great-grandson of the original designer, Charles Frederick Worth, ran the house by then, and his recent designs had revolutionized fashion. He was the consummately modern designer at the time, and Louise wanted to get Eleanor an exciting dress that would be different from everyone else's, while maintaining a look of dignified elegance. His prices were astronomical, but Charles had given her permission to buy whatever she wanted, as long as it wasn't too modern or outrageous. Worth's use of beading, metallic threads, incredible embroidery, and exquisite fabrics made everything he touched a work of art, and Eleanor's lovely slim figure lent itself perfectly to his sleek designs.

The dress he had designed for her was a narrow column which fell from her shoulders with a slightly lowered neckline in back, and a discreet drape below it. It was the most beautiful dress Eleanor had ever seen, beyond her wildest dreams when it was finished. He designed a headpiece to go with it that was the height of modern fashion, and set a halo of pearls and embroidery on her dark hair. It was perfection. They arrived back in San Francisco in late July, and

Wilson was holding the dress now. It was heavy from the intricate beading and embroidery.

Eleanor stepped into it, ready for this long awaited moment. Her dark hair was swept into a loose bun at the nape of her neck with pearls woven into it, which Wilson had done masterfully. The headpiece sat on the stylish waves which framed her face. The dress was both modern and traditional and used all the techniques that the House of Worth was famous for to create an unforgettable impression of high fashion.

Louise and Wilson stood back to admire the effect, as Eleanor beamed at them both, and could see herself in the mirror behind them. She barely recognized the elegant young woman she saw in the reflection. Her father hadn't seen the dress yet, and he stood still in the dressing room when he saw her.

"Oh no . . ." he said with a look of dismay and Eleanor was instantly worried.

"Don't you like it, Papa?"

"Of course I do, but so will every man in San Francisco. You'll have ten proposals before the night is out, if not twenty." He turned to his wife then. "Couldn't you have gotten something less spectacular? I'm not ready to lose her yet!" All three women laughed, and Eleanor looked relieved. She wanted her father to love her dress too.

"Do you really like it, Papa?" she said, her eyes bright as he leaned down to kiss her. He looked as elegant as ever in white tie and tails, and gave his wife an admiring glance in her green satin gown and the exquisite emeralds he had given her. As always, thanks to him, she would be wearing the most stunning jewels in the room.

"Of course I do, how could I not? You and your mama chose very well on your adventure in Paris." A less generous man would have paled at the bill. Worth was famous for charging a fortune, and even more to his American clients, and he had followed his usual tradition this time. But Charles thought the dress was worth every bit of it, and had no regrets. He could easily afford it, and wanted his wife and daughter to be happy. It pleased him to think that his daughter would be the most beautiful debutante of this or any season. And the attention they'd lavished on the ball was commensurate. He wanted this to be an evening that would be a memory Eleanor would cherish forever. Their magnificent mansion on Nob Hill was the perfect place for it.

Charles offered his daughter his arm, as they left her mother's dressing room. He and Eleanor led the way down the grand staircase, with Louise following right behind them. Wilson watched them, smiling gently. She was happy for them. They were good people, and after losing their son twenty years before, they deserved all the happiness life could give them. She would be waiting for Eleanor to help her undress at the end of the evening, at whatever hour, and she was sure it would be very late. They would be serving a supper at midnight, after a sumptuous dinner several hours before that. There would be breakfast at six in the morning for the young people who stayed late, including the bachelors who remained to dance with the young women and flirt with them. The older people would have left by then, but Wilson knew that the young would dance the night away.

There were a dozen footmen at the bottom of the stairs, waiting to serve champagne from silver trays. Half of the footmen worked for them, and the other half had been hired for the night. The champagne was of the best vintages from Charles's wine cellar, put there well before Prohibition began, so they had not had to purchase wine or champagne then for so many guests. And since it was a private party, there would be no problem. The kitchen would be teeming with activity by then, as their cook and three assistants prepared the meal, and dozens of footmen waited to serve them. Louise had planned everything meticulously. The house was filled with flowers, the candles lit the rooms brilliantly, the ballroom was ready to receive them. She had spent weeks on the seating to make sure that all the right people were placed where they should be. There was a long table for Eleanor and her friends, with all the most dashing young men carefully selected from the best families.

The guests began to arrive, with a long line of chauffeur driven cars outside, drawing up to the portico one by one. Additional footmen were waiting to take their coats and wraps the moment they entered the house. Charles, Louise, and Eleanor had formed a short receiving line to greet the guests, with their butler, Houghton, standing beside them to announce their names. The evening was no less formal or elegant than any similar event in Boston or New York. San Francisco society was every bit as impressive as its counterparts in the East.

Eleanor looked radiant as her parents introduced her to people she had never met, and their friends whom she knew embraced her and told her how ravishing she was in her exquisite gown. She managed to combine the elegance of high fashion with a look of distinction, and her parents watched her proudly as the crowd in the house grew and drifted into their reception rooms. It was fully an hour later when they left the receiving line to join their guests, and Eleanor whispered to her mother that it was just like a wedding without a groom, and Louise laughed.

"Yes, it is. That will all happen soon enough." But Eleanor was in no hurry for that, and neither were they. It was exciting to be part of society now, and Eleanor wanted to savor every moment and enjoy it for as long as she could. She had greeted many handsome young men on the receiving line, and the boys her age looked mostly silly and very young. Some blushed when they greeted her, and they were standing around in large groups with each other, admiring the young women present and drinking champagne. A few of the braver ones came up and asked Eleanor to put their names on her dance card, and she took out the exquisite little carnet de bal her father had given her earlier that day. It was a pink enamel book with ivory pages, and tiny diamonds and pearls on the cover, which had been made by Carl Fabergé at the turn of the century. The ivory pages could be erased at the end of the evening, so it could be used at the next ball she attended. It had a tiny pink enamel pencil with a small diamond at the end. She took it out of her evening bag and wrote their names in it. Once the other young men saw her do it, there was a crowd around her requesting dances with her. The little book was almost entirely full of young men's names by the time they went into the ballroom for dinner an hour later. They had asked other young ladies for dances too. Eleanor whispered to half a dozen of her friends as they walked into the ballroom together.

"They're very handsome, aren't they?" she said to some of her old classmates from Miss Benson's, and they all agreed. Her mother had chosen carefully who she included on the guest list, and the young men in the room seemed equally pleased. The table of young people she had seated with Eleanor was a lively group. They were talking and laughing and appeared to be having fun all through dinner, as the older guests in the room glanced at them, smiling with approval. A debutante ball brought back tender memories for most of them, and it was nice to see so many handsome young people enjoying each other and having fun.

Eleanor danced the first dance with her father, a waltz, and then everyone else danced when he led Louise onto the floor for the next one. Their oldest friends were seated at their table, and the band Louise had hired was very good. Charles complimented her on it. The music got livelier as the evening wore on. Eleanor had taken lessons to prepare her for this, and with all the names in her elegant carnet de bal, she didn't sit down for a moment until she finally left the room with a group of other young ladies. They took refuge in the library for a few minutes to catch their breath. Several young men followed them there, to pursue conversations, or meet the girls they hadn't danced with yet.

When they walked into the library, Eleanor noticed a tall, good-looking man with dark hair intensely studying a book he had removed from one of the shelves, and he looked up in surprise when she and her friends walked in. Her father had an excellent collection of rare books and first editions, and the man smiled at her as she walked past him to get some air at an open window. She noticed that he had serious, warm brown eyes as he watched her.

"You've been dancing all evening," he commented, as her friends drifted away for a moment, and he put the book back on the shelf. "Your father has some wonderful books here," he said, with admiration, and she smiled at him.

"He's gotten them from all over the world, and a lot of them in England, and New York." He knew who she was. Her father had introduced them on the receiving line. He was Alexander Allen, whom she knew by name but had never met before. He was of the other most important banking family in the city. He was considerably older than her contemporaries, and observed her with a fatherly air. He was somewhere in his thirties and seemed very grown up to her, and appeared to be at the ball alone. "I would have asked you to dance, but you were so surrounded earlier in the evening that I'm sure your dance card is quite full by now." He wasn't in the habit of chasing debutantes, but he didn't want to seem rude for not asking her to dance.

"Actually, I have three dances left," she said innocently, and he laughed. She was so new to all this that there was something wonderfully childlike about her.

"I'll sign up, but I'm afraid your shoes and your feet will never be the same." She was wearing elegant white satin shoes with pearl and rhinestone buckles which Worth had made as well. Worth had even made her little evening bag, entirely embroidered with silver flowers and encrusted with pearls. "Why don't you put me down for those three dances, and you can see how I did after the first one. If your shoes are damaged forever, I'll release you to find another partner for the last two." She laughed and took the pink enamel carnet de bal out of her purse.

He didn't want to seem rude to his hosts for not dancing with her. The evening was in her honor after all.

"That seems fair," she said happily and wrote down his name on two different pages. The first dance was somewhat earlier in the evening than the last two, which were one after the other. They chatted for a few more minutes and then her next partner came to claim her and led her back to the ballroom. As she left, she waved at Alexander Allen and he smiled, and helped himself to another book, which he thought was more fun than dancing, although he was looking forward now to dancing with her. There was something so fresh and easy about her, and she was pleasant to talk to. She had none of the agonized shyness of some young girls at their debut, nor the aggressive ambitiousness of girls desperate for a husband from the moment they came out. She was just having fun, she looked spectacularly elegant, and was a very pretty girl.

It was another hour before his turn to dance with her, and he wandered back into the ballroom shortly before. The dinner tables had been removed by then, and there were smaller tables where people congregated, drinking and talking. The mood was one of considerable animation, everyone seemed to be having a good time, and Alexander Allen stepped forward in time to claim Eleanor for their first dance. She seemed pleased to see him again.

"Is tonight everything you hoped it would be?" he

asked as they set off on the crowded dance floor. He was surprised at how thin she was once he held her, and what a good dancer she was.

"Oh yes," she answered, smiling broadly. "It's everything I hoped and more. It's so exciting. I've never been to a ball before."

"Well, you won't find many to measure up to this one. Your parents have provided a magnificent evening for all of us. I don't usually like balls, but I've had a wonderful time, especially dancing with you." He smiled at her, and she looked pleased. A few of her school friends noticed her in the arms of what they considered an older man and felt sorry for her. Her father looked at her mother and raised an eyebrow, surprised that Alex Allen was dancing with her.

He said something to his wife as they watched them. They made a very handsome pair. "I'm surprised you asked him. He's not really the sort to chase young girls. I hardly see him out anymore, except at my club for lunch once in a while. He's a serious sort, although he's a good man. I suppose he felt he had to dance with Eleanor." It showed excellent manners, and that he hadn't just come for the dinner and superb wines.

"I don't think he ever recovered from what happened. All the ambitious mothers invited him everywhere for a while. I don't think he went out for a year or two afterward. Someone told me he's a confirmed bachelor, but we needed men to dance with the women his age." There were always some spinsters and young widows at any party, and he was the right age for them. They couldn't just have a room full of married men and young boys.

"That was unfortunate," Charles agreed. He remembered the story, they both did. Alex had been engaged to one of the most beautiful young women in San Francisco, from one of the best families, eight years before. It had been one of those love stories that captured everyone's hearts, probably because they were both so good looking and seemed so much in love. Alex had served in the Great War in France, and two years later was madly in love and engaged. His fiancée succumbed to Spanish flu, and died five days before their wedding. His mother had died in the same epidemic, and his father had died suddenly two years later.

Alex ran the family bank now, at thirty-two, and was only twenty-six when he'd inherited it. He was doing a good job of it, Charles knew. "He's probably too busy with the bank to think about marriage, and an incident like that must have been so traumatic," Charles said sympathetically. "He's too old for Eleanor, but you were right to invite him. He's a good man. I liked his father. Terrible tragedy, all that. I think his mother and his fiancée died within a day of each other." They had lost several friends in the epidemic, which had ravaged the world, and taken more lives than the war itself. Twenty million people had died of Spanish flu before it was over. Louise hadn't let Eleanor leave the house for months. She had been ten then, and after losing their son to pneumonia, they were terrified of losing their only surviving child to Spanish flu.

"Well, how did I do?" Alex said, looking down at Eleanor's shoes as the dance came to an end. "I think I stepped on you at least a dozen times," he said humbly.

"Not even once," she said proudly, and pulled up her gown just enough to expose the elegant shoes, which had remained pristine. He noticed that she had small, narrow feet.

"That is lucky," he said, smiling broadly. "Does that mean I can stay on your dance card for the other two dances?" She nodded, smiling.

"I had a nice time talking to you," she said, shy with him for the first time. She looked so vulnerable and young that it touched him and made him feel protective of her.

"Even though I must seem a hundred years old to you," he said, sounding more somber than he meant to. It was easy to be honest with her. She blushed. She thought he was old, but not a hundred certainly. She wondered if he was one of those old bachelors her parents had warned her about, who preyed on young women. But she didn't think they would have invited him if he was.

"Why don't you go dancing more often? You're a very good dancer," she said earnestly and he laughed.

"Thank you. So are you," and then he grew serious again. "It's a long story, and not appropriate for an evening like this. I don't go to parties very often. And I'm definitely too old for debutante balls. I like your father very much, so I wanted to come to this one, and I'm very glad I did. I'll try not to ruin your shoes with our next two dances. I like talking to you too," he added, and she smiled at him.

"The boys my age get a little tiresome after a while, and most of them are drunk by now. They're the ones who will ruin my shoes!" They both laughed at that, and a minute later, her next partner came to claim her and they danced away, as Alex watched her with a smile. She had literally been dancing all night.

It was another half hour before his next dance with her. He was getting tired by then, but she was as lively and graceful as ever in his arms. When the dance ended, the midnight supper was set out, and they went to get something to eat, and sat at a table together. The guests were beginning to thin out a little, and the older guests had begun to leave. Her parents stood near the entrance to the ballroom saying good night to them, and Eleanor's table filled rapidly with old classmates and childhood friends. They looked at Alex like he was someone's parent, although he was only thirty-two. But they rapidly discovered that he was good company, and he teased several of them and made them laugh, telling them stories about debutante balls he'd been to where everything went wrong, and one where the debutante got so drunk, no one could find her. She was under a table, sound asleep. Eleanor's friends loved the story, and the way he told it, and after supper he claimed his last dance with her. He felt like an old friend by then.

"Thank you for being nice to my friends, and not treating them like silly children." He had treated them all like amusing adults.

"I'm a silly child myself sometimes," he said, smiling at her. "Even if I seem very grown up to them. I remember how annoying it was to be dismissed as an idiot at their age, by people the age I am now. I was barely older than they are. I was twenty-one when I went to war. That makes you grow up pretty quickly," he said quietly.

"My father wanted to volunteer. He was forty-one when America got into it. My mother didn't want him to go, and he was too old to fight anyway. They gave him a desk job and he never went to Europe. I think he was disappointed not to go."

"It was a nasty fight. I was in France for a year. I was an officer in the infantry. It was ugly. I went as a boy, and came back a man," he said with the memory of it in his eyes. And then their dance came to an end. "I had a lovely time with you, Miss Deveraux," he said, smiling at her again. "And I hope you thoroughly enjoy your first season." He bowed and she laughed.

"I'm sure I will. I hope we meet at another party sometime," she said, and he didn't answer, but had been thinking the same thing. He left her then, and she went off with her friends. He thanked her parents for a wonderful evening, and left, surprised by what a good time he'd had. He hadn't had so much fun in years. He couldn't remember the last debutante ball he'd been to.

The party went on long after Alex Allen had left. Eleanor danced until she felt like she couldn't anymore. There was still a good sized crowd of very young people when breakfast was served at six in the morning. The young men had had a lot to drink by then, and the substantial breakfast did them good. Then finally, at nearly seven A.M., the ball was over. The band had stopped playing, the servants still at their posts looked exhausted. Eleanor's parents had gone to bed around two in the morning, and were content to let the young people take over. There had been no problems or awkward incidents. Everyone was well behaved. Some of the older guests were a little less so and drank too much, but they'd gone home.

When Eleanor finally walked up the grand staircase after the last guest left, she found Wilson waiting for her in her bedroom to help her undress. She had been dozing in a chair, and woke up the minute she heard Eleanor come in.

"Well, how was it?" she asked, with eyes full of expectation and delight for Eleanor. "Did you dance all night?"

"Yes, I did." Eleanor smiled sleepily, and held her

arms out so Wilson could take off her dress, and then she gently lifted the headpiece off Eleanor's head. "It was perfect," she said happily, her eyes still dancing with the thrill of the magical evening. "I had the best night of my life," she said, kissed Wilson's cheek, and climbed into bed. Before Wilson could turn off the lights, or leave the room to hang up the dress, Eleanor was sound asleep. It had been an important rite of passage for her, not just a party. Her life as an adult, and a woman, had begun. Wilson smiled, thinking about it, as she quietly closed the door. And as beautiful as Eleanor was, Wilson was sure she'd be married soon. That was the purpose of it after all, wasn't it? Debutante balls were for young girls from good families to find husbands. And even in 1928, nothing had changed.

Chapter 2

Alex Allen found himself thinking about Eleanor Deveraux at his desk the next day. And for several days after that. He thought of her during Christmas, which he spent with his two younger brothers, Phillip and Harry, in the vast family home, which Alex had inherited from their parents, as the oldest son. They had left it to him, along with the bank, and all the responsibilities that went with it. Neither of his brothers worked at the bank. Their inheritance was more than adequate to support them, and neither of them had any ambition. They were eight and ten years younger than Alex was and seemed like children to him. At their ages he had been to war, and had almost gotten married, but as the eldest son he had grown up more quickly and his parents had expected more of him. And they had been barely more than children when they were orphaned, and Alex took care of them too.

Now Phillip spent all his time playing polo and buying horses. Harry spent it chasing women of dubious reputation and drinking too much. His brothers lived in a house he had bought for them, a few blocks from the home where Alex lived, with many of his parents' servants still working for him, though he never entertained, and hardly used most of the house now. He was always at the bank, or traveling for business. And his younger brothers preferred to live on their own, away from his supervision.

Alex spent New Year's Eve with friends, and thought about Eleanor again, which seemed foolish to him. She was barely more than a child, fresh out of the schoolroom, yet there was something very sensible and mature about her too. He was surprised by how much he had enjoyed talking to her at her debut ball. She was interesting and intelligent as well as beautiful. Against his better judgment, and despite her age, he dropped her a note two weeks after the ball, and invited her to dinner. She graciously accepted. They had dinner at the Fairmont, and she had been delightful company. Her parents invited him to dinner after that, and didn't seem to object to his taking her to a party at the home of people they both knew. They agreed to his taking her out to dinner again, although they questioned Eleanor about it, and she said they were friends.

Louise and Charles discussed it privately, and Charles thought they shouldn't make a fuss about it. There was nothing wrong with Alex Allen, neither his bloodline, nor his character, his profession, or his fortune. And he didn't seem to be trifling with her. He was certainly considerably older than Eleanor. They had assumed that she'd fall in love with a boy her age, but the more they thought about it, the more they liked Alex. So did Eleanor, although she was convinced that Alex had nothing more than friendship in mind, which suited her. She had fun with him and liked talking to him.

They'd been dating for a month when Alex told her he was in love with her, and kissed her for the first time. She was as startled as she was pleased, and shyly told him she was in love with him too, although she hadn't realized it before, or allowed herself to. He spoke to her father two weeks later, and assured him that his intentions were honorable.

"I never expected to marry, after . . . well, you know . . . after Amelia died. I've never met a girl like Eleanor. She's so honest and straightforward, with her feet on the ground. It makes me happy just being with her." Her father and Alex knew they were an even match economically, more than any other man in San Francisco would have been. Two great families merging, two banks allied by marriage, their histories similar, their backgrounds the same, their standing in San Francisco society of equal importance. There truly wasn't a better match for her anywhere, and Alex was a man of integrity and sound values, and was head over heels in love with Eleanor. Charles couldn't ask for anything more in a husband for his daughter. He had hoped she wouldn't marry too quickly, only because he didn't want to lose her, but he couldn't deny her the opportunity to be with a man who loved her so profoundly and would treat her so well. He wasn't some twenty-two-year-old boy who had years of growing up to do. Alex Allen was a man, and an honorable one, and Charles gave Alex his blessing with tears in his eyes and a firm handshake, and reported it to Louise immediately afterward. She cried for the same reason as Charles, sad to lose her daughter but delighted for her.

Alex didn't waste any time, and proposed to Eleanor that night. He proposed to her on bended knee before they went out to dinner, and presented her with his mother's engagement ring. It looked enormous on her hand, and was a very impressive ring for a girl her age. Eleanor gasped in astonishment when he asked her. She didn't know he had met with her father, and thought they would go along for some time, being in love, and dreaming of a distant future. She had no idea that the future would become the present so quickly, but as she stared at him with wide open eyes filled with love, she accepted and he kissed her. Then they went to find her parents and tell them. They celebrated with champagne, and after two glasses, she felt giddy when she and Alex went out to dinner. There was so much to talk about and think about now.

She was the first of her season of debutantes to get engaged. It was announced in the society pages of the newspaper that weekend. Floods of letters and telegrams of congratulations started pouring in immediately. It seemed fitting to everyone, and they were particularly pleased for Alex, who had mourned his lost fiancée for so long. Two royal banking families were about to form a sacred bond through marriage. What could be better or more suitable?

They set the date for the marriage at the beginning of October, to give her mother time to plan the wedding. Louise estimated that there would be eight hundred guests at the reception. They would hold it at home, but tent their large garden to accommodate the number of guests. Their garden filled most of the square at the top of Nob Hill.

In March, Louise told Eleanor that they would be going to Paris in April to order her wedding dress. She hadn't decided which designer they would choose this time, and she was studying fashion magazines while she thought about it. Eleanor was amazed at how quickly it was all happening. Three months before she had been looking forward to her debutante ball, and in seven months, she would be a married woman. The best part of it was she was going to be married to Alex. She could hardly wait. She didn't even want to go to Paris this time, and leave him for a month. But he encouraged her to.

"You'll have fun with your mother, and it will help pass the time." In June, the Deveraux family would be moving to their estate at Lake Tahoe for the summer, and Charles assured Alex that he would be welcome to join them there as often as he liked, and to stay as long as he wanted. They would be there from June until September, and come back to town to attend to the final details before the wedding.

They stayed in Tahoe every summer, and had thousands of acres on the lake, which Charles's grandfather had bought when it was worth nothing. They had a private train to take them there, and a beautiful property with a large main house, several guesthouses, and other buildings for the servants. They took a very large staff to the lake with them, to serve them while they were there, in addition to the staff who stayed on the property year-round, among them the boatmen who cared for the fleet of speedboats they kept at the lake. Charles was delighted at the prospect of having a son he could hunt and fish and enjoy masculine pursuits with.

The months ahead seemed extremely enticing to all of them, and Eleanor finally, reluctantly agreed to go to Paris with her mother to order her wedding dress, although she didn't like leaving Alex for so long. She'd be away for at least six weeks, a week of travel each way by train and boat, and a month in Paris to select the design, and for fittings. Charles booked passage for them on the French Line's SS *Paris* for the end of April. More than ever, Eleanor hated to leave Alex when the time came.

"You'll be back very soon," he reassured her, touched that she was so upset about leaving him.

"You'll never find a dress you like as much here, and Paris is wonderful at this time of year."

"I'd rather be here with you," she pouted the night before they left for New York to board the ship. "Besides, what if the boat sinks?"

"It's not the *Titanic,* it's the *Paris,*" he said with his arms around her, loving her more each day. She was sweet and loving and easy to get along with, intelligent, and surprisingly mature for her age. He couldn't think of a better woman to marry. "Besides, the *Paris* doesn't sink, it just runs aground," he teased her. The ship had had two embarrassing incidents in the past month. The SS *Paris* had run aground in New York Harbor and had been stuck for thirty-six hours. And eleven days later, she had run aground again in Cornwall, and was refloated two hours later. It wasn't reassuring. She was a fabulously luxurious ship though, as Louise and Eleanor had experienced the year before when they'd gone to Paris for Eleanor's debut dress. This time, their mission was infinitely more important. Louise wanted to order her the most spectacular wedding dress they could find, and Charles was fully in agreement, whatever the cost. They wanted the marriage to be the wedding of the century, and Alex was touched by all the fuss they were making. It was all even grander than his previous engagement had been.

Alex and Charles saw them off on the train to Chicago, where they would change trains to New York. Wilson was going with them. Louise had told her to take a few days to visit her family in Ireland while they were in Paris, as she had the year before too.

Eleanor's mood improved slightly once they left the station. They had a mission to accomplish and Alex had promised to write to her while she was away. She treated the trip to Paris more like a punishment than a pleasure, having to be away from Alex for so long. She cheered up considerably once they were in New York and visited her mother's cousins. When they were on the ship, the excitement of what they were doing finally caught up with her, and she began looking seriously at all the magazine clippings her mother had brought with them.

They were considering several designers this time. Louise felt that Jean-Charles Worth's designs had become too extreme in the last year, and too modern, which had been fine for her debut, but not a wedding. She wanted to visit other designers when they got to Paris.

Gabrielle "Coco" Chanel was making a sensation, but she was too controversial, also too modern, focused more on sportswear, and didn't seem appropriate to Louise for a wedding gown. Paul Poiret was a strong possibility, and had become very important on the Paris fashion scene. Also the houses of Doucet and Paquin. Elsa Schiaparelli had also become very noteworthy in the world of haute couture, but from the magazines Louise had brought with her, it seemed like she was more engaged in trend setting, with knitwear, tweeds, ski suits, swimsuits, and chic trompe l'oeil sweaters that were all the rage. But Louise didn't think her wedding gowns would be traditional enough, and she wanted to meet with Jeanne Lanvin, an important designer in Paris fashion. She had designed a number of exquisite gowns for her daughter, the Comtesse de Polignac, which Louise had seen in *Vogue,* and she had a feeling that Jeanne Lanvin might be the right designer for Eleanor's wedding gown. They were going to make an appointment to see her at her new boutique on Faubourg Saint-Honoré. They had serious work to do when they got there, and by the time they docked at Le Havre, Eleanor was ready to join her mother in their quest for the most spectacular wedding gown they could have designed.

They stayed at the Ritz, as they had the year before. After giving themselves one day to recover from the journey, they walked around Paris enjoying the spring weather, and the next day they embarked on their mission. Before they left the hotel, Eleanor got a telegram from Alex.

"Counting the days, and loving you more every day. Have fun! I love you. Alex." She left the hotel with a smile on her face, after asking the concierge at the Ritz to send her response. Then she and Louise began making the rounds of Parisian designers.

They started with Paul Poiret on the rue Auber, and looked over a book of his recent bridal designs. The sketches were beautiful but Eleanor wasn't excited about any of them, which was disappointing.

From there they went to Elsa Schiaparelli because Eleanor wanted to see her trompe l'oeil pullover sweaters. She bought four of them. They were Schiaparelli's signature pieces and the height of fashion. One was a pierced heart, there was a sailor's tattoo, a skeleton, and a black pullover with a shocking pink bow, the designer's favorite color combination. Eleanor was excited about the sweaters, which were a huge hit among fashionable couture clients in Paris, but not about the bridal designs they showed them. She used a lot of visible zippers and modern touches that Eleanor loved for day wear, but the wedding gowns didn't appeal to her at all.

They went to the Crillon for lunch then, and then to Jeanne Lanvin's new boutique on the Faubourg Saint-Honoré. The design house had been established for forty years, but the boutique was new. As soon as they arrived, both Eleanor and Louise knew they had come to the right place. Lanvin's designs were not overly modern, they weren't flashy or showy, but they were everything that haute couture should be. Aside from the exquisite workmanship, where every stitch was done by hand, the designs themselves combined elegance and youth, opulence without vulgarity or pretentiousness. They were incredibly chic, and exquisitely tasteful, and had a regal quality to them. Eleanor could see herself in a dress designed by Madame Lanvin. She knew it would be very special and just right for the most important day of her life.

The directrice of haute couture met them initially, and Madame Lanvin herself joined them halfway through the meeting. She spent some time talking to Eleanor, getting to know her, and listening to her describe how she envisioned herself on her wedding day, what her dream was, and what kind of bride she wanted to be. Then she made a quick sketch on a small pad, her interpretation of what Eleanor had said, with a little twist here and there, and additional suggestions, as Eleanor stared at the drawing in amazement. It was exactly what she wanted, but hadn't known before. It was as though Madame Lanvin had read her mind.

"That is *precisely* what I want," Eleanor said in a hushed voice, in awe of the famous designer.

"Yes . . . just so . . . and do we want satin?" The designer muttered to herself, "No . . . we want lace, with the design embroidered in tiny pearls . . . yes . . . yes . . . ah, *voilà* . . . *comme ça* . . . *non* . . . I think we make the waist very small," she glanced at Eleanor's slim waist and nodded, "*very* small . . . and the skirt wider to accentuate it." She looked at Louise and Eleanor then, "No chemise. Everyone is doing that now. Poiret, Worth . . . they're all doing it. I do it too, but not for brides. We make the skirt wider but not too wide, and a very, very, very long train, like for a queen. I did that for my daughter when she became a comtesse . . . and the veil over the face, to here," she indicated Eleanor's fingertips, "but long at the back with the same lace around the edges." Her pencil flew over the sketchpad, and a vision of a regal-looking bride appeared. Regal, and at the same time delicate and vulnerable, with long sleeves and a high neck, and a bell shaped skirt that would swing as she walked down the aisle and a waist so small you could put two hands around it. The entire gown would be embroidered over the lace and encrusted with tiny pearls. Both Eleanor and her mother could easily envision her in the wedding dress, as Madame Lanvin sat back and smiled at them.

"I will send you more finished sketches at the hotel in two days, and then we will talk about anything you wish to change. After that, we take your measurements and we get to work. Three fittings, one a week. We will put your dress ahead in the atelier so you can go home in a month or so. We will have the embroiderers begin to work on the lace as soon as you approve the sketches. The first fitting will be in muslin, until we are sure the pattern is right." She was speaking as much to herself as to them, and giving instructions to her assistant in French. "We have the perfect lace. I have been saving it for something very special." She smiled at them and stood up, and they all shook hands. Eleanor and Louise left the boutique two hours after they'd arrived feeling as though they had found the Holy Grail, and so easily and quickly. The decision to meet with Jeanne Lanvin had been inspired. They were both silent as they got in their hired car to take them back to the Ritz. It was almost five minutes before Eleanor spoke to her mother.

"That was fantastic. I can see the dress perfectly, Mama."

"You're going to be the most beautiful bride I've ever seen," Louise said as tears filled her eyes and she leaned over and kissed her daughter.

"Will it cost a fortune?" Eleanor asked with a suddenly guilty look, all the embroidery Madame Lanvin had talked about, and the pearls, the lace she had been saving, and the "very, very, very long train."

"Probably," Louise answered with a grin. "Your father will be disappointed if it doesn't. He wants you to have the best wedding dress we can have made here. I think we just found it. The rest is up to us, and Madame Lanvin." Eleanor nodded, feeling dazed.

They had room service for dinner at the hotel that night, and went to bed early. Eleanor had another telegram from Alex telling her how much he loved her and missed her, and she went to bed, dreaming of bridal gowns and the incredibly talented Madame Lanvin.

They went to the Louvre the next day, and wandered in the Tuileries Garden. And they went to Sylvia Beach's bookstore and the Librairie Galignani on the rue de Rivoli, to find some first editions to give Charles when they got home. And after their bookstore foray, they went to Angelina's tearoom, with its elegant interior, for a cup of hot chocolate and their famous Mont Blanc pastry, made of chestnuts, meringue, and whipped cream.

Two days after their meeting, the promised sketches arrived at the hotel. The drawings were beautiful, and the wedding gown was magnificent, with every detail they had discussed part of the drawing. Eleanor wanted to frame it. It was like seeing a dream come to life. She could already imagine herself in it, and Alex looking bowled over when he saw her on their wedding day.

They called the boutique and made an appointment for the next morning. They arrived on the Faubourg Saint-Honoré at ten and the work began in earnest. One of Madame Lanvin's premieres of the atelier, a highly respected position, presented the lace to them, as though showing them a jewel. It was the most beautiful lace Louise had ever seen. Then every inch of Eleanor's body was measured, in centimeters, the size of her wrists, her neck, her waist, the distance between collarbone and the point of her breast, the center measure from her neck to her waist, both front and back, shoulder to elbow, upper hip to lower hip, her chest above her breasts, then below her breasts, from her neck to the floor, in both front and back. The measurements took time, and would be vital for making the pattern, first for the muslin, and later, much later, for the lace. They could not make mistakes with the lace, so the early fittings would be in muslin until they got it absolutely right.

There was no margin for error, and there would be none. The beauty of haute couture was that it would be flawless when it was done. Perfection.

They had a week to spend exploring after that. They visited the Orangerie and the Jeu de Paume. The next day, they toured Versailles, which they had seen before, but it was still fascinating. And they visited Marie Antoinette's private chambers.

The week flew by with daily exchanges of telegrams with Alex, constantly expressing his love for her, and how excited he was about the life they would share. He asked her questions about the dress, which she didn't answer. She wanted everything about it to be a surprise for him.

On their second week in Paris, they ran into friends from San Francisco who were staying at the Crillon, and they met them for lunch at La Tour d'Argent before they left for the South of France. It was a nice distraction to help pass the time between fittings. Eleanor had started taking long walks every day, while her mother spent hours making notes about plans for the wedding.

A wedding for eight hundred people was a major undertaking, and was like planning a war with a happy ending. It was going to be the grandest wedding San Francisco had ever seen, and they would have friends and relatives coming from New York and Boston. She asked Eleanor for a list of the friends she wanted to invite, and she wanted the same from

Alex, but most of the guests would be her and Charles's friends, which was the tradition.

The first fitting of the muslin was very exciting. Two of the premieres were there to make adjustments and copious notes, the directrice of haute couture, and of course Madame Lanvin herself, who arrived frowning, in anticipation of all the things she knew she wouldn't like. She embraced Eleanor and shook hands with her mother, and then the muslin was fitted to Eleanor's body. It looked like a finished gown, in a fine cotton. It fit her like a glove, with barely a ripple here and there, which Madame Lanvin pointed to immediately, and the premieres corrected with pins. The premieres and Madame Lanvin stood staring at every inch of the muslin, looking at flaws that would betray them later if not altered on the muslin. It took them an hour. And then they had Eleanor choose the style shoes she wanted. Eleanor chose the style which Madame Lanvin preferred for the gown, with the heel height she felt was right for it. Then they measured Eleanor again for the undergarments that would be made for the dress. Nothing was left to chance. She would be wearing haute couture from the inside out and from head to toe.

They took several road trips that week, to explore some of the chateaux outside Paris, Chateau de Cheverny, where they loved the tulip garden, and Chateau de Villandry, with beautiful formal gardens.

At the next fitting, the muslin fit perfectly. There was only one tiny detail Madame Lanvin wanted changed. She felt the waist was a centimeter too high, and wanted it lowered. Other than that, she seemed satisfied and disappeared quickly.

At the next fitting, the panels of lace had been basted into place. It looked like a finished dress to Eleanor, but to Madame Lanvin, it was far from it, and still a work in progress. The fittings with the muslin had paid off. The dress fit Eleanor without a single flaw or ripple. There was nothing to change, and the next week felt like waiting for a baby to be born. Eleanor could hardly wait to see it, and Louise was as excited as she was.

The final fitting, when it came, made every moment they had spent in Paris worthwhile. Eleanor stood before them looking like a vision in her incredibly beautiful wedding gown. Every detail was flawless, the embroidery was exquisite. All the tiny pearls sewn on the lace were perfectly placed. There were a hundred tiny buttons down the back. The undergarments fit her like a second skin, and when they placed the veil on her head, both Eleanor and her mother cried. Eleanor had never felt so beautiful in her life or looked so spectacular. It was the wedding gown to end all wedding gowns. Madame Lanvin smiled when she saw her.

"Yes . . . yes . . . it is very nice. The lace is just the right one for this dress," and then she looked at Eleanor seriously, and said, "You are a beautiful bride, and a beautiful woman. You will look wonderful on your wedding day."

"Thanks to you," Eleanor said in a hushed voice. She stood there staring at her reflection and couldn't believe it was her in the mirror. She couldn't wait for Alex to see her in the dress.

"We will have a box made for it. It will be delivered to your hotel before you sail," Madame Lanvin promised. She kissed Eleanor on both cheeks then, and wished her a happy wedding, and the magician who had created the miraculous gown disappeared. Louise made the final arrangements with them, which Charles was handling from the bank, through a correspondent bank in Paris, and they left a few minutes later. Eleanor felt as though she were walking on air.

"Mama, how can I ever thank you for a dress like that? It's so beautiful I'm almost afraid to touch it."

"You will touch it, and wear it, and you'll be the most beautiful bride anyone has ever seen. And you and Alex will live happily ever after." She smiled at her daughter as they held hands and walked down the street. They had done what they came to Paris to do. And Jeanne Lanvin had created the most magnificent bridal gown in the world.

When the box with the dress in it arrived at the Ritz, it was three times the size of any of their trunks, and had a wooden crate around it that had been made especially to protect it. Now they could go home to Alex, and Eleanor's father. They had been gone for five weeks by then, and they still had to get to California by train, after they docked in New York. Eleanor could hardly wait until October. It was going to be the happiest day of her life, in the most beautiful dress in the world.

"Ready to go home?" Louise asked her after two men carried the crate to their suite on the ship. Eleanor smiled as she nodded. Ready indeed, and Alex would be waiting for her, which was the best part of going home.

Chapter 3

The trip back to New York on the luxurious SS *Paris* was uneventful. Every time Eleanor walked into her cabin and saw the huge crate from Lanvin there, it gave her a thrill, knowing what was in it. For the moment, it was the symbol of her future with Alex. She could hardly wait to wear the dress. It made her debut dress by Worth seem plain by comparison. Her wedding dress was going to look absolutely regal, and innocent and feminine at the same time. Jeanne Lanvin was a genius with immense talent, and had been the perfect choice for Eleanor's wedding dress.

Eleanor had told Wilson all about it, and she couldn't wait to see it. She had spent a week with her family in Ireland, and was grateful that Louise had let her go. She had her own cabin in second class on the ship, which was a nicer accommodation than most lady's maids were given by their employers.

They only spent two days in New York, and stayed at the Sherry-Netherland as they had on the way to Paris. It was a beautiful new hotel that had opened two years before. It was late May. The weather was warm and balmy, and Eleanor and her mother couldn't wait to get home. They boarded the train to Chicago in a first-class compartment, with a second one for Wilson, and all their trunks and the crate from Lanvin. They changed trains in Chicago, and Eleanor could hardly sleep on the last leg of the trip. All she could think about was Alex, and the months ahead. She wanted time to speed up now until their wedding. Five months seemed like an eternity to wait for the big day when she would become his wife. It was hard to imagine how much she had come to love him since they met at her debut five months before.

As the train pulled into the station in San Francisco with Eleanor and Louise looking out the window of their compartment, Eleanor in one of her Schiaparelli sweaters and a new red hat she'd bought from a talented milliner on the rue du Bac on the Left Bank, they saw them waiting on the platform. Alex and his future father-in-law stood side by side, Alex with an armful of red roses, and both of them smiling broadly. Eleanor dropped the window and waved, and the men saw them. Charles beamed happily at the sight of his wife, and Alex looked as though he might explode with joy. The serious, slightly somber young man he had been for nearly a decade had disappeared, and he was wreathed in smiles. Eleanor rushed down the steps as soon as the conductor opened the door of their carriage, and flew into Alex's arms. He dropped the roses on the platform and held her tight and kissed her, as Louise and Charles hugged a little more circumspectly but were obviously pleased to see each other. There were porters waiting to collect their bags and trunks, and Charles instructed them. The car was waiting for them outside, with two additional cars for their luggage and to give Wilson a ride back to the house. He smiled when he saw the enormous crate from Paris emerge from the train.

"Is that it?" he asked Louise, and she nodded with a smile.

"You've never seen anything so beautiful." The dress was perfectly simple in its lines, but laden with embroidery and pearls, which had cost a fortune. Both of Eleanor's parents had no doubt that what Charles had paid was worth it. Madame Lanvin had outdone herself, and Eleanor would do honor to her design.

They went home to the house on Nob Hill, and both women were happy to be back. Wilson disappeared quickly to go downstairs before going to Louise's dressing room to unpack her bags. She told the other servants about her week in Ireland to visit her relatives when she got to the servants' hall and had a cup of tea and some warm biscuits the cook had just taken out of the oven. She had been seasick on the ship, but they envied her anyway for the trips she was able to take with the family, and she had bought herself a stylish new black hat in Paris too. They all asked if she had seen the wedding dress, and she admitted she hadn't, but had seen the sketches of it and a sample of the lace and it looked beautiful.

She went upstairs after that with two of the maids to help her unpack Louise's trunks and then Eleanor's. The wedding dress was to be left in its special box and put in a guest room, which would be kept locked. Louise and Eleanor were having lunch in the dining room with Alex and Charles, who looked happy to have their women home. They had been gone for a long time. The engaged couple couldn't keep their eyes off each other, and held hands at every opportunity. Charles went back to his office after lunch, after kissing his wife, and Alex stayed to walk in the garden with Eleanor. They sat on a bench for a few minutes, talking about their honeymoon. Alex was planning to take her to Italy, and they were excited about it. She had never been there, only to France with her mother for her debut dress and her wedding gown, and this would be her first trip with Alex, as his wife. It sounded like a wonderful adventure to both of them.

"I missed you terribly," he admitted, with an arm around her as they sat on the bench. "Are you happy with the dress?"

"Ecstatic. I hope you like it too."

"You could get married in a sack, and I would be

happy, as long as you're my wife at the end of it." He knew the wedding was going to be an enormous production, and had heard wisps of it from Eleanor and Charles. Charles was content to let his wife plan it, and make all the decisions, and he would pay the bills. Planning a wedding was a mother's job, and Alex was content to be surprised on the day.

Eleanor told him a little of what she'd done in Paris with her mother, the museums they'd been to, and the chateaux, and she caught up on his news. They had written to each other daily while she was in France, and had sent countless telegrams. She had saved all of it, and was planning to put them in an album as a souvenir of their love for each other during their engagement, to show their children one day. They hoped to have many of them, and had spoken of it shyly a few times. Eleanor had confessed to her mother that she hoped to get pregnant on their honeymoon. They were so in love that they didn't want to wait, and wanted to start their family immediately and Louise approved. Alex would make an excellent father and she knew he would take good care of Eleanor. She and Charles both felt confident entrusting their precious daughter to him.

"Your father says you're leaving for Lake Tahoe in two weeks," Alex said with a sigh. He had never seen their estate at the lake, and he was looking forward to it. "He very kindly invited me to come and stay with you. I can take a few weeks off in August, since almost everyone does, and the office is quite slow then, but in July I'll have to go back and forth a bit."

"Papa does too," she reassured him, "and he spends all of August at the lake with us." They invited other friends too, and often had big house parties over the weekends. People loved visiting them there, in the healthy mountain air. They took long walks, played badminton and tennis and croquet. The men went fishing, and everyone loved going out in the boats, and swimming although the water was very cold. They visited other families at the lake, and it was a good respite from social life in the city, although at times they were just as busy at the lake.

The main house was almost as big as their mansion in the city, although life there was slightly less formal. They wore black tie for dinner, rather than white tie and tails, and sometimes had as many as twenty houseguests on the weekend. There was an outdoor dining room and an indoor one. Charles had encouraged Alex to invite his two younger brothers up as well, which Alex was loath to do, and admitted to his future father-in-law that they were young and sometimes quite badly behaved. They were planning to visit friends in the East that summer, and he knew that his horse-mad brother Phillip was planning to play polo in Mexico. They were a handful, and he didn't want to inflict them on his in-laws, and he knew that in a respectable older group, both boys would be bored, and he would end up scolding them all weekend for drinking too much or sleeping with the maids. They were too old for him to control now, and not old enough to want to settle down, so he turned a blind eye to their antics, and got them out of trouble when he had to. It was relatively harmless, though tiresome.

As head of the family by the time he was twenty-six, Alex had grown up at an early age, which Phillip and Harry hadn't achieved yet, and had no reason to since they didn't work. Their inheritances supported them lavishly and allowed them to indulge whatever prank they could dream up, which they did frequently, much to their older brother's dismay. They knew every speakeasy in San Francisco. He loved them but they tested his patience. Eleanor had met each of them once, briefly, before she left, and they thought she was nice, but too circumspect for them. They couldn't imagine why Alex wanted to get married and thought he should have some fun first. They thought him very dull, although they were fond of him, but had little in common with him, or his interests, particularly now that he was engaged. They were coming to the wedding of course, but Alex doubted that they'd behave. At least in a crowd of eight hundred guests, no one would notice what mischief they got up to, unless they did something truly outrageous, which they were capable of too. They had never been forced to be responsible and Alex often wondered if they ever would be. So far, his occasionally stern lectures fell on deaf ears.

Alex and Eleanor sat for a little while longer in

the garden, basking in the joy of her return. He had to tear himself away and force himself to go back to the office. When he left, Eleanor went upstairs to look over their unpacking. She had bought a lot of pretty new things in Paris, and some summer evening dresses, and bathing suits by Elsa Schiaparelli to wear at the lake. She loved to swim in the icy cold water and then lie in the sun on the dock, or go out in the boats. She had learned to drive them, with one of the boatmen next to her, and she had learned to water-ski the summer before. Alex said he wanted to learn too. A million happy discoveries lay ahead of them. Eleanor could see her life ahead of her now, with Alex, and their children, spending summers in Lake Tahoe with her parents. Her father wanted to redo one of the houses on the property for them, and to have it ready by the following year. They were excited about that too. Her father was going to have an architect draw up some plans for her to look over with Alex. Eleanor wanted at least four bedrooms for all the children they hoped to have.

The move to Lake Tahoe, two weeks after Eleanor and her mother returned from France, looked like the migration of an entire village. Eleanor and Louise took endless trunks, they kept clothes at the lake house but added to them every year with new fashions they couldn't live without. Charles was happy to indulge them. "You know how women are," he had said to Alex more than once. Louise and Eleanor went up on the private train before the men did to get organized and settled. They didn't have guests coming on the first weekend, but had invited many for the rest of July and August. Their dining room was as large at the lake as it was in the city, and they had more than twenty guest rooms, including the guesthouses near the main house.

Louise met with the gardeners when she arrived, and told them what flowers she wanted every day from their gardens. She brought the cook from the city, with her assistants, and many of the maids. They hired some local girls to help every summer. The boatmen had the boats ready. They kept horses in the stables for their guests to ride. Louise rode, but wasn't enthusiastic about it. Eleanor enjoyed riding up into the hills with her father. All the fishing gear was at the ready for Charles and their guests. By the time Charles and Alex arrived on the weekend, everything was in order and waiting for them. Louise ran an extremely efficient home.

The four of them enjoyed a quiet dinner together the night the men arrived on their private train. They had their own small station not far from the house. They went to bed early and Eleanor and Alex went riding the next morning, before her parents were up.

"This is a wonderful place," Alex said, looking enthusiastic. There was so much to do. "My parents had a ranch in Santa Barbara where we used to go in the summer. I sold it when they died. My brothers didn't like it, and it was too much for me on my own. I thought I'd buy something smaller, but I never have."

"Well, you don't need to now." She smiled at him, comfortable on the horse she rode every summer, a gentle mare. She had given Alex one of her father's hunters who was a good ride as well. "We have this," she said peacefully, looking out at the vast expanse of their land, which included a forest, and part of the mountains behind them, as well as a long stretch of lakefront, where they had their boathouse and the dock, and a narrow beach. "I like coming up here. It's nice to get away from the city. I hope you'll love it here."

"I'll love any place where I am with you and it will be wonderful for our children one day," he said, and she blushed. It embarrassed her to discuss things like that with him, but it was her dream too, and she could envision it easily. The property had been in her family for four generations, and would continue to be in the future.

"I'm sorry," he said gently, "that was indelicate of me, but I can't think of anything more wonderful than having children with you." She nodded, unable to speak for a minute, and he leaned over and gently touched her cheek. "I want you to be happy, Eleanor, and to give you a perfect life." Her life was already perfect, but he was the added blessing now. She had never expected to love a man as she did him, and they seemed to love each other more every day.

They rode for an hour, and then took the horses back to the stable and joined her parents for breakfast in the morning room that looked out at the lake.

"Have you been out in the boats yet?" Charles asked Alex over a hearty breakfast.

"Not yet. We thought we'd go down to the boathouse after breakfast." Charles nodded with a smile, knowing the pleasant surprise in store for him. He joined them and walked to the lake with them after breakfast, while Louise went to confer with the cook. They were going to have crayfish from the lake for lunch, and trout. The boatmen fished for them and the cook did wonders with their catches.

When they reached the boathouse, Alex was stunned by the beautiful speedboats they kept there. They had a sleek Gar Wood racing boat, a Fellows & Stewart "marine sedan." They got into Charles's favorite one, *Comet,* with a Hall-Scott engine, and then sped across the lake, and took a tour for an hour at full speed, before returning to the dock. Eleanor wanted to change into a swimsuit, and lie in the sun, and they were going to water-ski that afternoon.

The days at the lake passed easily, and Alex and Charles spent considerable time discussing the recession that had begun that summer and concerned them both. The stock market was continuing to rise and both men were afraid that the bubble would burst. Stock prices had reached a high which could no longer be justified. Alex hated to leave on Sunday night to return to the city to work. Eleanor drove him to the station on their property. She didn't have a license, but their chauffeur had taught her to drive two years before. Alex took her in his arms and kissed her, while the train waited for him. Charles wasn't going back to the city until Monday night, but Alex felt he should get back sooner.

"You're going to make a lazy man of me." He smiled at his future wife. "It's too wonderful being with you. Our life is going to be better than I ever dreamed," he said in a soft voice, and kissed her again. He felt as though he was going to burst with happiness. He was meeting with an architect the next day to make some changes to his own mansion on upper Broadway, where they would live after their honeymoon in Italy. He wanted to redo his mother's dressing room and modernize the bathroom as a surprise for Eleanor. She was going to be moving from one very large, stupendously beautiful home to another. The house Alex's grandfather had built was almost as grand as the Deveraux mansion, though slightly more austere, but they had a spectacular view of the bay, which the Deveraux home didn't have. Alex thought the garden needed redesigning, and he was going to ask Eleanor to do it once she moved in.

"I hate to leave you," he whispered, and then with a sigh, "I'll be back Friday night with your father. It's going to be a long week without you. I'm afraid I'm not going to let you out of my sight once we're married, except possibly to come up here in the summer.

My life is just too lonely without you." He could no longer imagine how he had lived without her for thirty-two years. But the timing had been just right, and providential. She wouldn't have been able to be with him before her debut anyway, so things had worked out as they were meant to. He had been in hibernation, waiting for her to grow up, and hadn't known it. Amelia had died when Eleanor was ten years old, and he wouldn't have wanted any other woman. She smiled at the sweet things he said to her, kissed him again before he boarded their train, and waved as they pulled away until the train rounded a bend and was out of sight.

The next weekend she knew that her parents were having a dozen houseguests so they would all be busy playing tennis and croquet, and whatever entertainments her parents devised for their guests. They often played bridge or other card games at night, and sometimes charades, which was a good icebreaker. They were starting with a smaller group than usual for the first weekend of the summer.

She and Alex thoroughly enjoyed the time they spent at Lake Tahoe that summer. They both became proficient water-skiers, as her parents watched them from the dock and waved as they went by. Charles developed a strong rapport with his future son-in-law, which for Charles filled the void of having lost his own son so many years earlier. And Alex had lost his father. The two men rode and fished together, talked about banking and the world economy, and shared similar views on many subjects. Whenever possible, Alex stole a few moments alone with Eleanor, savoring the excitement of the pleasures in store for them once they were married. It excited him just looking at her and talking to her, and he could hardly wait until she was truly his.

By the time they went back to the city after Labor Day, their wedding was only four weeks away. It was set for Saturday, October 5, and all of San Francisco was talking about it as the wedding of the century. Louise was constantly busy now, and Eleanor helped her where she could. They were working on the seating of nearly eight hundred guests. There was going to be a full orchestra and a singer for the dancing. Flowers were being shipped in from all over the state for the garlands and table arrangements. They were going to hang chandeliers in the massive tent, which was unheard of. The huge dance floor was being made. The guests had responded as soon as they'd received the coveted invitations.

The exquisite Jeanne Lanvin gown was hanging in the locked guest room, where it had been since they returned from France. Only Eleanor and her mother had the key to it. They didn't want anyone to see it before her wedding day, or for one of the servants to take a photograph of it and sell it to the newspapers. They trusted Wilson but none of the others to resist that kind of temptation if the social columnists offered to pay them for it. There was speculation all over town, among fashionable women, about what the dress would look like. Those who knew that she and Louise had gone to Paris for it were guessing it was by Worth or Poiret. They were sure she had gone modern, and might even have gotten a sleek gown by Chanel. No one knew the designer of the dress or what it looked like. And even Alex was curious about it now, but knew better than to ask questions. Wilson, when questioned by her coworkers in the staff dining hall, told them honestly that she had never seen it.

Eleanor and her mother had opened the crate themselves late one night, and took the dress out of its huge box. Two full-grown people could easily have hidden in the box, and it was stuffed with reams of tissue paper. Louise had cried when she'd seen the dress again, and Eleanor felt breathless as she looked at it. She still couldn't believe how beautiful it was, and that she would be wearing the exquisite wedding dress when she married Alex.

"Mama, can you imagine me in it?" she said, looking like a child at Christmas.

"Yes, I can, my darling. I can imagine it perfectly." Eleanor had looked exquisite in it at the final fitting in Paris. "It won't be long now." The wedding was only a week away, and the time seemed to be flying.

"It seems a terrible shame to wear such an amazing dress only once," Eleanor said in wonder as she touched it reverently.

"That's always true with a wedding dress." Louise smiled at her. "I think every bride feels that way. I hope your daughters will wear it years from now, or maybe even a granddaughter."

"I hope so," Eleanor agreed with her. And hopefully not in too many years, if she and Alex began having children quickly, which was their dream.

They left the dress in the locked room, and went back downstairs to their own rooms, each of them thinking about Eleanor's wedding day. Much to her annoyance, Eleanor got a cold that week, and on Monday night she felt ill, and had to cancel dinner with Alex. She wasn't seriously ill, but she wanted to nip it in the bud before the wedding. She left a message with his secretary that afternoon saying that she had to cancel dinner, because she felt ill. She was shocked when he appeared at the house less than an hour later, looking panicked and deathly pale. Houghton told Eleanor Alex was downstairs in the drawing room, and she went down in her dressing gown to see him. He appeared to be on the verge of tears.

"What's wrong? Have you called a doctor?" She was shocked by his extreme reaction, and how ravaged he looked. He had walked straight out of a meeting when he got the message, and driven directly to the Deveraux home on Nob Hill.

"No, of course not. I'm fine. Wilson has been making me lemon tea with honey in it. I just don't want to get sicker before the wedding, so I thought I should stay home tonight." They'd been planning to have dinner with friends and go dancing. There had already been several dinner parties for them, and hostesses all over the city were dying to entertain them. As she looked at Alex, she realized what had happened. Her canceling the evening with him six days before the wedding was all too reminiscent of his past fiancée, Amelia, dying of Spanish flu five days before their wedding. Eleanor held her arms out to him and he flew into them and held her so tightly she could hardly breathe.

"I don't want anything to happen to you," he said in a choked voice. "I couldn't bear it, Eleanor. I love you so much."

"I love you too," she said gently and pulled away to smile at him. "I'm fine, it's just a little cold, but I don't want to have a red nose at our wedding."

"Oh my God, I thought . . ." He couldn't even say the words.

"Nothing bad is going to happen, Alex. I'm fine. I promise."

"Please, please take care of yourself. I think you should call a doctor," he said miserably as Louise walked into the room and was surprised to see Eleanor in her dressing gown with Alex. She could see how distressed he was, and had heard him tell Eleanor to call a doctor.

"Did someone get hurt?" She seemed surprised, and Eleanor looked fine to her, although Alex looked dreadful and as though he was about to cry.

"Eleanor's sick," he said, obviously in anguish. And Louise understood even more quickly than Eleanor had. The ghosts of the past had come back to haunt him, and he was terrified.

"Are you?" her mother asked her matter-of-factly.

"I think I have a cold, Mama. I just wanted to be careful I don't get sicker, so I thought I'd stay in tonight."

"Excellent idea." Louise nodded her approval. "We can't have you sneezing and coughing in that dress or with a red nose."

"That's what I said to Alex." Eleanor smiled at him, and in the face of both women looking unconcerned, he started to relax.

"You're sure it's nothing?" he asked her again.

"Positive. I'll be fine by tomorrow or the day after if I stay home tonight. I promise." He sat down in a chair looking as though he'd been run over by a bus. Charles came home from the office at that moment, saw the three of them in the drawing room, and wondered why Eleanor wasn't dressed. She explained it to him, and he looked at Alex sympathetically.

"Come into the library, and I'll give you a brandy," he said to him, winking at his wife, and Alex followed him meekly.

"She canceled dinner and said she was ill. I thought . . ."

"I can imagine," Charles said, cutting him off from the unhappy memory and handing him a snifter of brandy, which Alex downed in a few swallows and thanked him.

"Sorry, it seemed like a nightmarish déjà vu for a moment." He looked serious.

"I'm sure it did. We all get a bit high strung before a wedding. I had a bit too much to drink at my bachelor party, passed out, and hit my head on the bar on the way down. I still had a headache the day of the wedding." He smiled at him. "What about you? Any mischief planned for your bachelor party?" He vaguely remembered that it was on Wednesday, although he had declined. He felt too old for evenings of that nature.

"I hope not." Alex smiled at him, feeling better after the brandy, and a little foolish for panicking. He could see that Eleanor wasn't direly ill, and was just being cautious with a sniffle, which was sensible of her. "My brothers are in charge of my bachelor party, which was not a good idea. Knowing them, I may be calling you to bail me out of jail, or something equally unpleasant."

"Count on me." Charles laughed. "Just call me. I won't say anything to the ladies if you've been arrested."

As it turned out, Alex wasn't far off the mark. His two younger brothers had invited more of their own friends than Alex's, and had hired a dozen prostitutes to entertain twenty young men who'd been drinking heavily for several hours before the girls got there. As soon as Alex saw the girls walk in, he slipped away quietly through a side door, and when he spoke to his brothers the next day, they didn't even realize he hadn't been there for the "fun." It had apparently gone on until morning, while Alex was peacefully at home in bed.

"Marvelous evening, wasn't it?" Harry, his younger brother, said, severely hungover when he called Alex the next day.

"Absolutely wonderful," Alex confirmed.

"I knew you'd enjoy that."

"Right." At least none of them had gotten arrested for disorderly conduct or hiring prostitutes, both of which had happened before, and Alex had had to bail them out of jail. "See you at the wedding, and don't bring any of the girls with you."

"Of course not. But we can drop in to see them anytime. I got them at a house on Market Street. They're good girls."

"I'm sure they are. I'm going to be married now, though," not that he had consorted with prostitutes as a bachelor either, but his brothers did, frequently. More than anything, the boys were bored and looking for amusement in any form.

"You need to have more fun, Alex," Harry said. "At least you had a good time last night."

"I certainly did." He had been home in bed and sound asleep by ten o'clock. He was glad he hadn't stayed.

He had dinner with Eleanor and her parents on Nob Hill that night, and Charles whispered that he hadn't called to get bailed out of jail, and smiled at Alex.

"I left just as the fun started. I know my brothers," he said with a wry grin. "I just hope they behave at the wedding."

"No one will notice if they don't, in a mob of eight hundred people."

"They're liable to chase each other through the tent on horseback on a dare, or some other unpleasantness or childish prank. They're a handful. They were so young when my parents died, and I'm afraid I wasn't stern enough with them, and assumed they'd be sensible. Instead they went wild." He felt that he should have kept a tighter rein on them, but he hadn't, and now it was too late.

"They sound relatively harmless." Alex rolled his eyes and Charles laughed.

They made it an early night, and on Friday, Alex had a peaceful dinner with his closest male friends, none of whom had been invited to the orgy by his brothers. Eleanor stayed home with her parents, to have a quiet night and get ready for her big day.

She lay in her bed, thinking that it was her last night in her childhood room as a single woman. She was excited about getting married, but there was something bittersweet about it too. She would be leaving her parents' home and going to her husband's after their honeymoon, and she would never be a young girl again, as she was now. On her wedding day she would discover the pleasures and pains of being a married woman. She was nervous about it, and not entirely sure what to expect. Her mother had explained it to her, but so discreetly that Eleanor was not entirely sure how it all worked and it sounded painful to her. Her mother said she would enjoy it after the first time. But the first time sounded somewhat terrifying, even with a gentle, loving man like Alex. None of her friends were married yet, so she had no one to ask. And she would have asked Wilson, but she had never been married either, so Eleanor assumed she knew as little about it as Eleanor did herself.

They were going to stay at the Fairmont on their wedding night, and take the train to New York the next day, then board the ship to Italy for their honeymoon. So this really was her last night at home, in her bed as a young girl, and the next day, after wearing her incredible wedding dress, she would be expected to act like a wife. She had no idea what that would be like. All she knew was how much she loved him, and hoped that would help make it easier. She lay in bed thinking about it for a long time that night, until she fell asleep at last. When she woke up, with the sun streaming into her room, it was her Wedding Day and her dreams were about to come true when she married Alex. She couldn't think about the rest of it now. This was her moment, when she was finally going to wear The Dress! And in a few hours, she was going to be a bride.

Chapter 4

The house was buzzing with activity from the moment Eleanor woke up. One of the maids brought her breakfast on a tray but she couldn't eat it, she was too excited. She stayed in her room, and tried not to get in the way. Her mother came to check on her several times, and told her everything was going splendidly, without a hitch. They were setting the dinner tables in the main tent by then, the dance floor had been installed, and the microphones for the band. The activity below stairs in the kitchen was massive and a small army of footmen had been sent to Charles's cavernous wine cellars under Houghton's supervision. He had enlarged the cellars before Prohibition came in. And they were going to do what they had for Eleanor's debut ball. Charles had a vast stock of fine wines and spirits, all of which were legal to serve at a private party in their home. They had more than enough for the number of guests and other parties in the years to come. He had selected some of his finest wines for the wedding. As long as Charles had owned the wine and spirits before Prohibition came in, it was legal to serve it. There was also a fleet of hired footmen being instructed in service.

At last, Wilson came to do Eleanor's hair. She had just done her mother's. She always did Eleanor's for special events, like her debut, or her parents' parties when she was younger and allowed to see the guests, or her graduation from Miss Benson's. Wilson did it with special care today, in the small chignon they had agreed on, with the waves around her face, and her mother walked into the room, while Wilson was using the curling iron to create the fashionable waves that Madame Lanvin had agreed would be the right style to wear with her veil.

"Oh you look lovely, dear." Her mother smiled as she looked at her in the mirror. She was carrying a large square box in her hands.

"What's that?" Eleanor asked her, intrigued. It looked like a jewelry box, only larger.

Louise sat down on a chair next to her. "This belonged to my grandmother, your great-grandmother. I wore it on my wedding day. I mentioned it to Madame Lanvin in Paris and she thought it would be pretty." She handed the box to Eleanor, who opened it carefully, and an exquisite pearl and diamond tiara lay nestled in the custom-made box. Louise had warned Wilson about it, who had been doing Eleanor's hair accordingly, and they gently set the tiara on her head. It was perfect, not too tall and not too showy. It was just the right thing for a bride.

"Oh, Mama, it's so beautiful." Eleanor had tears in her eyes as she hugged her mother. She was already wearing the underwear that the house of Lanvin had made for her, silk stockings, and the shoes that went with the dress, and a pink satin dressing gown. All three of them stood admiring the tiara, and Eleanor sat down so Wilson could finish her hair. She was keeping it very simple, though still stylish. She didn't want to distract from the tiara or the veil. She had just put the last pin in it, when one of the maids came to the door with a box, wrapped in white paper with a white satin ribbon tied in a bow, with a note tucked into it. Eleanor looked surprised, opened the card, and turned to her mother. "It's from Alex." The card read only, "To my wife, on our wedding day, with all my heart and soul. Alex." She could feel her heart pounding as she opened it, and she gasped when she saw it. It was a very important diamond necklace, made up of large perfectly matched round stones, and she could tell it must have been his mother's. It was even bigger than the one her mother had and seldom wore because the stones were so large. It was an amazing piece of jewelry. Her eyes opened wide as she looked at it and then at her mother. "Oh, Mama!"

"That is an extraordinary wedding present from your husband," Louise confirmed to her with a smile.

"Should I wear it with my dress?"

"Of course. He would be very hurt if you didn't, and it will look wonderful. It's just right for the neckline." It was a dazzling piece of jewelry, and with her great-grandmother's tiara, it would be even more impressive. Her mother put it on her carefully, and the necklace sparkled on Eleanor's neck, as Wilson went to get the dress.

It was so beautifully made that it was easy to get into. There was a concealed zipper, a number of hooks and the buttons down the back, but there was no mystery to it, and it glided onto Eleanor's shapely young body as smoothly as it had in Paris, and fell just as it was meant to, with the long train behind her. It took both Wilson and her mother to put the veil in place, however. It sat just behind the tiara, with a thin film of tulle which came forward over the tiara and Eleanor's face to her fingertips. She put on gloves which she would remove at the beginning of the ceremony. The final touch was her bouquet of lily of the valley and white orchids. The effect of all of it together was breathtaking, especially with the necklace and the tiara. Louise gasped as she looked at her and tears filled her eyes. She was wearing a deep sapphire blue gown herself that she had had made in Paris by a well-known dressmaker, but not an haute couture designer. Her dress was very elegant too, with a matching coat, and she was wearing sapphires that Charles had given her. The two women standing together looked incredible, and when they emerged from Eleanor's bedroom, Charles looked up and stared at them as they came down the stairs. He was speechless, he was so moved.

It was just after six o'clock, and the wedding was to begin at six-thirty at the temporary church on the site of Grace Cathedral, on Nob Hill, directly across from the Deveraux mansion. The original church had burned in the 1906 earthquake. The new church had been under construction for two years and was due to be finished in another year.

Charles kissed his wife with an appreciative glance and told her how beautiful she looked, and for a moment they both admired the gown Eleanor was wearing. It was every bit as splendid as Louise had promised it would be.

"I don't think I've ever been prouder in my life," her father whispered to Eleanor as they left the house to get in the Rolls-Royce that had been sent from England by ship the year before, while Louise left in their Packard, to go ahead to the church. Charles and Eleanor would be going to the rectory, where she would stay until she walked down the aisle on her father's arm. She had chosen not to have any brides-maids, only her father at her side, and Alex waiting for her at the altar. His two brothers were his best men, and had sworn to behave, and he was holding them to it.

Louise and Charles had appointed several ushers among their friends, and one of them led Louise to her seat, as they waited for the wedding to begin.

The music they had chosen began playing once

Eleanor was in the church, and Louise held her breath waiting to see her walk down the aisle. Everyone fell silent as they waited and then stood up as Charles and Eleanor walked in. The dress was the most spectacular one that Louise had ever seen, and Eleanor was equal to it. She looked stunning in her tiara and wedding necklace from Alex. Louise glanced at him, and he looked as though he might faint. Charles looked serious, as he and Eleanor made their way down the aisle to the altar at a dignified pace, and then at last she had reached him, and stood looking into Alex's eyes, as her father helped her lift the delicate veil which covered her face.

"Oh my God, Eleanor, I love you so much," Alex whispered, as the ceremony began. She was a vision of beauty like a creature in a dream. He barely heard what the minister was saying, until they exchanged their vows. Alex spoke up in a strong clear voice, and Eleanor's quavered with emotion, and they both cried when Alex slipped the simple gold band on her finger, and she put the ring on his, which his brothers had managed not to lose.

Then they were declared man and wife. Alex kissed the bride and they floated down the aisle through the doors of the church, and were driven the short distance to her home, where Alex finally had a moment alone with her before her parents and the guests arrived.

"Oh my God, is this happening?" he said as he looked at her. "Could I truly be this lucky?" He had never seen a more beautiful woman or bride in his life. "You look incredible, and I love you so much."

"Alex, the necklace . . ." she said, touching it, as she remembered, and he kissed her with all the longing and passion of a man so deeply in love he couldn't believe his good fortune to be married to her. And she was just as grateful to be his wife, and responded to his kisses with equal passion. It made her wonder for an instant if her mother was right, and those things took care of themselves. She felt as though she belonged to him now, and her place was at his side.

They kissed and whispered for a few more minutes, and then had to join her family and their guests in the enormous tent, while everyone exclaimed at how remarkable it all was, how exquisite her wedding dress was, how happy she looked and they had never seen a more beautiful bride in their lives. And they posed for photographs.

They spent what felt like hours on the receiving line, while people kissed her, and others squeezed their hands, and congratulated them and her parents. And at last, when the orchestra began playing, she danced the first dance with Alex, and then with her father, while Alex danced with his mother-in-law, and the guests smiled at them, touched by the obvious love between the bride and groom. It was the most impressive, dazzling wedding San Francisco had ever seen. Their friends were at the bridal table with them. Eleanor's father made a speech about how much he and her mother loved her that brought tears to Eleanor's eyes, and they welcomed Alex warmly into the family.

People ate and drank and danced all night. Alex saw his brothers leave with two very pretty young women, which was something of a relief. Guests commented on how good the food was, and the wine, no small feat with eight hundred wedding guests, and at two in the morning, Alex and Eleanor shared a last dance, circling the floor with her in the magical wedding gown with her train attached to a narrow satin loop on her wrist. And then he whispered to her and asked if she was ready to leave. She was. She wanted to be alone with him, and it had been a long, unforgettable night. She was slightly afraid too, but didn't tell him. He could see it in her eyes.

They had cut the enormous artistically decorated wedding cake hours before, and all that remained was for her to toss the bouquet. She stood on the stage with the orchestra for a moment, turned her back and threw it over her shoulder. She laughed when she saw that a classmate from Miss Benson's had caught it and was thrilled. She had confided to Eleanor recently that she was hoping to become engaged soon, and Eleanor hoped that the bouquet would bring her luck.

Alex and Eleanor thanked her parents profusely before they left.

"It was the most beautiful night of my life," she

said to both of them with everything she felt for them and Alex, and the wedding they had given her.

"And mine," Alex echoed with feeling.

"Thank you, Mama . . . Papa . . ." she said again as she kissed them. She was going to drop the tiara off at the house the next morning when they left for the train station at nine A.M. Her trunks were already packed and at the hotel, and she was going to take her wedding necklace with her to wear on the ship. Alex was pleased. As she had guessed, it had been his mother's, and one of her favorite pieces, he said. She had been much older than Eleanor when she received it, but Alex wanted her to have it, and it was perfect on her. His father had bought it at Cartier in Paris before the war.

Alex's chauffeur dropped them off at the hotel, just across from the house. He had reserved the largest suite in the Fairmont for them for their wedding night. They were both wide awake despite the late hour. Eleanor had stopped drinking champagne hours before. She didn't want to get drunk or sick at her wedding, and Alex had drunk in moderation for the same reason. He didn't want to be blind drunk on his first night with his bride. But they opened a bottle of champagne when they got to their suite, and Eleanor sipped it. They talked for a while about what an extraordinary wedding it had been. They had been posing for photographs all night long, and Eleanor couldn't wait to see them.

"Shall we retire?" he asked gently. They had to be

up at seven, to leave the hotel at nine. Wilson was to
come for the dress right before they left in the morning. They had a long journey on the train ahead of
them, after a big day and a late night.

Alex carefully helped her undo the fastenings on
the dress, and she disappeared into the bedroom of
the suite to finish undressing. It made her sad as she
carefully stepped out of the dress. She hadn't even
noticed how heavy it was with the pearls carefully
embroidered onto it. It was so perfectly made that
the weight of it was never uncomfortable, and it saddened her to realize that the big moment was over,
and she would never wear the dress again. She wondered who would, which of her children, a long time
from now. She laid it out carefully, with the shoes,
and disappeared into the bathroom where Wilson
had left a beautiful lace nightgown Madame Lanvin
had given her as a gift for her wedding night, with
little white satin ribbons on it. It molded her body as
Madame Lanvin had meant it to, without being vul-
gar, but exquisitely sexy and alluring, as only a
French designer could do. She took her hair out of
the chignon, and it cascaded past her shoulders, as
she stood in the white lace nightgown, looking lost
in the middle of the room, as Alex walked in, in his
dressing gown. There was a separate dressing room
for him, and he had undressed while she did. He
looked strikingly handsome, powerful and tall and
his heart went out to her the moment he saw her,
looking frightened and so young. He put his arms

around her, led her gently to the bed, and sat down with his arm still around her.

"We don't need to do anything tonight," he said in a whisper. He didn't want to frighten her more than she was. "We have a lifetime ahead of us," he said gently and she nodded and kissed him.

"But I want to . . ." she said softly. "I want to be your wife."

"You are my wife." He pointed to the ring on her finger and smiled as he showed her his. "And I have never been prouder or happier." He kissed her as he said it, and she responded with passion he hadn't expected, which aroused him instantly. He slipped off her nightgown and lay her on the bed, so he could admire her and kiss her, as she put her arms around his neck and arched her body up toward him, and he could no longer hold back. He dropped the lace nightgown to the floor, and entered her as gently as he could, but their joint passion overtook them both, more than he intended. She cried out once, but moved even closer to him and didn't pull away. He waited as long as he could to inflame the passion in her, and she was stunned when they both exploded at the same time. She looked shocked for a minute and gazed at him as they lay breathless in each other's arms.

"What was that . . . was that all right?" No one had told her anything about it, and her mother's genteel allusions hadn't included what happened when men and women made love and desired each other.

"That's what's supposed to happen," he said gently, and ran a finger down her body and up again, stopping in all the places that excited her. They made love again a little while later, and she was even more passionate the second time. He let his own desire for her go unbridled this time, and they both shuddered at the end of their passion again. Alex felt as though the earth had exploded in a million stars, and Eleanor looked sated and drowsy as she smiled at him afterward.

"I like being married," she said sleepily, ". . . very much," and drifted off to sleep in his arms as he smiled. He liked being married to her very much too. For Alex, it was the dream of a lifetime, and he intended to make all of her dreams come true. And he knew they would cherish the memory of this day forever.

Chapter 5

Wilson came to the Fairmont the next morning while Alex and Eleanor were having breakfast, before they left for the train. She took the wedding dress, the tiara, and all the accessories with her, and she congratulated them again. She said that Eleanor's parents were still asleep when she left the house. Some of the guests had stayed until five in the morning, and her parents had danced until nearly the end. They had enjoyed the evening too. Eleanor was wearing a pale blue wool dress and coat the color of her eyes that they had bought from a dressmaker in Paris between fittings at Lanvin. It looked lovely on her with a matching hat. They had made love again before they got out of bed that morning, and Alex was happy and surprised that she was such a willing partner, and by the morning, she wasn't even shy with him. He was her husband, and she said she wanted to be a good wife. He could tell that she wasn't sacrificing herself, she genuinely enjoyed their lovemaking, even though she had been a virgin when she came to him the night before. She had no hesitation about giving herself to him, which made her all the more appealing. He could hardly keep his hands off her, as they hurried to leave the hotel and catch the train to New York, which was to leave at ten. They were following the same route to New York she had taken with her mother in April to go to Paris for her wedding dress.

Only this time they would be sailing on the RMS *Aquitania,* disembarking in Cherbourg, and then on to Rome by train to begin their honeymoon. She was a British ship, made a stop in Southampton, and carried mail as well, and was the fastest ship afloat. She was called the "Millionaires' Ship," had served in the Great War, and had been refitted for military service three months after she was launched, and had been used as a hospital ship. And for the past ten years had returned to service as a luxury liner with three classes. She was the last of the four funneled ships, with glass enclosed promenade decks and magnificent public rooms and staterooms, a gym, and theater. A thousand crew members served the nearly three thousand passengers with impeccable service.

After Rome, they were going to Florence and Venice, with a few days at Lake Como at the end. They planned to stay in Italy for almost four weeks, and then sail back to New York, and return to San Francisco in early November. Eleanor couldn't wait for the trip to begin, and she looked like an excited child as they boarded the train. Alex smiled at her.

"You have made me the happiest man in the world, my wonderful wife." And she had been the most extraordinarily beautiful bride he had ever seen.

They settled into their compartment, read, played cards, talked, and made love. They ate in the dining car, and lay in each other's arms at night. They passed the time at ease with each other, changed trains in Chicago after the three-day trip, arrived in New York the next morning, and checked into the Plaza hotel.

The *Aquitania* was sailing the next day. She was excited to be sailing with him. They had wanted to sail on the SS *Paris* but she had been severely damaged in a fire in August in Le Havre, and was not back in service yet in October, after the smoke and water damage. It was fun exploring the *Aquitania* with Alex when they boarded. They had a huge luxurious cabin, with enough room for Eleanor's trunks, with her trousseau for the trip. She had been buying clothes for months to wear on their honeymoon. And when they wore evening clothes at night, she wore the diamond necklace Alex had given her as a wedding present. He was pleased that she liked it so much. It dazzled everyone who saw it.

They played shuffleboard on deck, and lay in the sun in deck chairs, reading, then went to the swimming bath or the gym, and afterward went to their cabin discreetly, several times a day to make love.

They chatted with other couples and dined at the captain's table, and danced and drank champagne. They were in high spirits when they docked at Cherbourg in France. They'd already been traveling for ten days together by then, and Eleanor was totally at ease with Alex, as though they had always been married. She wasn't shy with him at all, and was excited to board the train to Rome.

They stayed at the Excelsior hotel on the Via Veneto in Rome, in an elegant suite, and took a horse drawn carriage around the city, looking at the monuments. Eleanor was enchanted with it, and Alex was enamored with her, more so every day. She couldn't help wondering if a baby would result from their honeymoon. They made love constantly, several times a day. She initiated it as often as he did, which pleased him no end.

They ate at elegant restaurants recommended by the hotel and particularly loved the Al Moro restaurant, which had just opened behind the Trevi Fountain. They went for long walks, bought pretty things. He got her an emerald bracelet at Bulgari, and she bought him a Fabergé box at a famous antique store. They explored all the shops and small churches, and left Rome reluctantly after a week. It was the twenty-second of October, and they went from Rome to Florence, for four days, and admired the wonders of the Uffizi, and more churches.

Two days after they got to Florence, Alex received a flood of telegrams from his bank, that the stock market bubble had begun to burst. Investors had dumped shares en masse. Twelve million nine hundred thousand shares were traded that day, and they were calling it Black Thursday. Alex was concerned by the reports.

They went to Venice two days later, which Eleanor fell in love with the moment she saw it. They stayed at the Danieli and walked everywhere, got lost, and found their way again. They took a gondola beneath the Bridge of Sighs, while the gondolier sang to them. It was the most romantic place she had ever been. Alex was enchanted being there with her. They had had the most perfect honeymoon he could have imagined, and Italy had been the right place for it.

They were planning to spend a week in Venice, and several days at Lake Como, before returning to Cherbourg to sail back to New York. They had been in Venice for three days, it was October 29, 1929. They had just returned to their suite at the hotel after a day of shopping and exploring. It was six o'clock and they were going to rest for an hour or two, before going to dinner at the best restaurant in Venice.

They had just walked into the room, when there was a knock at the door and Alex opened it, and one of the hotel's young runners handed him a telegram. He took it and tipped the boy, lay down next to his wife on the bed. He assumed it was from his office at the bank, which would have just opened at that hour. He was right, it was from the assistant manager, in charge in Alex's absence, and Alex frowned at what he read. "Disastrous situation. General economic crisis is coming to a head. Mass panic. Shares being dumped on the stock exchange in New York. Millions being lost. The economy is falling into the abyss." Alex couldn't believe it was as bad as he said. He wrote two quick telegrams, one to his manager and told him to sit tight, the other to a friend of his in New York, a stock market analyst, to ask him what he thought. He told Eleanor he'd be back in a minute, went to the front desk, and sent the telegrams. He got their responses before they left for dinner.

His friend in New York confirmed that disaster had struck. Panic had hit Wall Street. Stocks were being dumped by the million. Billions of dollars were being lost. Sixteen million shares were traded that day in the second wave of panic in five days. Millions of shares had become worthless. It was becoming a crisis from which the country could not recover. It was the biggest stock market crash in the history of the stock exchange. Investors who had bought on margin were instantly wiped out. Black Tuesday was even more deadly than Black Thursday had been five days before.

It didn't make sense to Alex. How was that possible? Surely they were exaggerating. He sent a telegram to Charles Deveraux then, and they left for dinner. He didn't say anything to Eleanor. He didn't want to worry her, and he still didn't believe that what had happened was as bad as they were saying. It just wasn't possible.

Eleanor thought he seemed distracted at dinner. He was unusually quiet, but she also thought maybe he was just tired. They had made love into the morning hours the night before, had gotten very little sleep, and had run around all day. She didn't make the connection between the telegrams he had received and his silence. She just assumed they were messages from his office about ordinary things. And he said nothing to her of the panic on Wall Street.

When they got back from dinner, he had a telegram from Charles, and several others. He read the one from Charles first.

"It's worse than you've been told. I am ruined. Many are. Banks are failing. Entire fortunes have been lost. The country is on its ear. We won't recover from this in our lifetimes, mine anyway. Disastrous situation. Sixteen million shares traded today. Billions lost. The country is wiped out. Economic crisis of Olympian proportions. Charles." The country's overspending had finally caught up with it and the stock market bubble had burst with disastrous results. Banks that had been overextended would go under.

Alex said nothing to Eleanor that night. The other telegrams he had received said pretty much the same as Charles's, some worse. The manager of his bank said that, too heavily invested, they had been wiped out. They had also extended too much credit. Alex needed to know if it was true. He couldn't imagine that Charles was really ruined, with a fortune that size. He went downstairs to read the newspapers in the morning before Eleanor woke up. He got the Italian, British, and international American newspapers. It was the headline on every paper. The crisis had reached Europe and the world, although for now, the most severe losses were in the United States. The stock market crash was front page news in every language, and the clerk at the reception desk looked concerned, as Alex wrote out more telegrams. When he went back upstairs, he told Eleanor that there appeared to be a stock market crisis in New York, but not that it had crashed and the country was wiped out. He didn't believe that himself yet, and still thought they must be exaggerating. But sixteen million shares traded the day before could not be denied. He told her he wanted to stay close to the hotel and see the responses to his telegrams when they arrived. She went for a walk on her own, and when she returned, she could see the seriousness of it by how Alex looked. Every mention was the same. The country was in extremis and entire fortunes had evaporated in a day. He wondered if his had too. It was beginning to seem likely, and he told Eleanor with regret that he thought they should get home and cut the trip short. She looked disappointed but said she understood.

"Is Papa all right?" she asked him, worried, and

he remembered the telegram he'd received from Charles that said he was ruined.

"I'm not sure anyone knows yet. I think we need to go home and find out."

The reception desk helped them to book passage on the *Aquitania* almost two weeks earlier than the passage they'd planned to be on for their return, before they shortened the trip. Alex and Eleanor spent a quiet night at the hotel, discussing what had happened, and how bad it really was, and the next morning they left Venice by train to reach Cherbourg in time to sail. She put her arms around his neck before they left the hotel.

"I had a fantastic honeymoon, Alex. And I want you to know that whatever happens when we go back, we'll deal with it together. There are two of us now." She sounded strong and sure and unafraid. He was beginning to believe the dire messages he had received, and fear had corroded his confidence that reports had been exaggerated. From what the newspapers were saying, the entire American economy had collapsed. It seemed impossible, but he had begun to fear it was true, and he was anxious to get back.

Their return to New York on the luxurious *Aquitania* was stressful for Alex and filled with anxiety. He no longer felt like celebrating or dancing at night. The more he heard, the more desperate he was to return to the States. He was planning to spend a day in New York when he arrived, to see people he trusted who were involved with the stock exchange and the bond and commodities markets. He wanted real information, not the voices of panic. The last telegram he got before he boarded the ship was from his manager at the bank, informing him that their largest bank client, a man with an enormous fortune, faced with ruin, had committed suicide the night before. Matters were indeed grave and Alex was no longer sure of his own holdings. In fact he was almost certain he had lost the bulk of his fortune if what they were saying was true, and he was concerned about Charles Deveraux's situation too. If what Charles had said in his telegram about being ruined was true, it meant that the two most solid banks in San Francisco would be obliged to close. It was a terrifying thought. He shared as little as possible with Eleanor on the trip back on the ship. He didn't want to worry her unduly, or panic her unnecessarily. He wanted hard facts, not rumors, but she could sense that he was worried and the situation was serious. She said very little, and didn't question him on the trip. She instinctively sensed that interrogating him would only heighten his anxiety, so she remained silent most of the time and kept their exchanges light.

Alex got the hard facts he was seeking when they reached New York. He met with his stockbroker friends and several bankers. They and their clients had been wiped out. Some fortunes had vanished entirely in a matter of hours, others were left with some small remnant of what they had had. Banks had closed, businesses were cleaned out. Houses would have to be sold. Rich men had become paupers overnight, and possibly he among them.

It was a tense train ride back to San Francisco, and he tried to prepare Eleanor for bad news when they arrived. But even he wasn't prepared for how dire it was. He dropped Eleanor off at his home, and went straight to his bank. There was no question according to the manager he had left in charge. Heavily invested, the bank had lost everything and had to close. The clients' fortunes had been lost. Their own funds were gone. Panic had led to mass withdrawals, loans had to be liquidated. And when Alex checked his own personal situation, he had lost everything. *Everything!* He was penniless as a result of the crash. Everything he owned would have to be sold. He would have to find a job. And he had a wife now, and was going to drag her into the abyss with him. He couldn't bear the thought.

He went to see Charles. The bank was closed and he found him at home. His situation was the same, though not quite as desperate as Alex's. The bulk of Charles's fortune was gone, however, he had some small funds that had plummeted, but weren't entirely gone. But most of his holdings had been swept away by a tidal wave. By the time Alex returned to San Francisco ten days after Black Tuesday, several of their more important bank clients, and three of his friends, had committed suicide, unable to face the fact that they had nothing left and no way to live. A number of those who had killed themselves had left widows and children, who were destitute now. Alex couldn't imagine it. The country had been plunged into a depression.

"What are you going to do?" Alex asked Charles, closeted in the library with him, as they both drank straight scotch and looked like desperate men.

"We have a pittance left. I'm too old to get a job. I'm fifty-two years old and no one will hire me," Charles said bluntly. "We have to sell everything, this house, Tahoe, jewels, cars, art, furs. It's all selling for nothing now, but we'll have to take what we can get. We're going to keep a corner of the Tahoe property where the servants' quarters are and a small cottage. Louise and I can live there. The servants will have to go of course, we've already given them notice, but they're in a bad spot too. No one can afford to hire them now, after years in service, faithful to their employers in many cases, their jobs no longer exist. We'll have to become servants now," he said, giving Alex a black look. "What about you?"

"Nothing left. I'm going to tell Eleanor tonight. I'm going to give her the opportunity to annul the marriage, if she wishes to. I'm not the man she thought she married. I'll be lucky if I get a job as a janitor somewhere, and live in a shanty. I can't do that to her. At least she could go to Tahoe with you."

"So can you," Charles said in a hoarse voice.

"I need a job. I can't find one at Lake Tahoe, except as a gardener, and there'll be no one to hire any of us. We're a nation of ruined men and paupers now."

"If I know my daughter, she won't leave you. Louise has been wonderful about it. She's been contacting auction houses to sell the jewelry. We're putting the city house on the market next week. We'll sell it with everything in it, if someone will buy it. I had some money in the safe. We'll live on that for a while, but it won't last long." Alex couldn't believe what he was hearing, and he was half drunk by the time he went home to talk to his wife.

He told her where things stood without dressing it up, and he made her the offer he told her father he would. She looked baffled when he said it, as though she didn't understand. There was a lot to absorb right now. Their whole world had crumbled around them, and their way of life. An entire element of society had suddenly crashed to the ground, like a ship that had sunk. Their lives and their fortunes, their lifestyle and everything they knew had disappeared in the blink of an eye and a single day, and not through any fault of theirs.

"What are you saying to me?" Eleanor asked him, squinting as she looked at him, as though she couldn't see him clearly. "What do you mean?"

"I'm offering to have our marriage annulled, or to let you divorce me, to free you, Eleanor. You married a rich man who was going to be able to take care of you and our children for the rest of your days, as your father had until then. I have nothing now. There's nothing left. It's all gone. I have some cash in my vault here at the house. When that's gone, I can't buy food for you. We'll starve. I have to find a job if I can. I have to sell everything. You don't have to be part of this. I don't want to drag you into it, to live in squalor somewhere, and take in laundry or scrub floors. You need to jump ship, Eleanor. I love you. I won't take you down with me. Your father says he'll have enough to live on carefully in Tahoe, after he sells everything. You should go with them. I can't provide for you, or do any of the things I promised when I married you. I won't do this to you. You need to go back to your parents and forget me." There were tears in his eyes when he said it, but his voice was strong. He loved her too much to take her down with him, and her father's situation was slightly better than theirs, although not much. Alex would have something after he sold everything, but it wouldn't last forever. And there was no telling how long the country would take to crawl out of the biggest depression that had ever hit it. America was on its knees, and millions of people along with it, and Alex was one of them.

"What happened to better or worse? Didn't you mean that? I did," she said angrily. "It's very nice living in a house like this with servants and fancy cars and jewels and nice clothes. But that's not why I married you. I married you because I love you 'for richer or poorer, in sickness or in health, for better or worse.' I meant it, Alex Allen. Didn't you?"

"Yes, of course, but this is different," he tried to ignore what she said.

"Why is it different?"

"Because it's so extreme. I have nothing left."

"I heard that. So now that you're poor, you're abandoning me?" She made him sound worse than he was, when he was trying to be noble, for her sake, not his own.

"I won't take you down with me!"

"From what I understand, everyone's down. So what difference will it make?"

"A big difference. Your father has a little something left. You'll starve with me."

"Then we'll both starve. Besides, I can get a job if I have to," she said bravely, squaring her shoulders and meeting his gaze.

"What kind of job? You have no training for anything."

"I can be a lady's maid," she said, jutting her chin out, and he smiled.

"There won't be any lady's maids. The people who could afford them no longer can."

"I'll become a nurse, or a doctor, or a teacher," she said, refusing to give up. She loved him, and was not going to lose their marriage because he'd lost his money. "What will you do?"

"Look for a job in a bank, not like the one I had.

Bank presidents will be a dime a dozen, I mean like a bank teller or a clerk."

"Fine, then I'll be a secretary or a maid or something, or a waitress." He came to put his arms around her then.

"Eleanor, I love you. I can't support you now. I have nothing. I have to sell everything. I'd rather know that you're safe with your parents in Tahoe, and eating, than starving with me."

"I'd rather starve with you," she said, her voice quavering. "I'm not afraid to work. I won't leave you. I love you." He hesitated for a moment and looked at her.

"You're a stubborn woman, Eleanor Deveraux Allen."

"I'll sell my wedding dress," she said gamely, although it gave her a twinge to say it. It was a symbol of the best day of her life, but now hard times had come, and she wanted to prove to him that she was equal to them.

"Don't do that," he said seriously, "you won't get anything for it. Save it for your daughter one day." He meant it. It broke his heart that she had offered to sell it for them.

"If you divorce me, I won't have a daughter," she said sadly, and he held her tight.

"I have to sell everything, this house as soon as I can get rid of it. Everything we have. I have to close the doors at the bank. We're bankrupt."

"It's all right. We'll manage," she said. The way

she said it told him she meant it, and her dogged determination gave him hope that they would figure out something. But there were hard times ahead for the whole country. People with immense fortunes would be starving now, and living on the streets, and he and Eleanor might be among them, if he let her stay with him. But he didn't have the heart to turn her away. She was so young and innocent and loving and her love for him was so pure. She went to the kitchen then to rummage for something for them to eat, and came back with fried eggs, some ham, and slices of toast. It was all they had in the house at the moment, and she put a familiar leather box down next to him on the table. He recognized it immediately. It was the diamond necklace of his mother's that he had given her as a wedding present. "If we're selling jewelry, you should sell that." She smiled at him, and he kissed her.

"Some husband I am, selling your wedding present."

"I have you. I don't need diamonds. It was fun wearing it, but you should get a lot for it."

"Probably not. Everyone will be selling their jewels now. I'll see what I can get for it." He sighed and picked at his dinner, and she did too. But he didn't mention annulling their marriage again, or divorcing her. She had made herself clear. She was going down with the ship if she had to, but she was not getting in a lifeboat. She was not leaving him, and she was

willing to do whatever she had to, to stand by him.
He had never loved her more in his life.

They clung to each other that night in bed, like
two frightened children, and he had a dream that
they were drowning and he couldn't save her. He
woke up in a sweat in a tangle of sheets as she slept
peacefully beside him, unaffected by his dream. He
wondered if they would survive the changes that
were happening to them. He wanted to protect her
and take care of her, but how would he be able to do
that now? He held her as she slept, and tears rolled
down his cheeks. The future looked very bleak. He
thought of the vow they made only a month ago. For
richer or poorer . . . little did he know then that it
would come to this, and how true it would be.

Chapter 6

The early days of November were surreal, for the entire country. No one was untouched by what had happened. Fortunes evaporated, jobs disappeared. Businesses collapsed, unemployment was skyrocketing. People didn't trust their banks not to fail and withdrew whatever they had left. People in the Deveraux and Allen strata became indigent at a moment's notice. Both the Deveraux mansion and Alex's home were on the market, along with other stately homes, at absurdly low prices. There were dozens of important homes for sale, none as grand as theirs, but some quite beautiful and luxurious. For those who had a little money left, there were incredible deals to be made. Louise had sacrificed all of her jewelry to be sold at auction, even family heirlooms, and all that Charles had given her over the years. They had no other choice. They had stripped their walls of valuable paintings, and sent them to auction houses in New York too. The auction houses were flooded with art from well-known families and sellers. Prices had plummeted, and once the auctions began, priceless art and extraordinary jewelry were selling for a fraction of what they were worth, which was small consolation to the sellers who needed the money desperately. Alex had sent all of his mother's jewelry to auction too, including Eleanor's wedding necklace.

The Deveraux family had given all of their servants notice. They were only keeping two or three for the moment, which was all they could afford, and they could barely pay them for much longer. They didn't want to turn the others out into the street with no job market for them, so they allowed them to live at the house for free until it sold, but they could no longer pay them. Once they moved to Tahoe, the last of them would have to go. They would hire a local girl in Tahoe to help Louise clean the houses they kept there. They were selling their thousands of acres in Tahoe, and the main houses. Charles had carved out a small slice of the property for them to keep, where they would live. They were going to live in the main servants' house, which was small and rudimentary, and a tiny cottage, which they thought Alex and Eleanor could use when they came to visit them. There was an enormous barn they were going to use for storage of whatever they kept. The boathouse would go with the main house for the new owner. And Charles had put their boats up for sale.

He had already sold his horses to a neighbor. They could no longer afford their upkeep, the grooms, or their feed.

Wilson knew that once they sold the house on Nob Hill and moved to Tahoe, there would no longer be a job for her. She, Houghton the butler, and one of the maids were the only employees they were still paying, but they couldn't do it for long. Wilson had contacted her relatives in Boston, and they said the situation there was just as desperate, and there were no jobs available. She was going to use her savings to go back to Ireland, and get whatever work she could there.

The cook had just gotten a job in a restaurant for abysmal pay, but at least she was employed. Houghton was thinking of going back to Europe, like Wilson, and hoped for a job with a family there, after years of faithful service to the Deveraux. The only maid they were still paying was trying to find a job in a hotel, but no one was hiring at the moment. Most of the country appeared to be unemployed. Alex spent hours every day trying to find a job in a bank, however lowly. The interviews were depressing, and those who were still employed seemed to gloat at how the mighty had fallen. The interviews were all humiliating for Alex, and he got turned down every time, for being vastly overqualified for the meager jobs he was applying for.

In the end, Eleanor was the first to get a job. She had gone to her old school, Miss Benson's School for

Young Ladies, and literally begged for a job. She had been candid about her situation, and they hired her for a very small salary to teach French, drawing, and art. She had been a good student herself, had some talent with watercolors, and her French was fluent. The teacher Eleanor was replacing was having a baby in January, so the timing of her application was fortuitous, and she would be starting after Christmas. She had just turned nineteen and would only be a few years older, if that, than the young women she'd be teaching. Their enrollment had dwindled dramatically in the last two months, since many of the families whose daughters attended the school could no longer pay the tuition. They were happy to get Eleanor's services for a fraction of what they normally paid their teachers. But she was grateful to have found work, and Alex was proud of her. She said she was looking forward to it, and sounded enthusiastic for his sake. She and her mother had had a long talk about their current situation and Louise had reminded her that it was up to them now to bolster their men and give them strength. Charles was not doing well, and looked as though he had aged ten years in two months.

Alex's house sold first, before the Deveraux's. It was bought by a speculator, who wanted to turn it into a hotel. He bought it with all its museum quality contents, so he didn't have to furnish it, and the price he paid Alex was shameful it was so low, but Alex had his back to the wall and needed money from somewhere. It was his only option for now. The house and contents were worth fifty or a hundred or a thousand times what the purchaser paid for them, but Alex had no choice. He took it, and cringed at the thought of the beautiful home his grandfather had built being used as a hotel. His mother's jewelry had brought pathetically little at auction, and he needed some kind of cushion in the bank for him and Eleanor to live on. The house was the only important asset he had now. All of his investments and fortune had been lost in the crash.

The purchaser of the house took possession immediately, and in December, Alex and Eleanor moved in with her parents. It was cheering to be in their familiar home, after losing his, but it was only a matter of time before theirs would sell too.

His brothers, Phillip and Harry, had left San Francisco by then, and gone to live with cousins in Philadelphia who still had their home and had offered to house them. Neither of them had jobs, or anything to live on, and no skills to sell. Alex had gone to the train station to see them off. All three of them had cried, not knowing when they would see each other again. The boys would be forced to grow up now, and find some way to earn their keep. Alex was sad to see them go, but he couldn't house them or support them. They would be under their cousins' roof, but financially on their own, and Alex knew only too well how ill prepared they were, and blamed himself for it. He felt the pain of separating from them as he hugged them tight.

It was a time of losses and goodbyes. Christmas was a grim affair, with reports of more suicides among the people they knew, mostly by older men who couldn't face the loss of their entire world.

Charles had sold the cars, except for the one he drove himself. Eleanor and Louise cooked their Christmas dinner with Wilson's help, and it was surprisingly good. There were no debutante balls or Christmas parties this year. Louise felt sure there would be again one day, but certainly not now. There was nothing to celebrate with the whole country in mourning for their jobs, their savings, their homes, and their way of life.

In January, Alex found a job, as the lowest clerk at a commercial bank. The man who hired him was a particularly unpleasant person, whose eyes gleamed every time he reminded Alex that he was no longer a bank president, but a lowly clerk. Alex came to work every day looking distinguished and elegant, which only enraged his new boss more. The pay was poor, but he was grateful to be employed. He had the money he'd gotten for his house on upper Broadway and his mother's jewelry, Eleanor's salary and his own, and it would have to last them until the economy turned around again and he could get a better job, and there was no telling when that would be. The Depression seemed to worsen day by day, with unemployment constantly rising. It was a dark time for all.

Alex and Eleanor were still living with her parents, in the grandeur of the Deveraux home. Many of the walls were bare now that the paintings had been sold. And all of Louise's jewelry was gone, except the wedding tiara which she kept. She was determined to be cheerful about their losses for her husband's sake. Charles was struggling with the changes that had been forced on them, and the loss of the bank that had existed for seventy years before it went bankrupt. He blamed himself for not being better prepared, and for the investments that hadn't survived the crash. He was as depressed as the economy, despite Louise's efforts to cheer him. He and Alex talked about the economy and where the country was headed every night. Charles said frequently that only another war would save them, which Alex thought was a dismal point of view.

At the end of the month, a purchaser appeared for the Deveraux mansion. A group of investors wanted to buy it to use as a school, and knew this was the ideal time to buy. It was an opportunity that would never come again at an absurdly low price. They walked through the house trying to figure out how they could use it, and it was painful listening to them. But they were the only buyers who had appeared. The price they offered was painfully small, but in the current market it was the best the Deveraux could hope for, and the house had to be sold.

They could no longer afford to maintain it or staff it, and Charles needed to put some money back in their empty coffers to live on, since at fifty-two he couldn't find a job. He discussed it with Louise and accepted their offer the next day. They gave him thirty days to move out, and Louise got busy packing immediately. Charles wanted to send the furniture to auction, but Louise insisted on keeping some of it. They had room for quite a bit in the barn in Tahoe, and furniture and fine antiques like theirs were selling for pennies. She decided to keep as much as they could store in the barn, and sell it later if they needed to.

She and Wilson packed the entire house in a matter of weeks. Charles insisted that they sell some of the silver, that was selling for pennies too, but Louise held on to as much as they needed to turn the servants' house in Tahoe into a decent home for them, with familiar objects around them. She seemed to have a plan as she sent furniture and many paintings to Tahoe, her favorite rugs, the china she loved which wasn't worth selling, as many of their linens as she could take with them. She made several trips, with young men to drive the five hours from the city, and unload the truck they borrowed. And little by little she filled the house they were keeping, the cottage, and the barn with beautiful antiques and treasured objects from their home. There was no market for them now anyway, except at bargain prices, and they were making enough from the house sale not to be desperate for a while. They still had the main property at Lake Tahoe to sell, so Charles let Louise fill the barn with whatever she wanted. They could always sell it later if they needed to, and everyone was selling everything now. The market was flooded and Charles still had some minor investments which had dropped in value dramatically and he was hanging on to, convinced that they might revive again one day.

Their preparations to move to Lake Tahoe put Alex and Eleanor in a quandary about where they would live, once her parents turned the house over to the people who had bought it as a school. They had gotten it at a bargain price, and had been looking for a proper building for years, and the location on the top of Nob Hill would lend dignity to the institution they planned to establish, the Hamilton School. They were planning on opening an exclusive girls' school, which would go from kindergarten through twelfth grade, which was a very progressive idea.

"We have to find an apartment before your parents leave," Alex said to Eleanor one night. "We can't stay here after that." They'd been given thirty days by the new owners to vacate the house, and time was flying.

"Can we afford to move into an apartment?" Eleanor asked him. She liked her new job more than Alex liked his. She liked the girls she was teaching at Miss Benson's, and the school was familiar to her since she had gone there herself. The headmistress was sympathetic with her situation. Her own family had lost their money when she was a young girl, and she knew how painful it was when life changed suddenly. Both their salaries were meager, but they had to live somewhere to keep their jobs, and Alex didn't want to be a burden to Eleanor's father.

"We don't have any choice," Alex said. "We can't afford Pacific Heights. Maybe something downtown." They combed the paper for apartments, and visited several of them that weekend. Many of the buildings were awful, most were filthy, and even dangerous. They found one on the fringes of Chinatown, above a restaurant. The building appeared to be full of families. No one spoke English, and the apartment was cheap, but the living room was big and sunny, the bedroom was cozy and pleasant, and the kitchen and bathroom were clean. They agreed to take it. Eleanor asked her mother for some of the furniture she was planning to send to the barn in Tahoe. Louise told her to take whatever she wanted, and helped her pick enough to furnish the apartment, from an upstairs sitting room they rarely used, and from Eleanor's own bedroom, which would be familiar to her. They picked two sets of china Eleanor thought they'd have room for, all the kitchen equipment she needed and some silver and linens, and some of the paintings that hadn't gone to Tahoe yet. None of it had great value in the current market, but they were handsome pieces, and some truly beautiful.

The following weekend they hired two of their

old hall boys who were still living at the house, but no longer working for them, and Alex and Eleanor installed everything in the apartment. Alex looked around in amazement when they were finished.

"You are a magician," he said, beaming at her. The apartment actually looked elegant, as soon as one entered. The paintings looked lovely, the furniture fit and was covered in rich damasks and velvets. "It looks like your parents' house." He laughed with pleasure at their new home.

"It's a bit smaller," Eleanor said, grinning. She was happy with the result too. She and her mother had chosen well, and they had plenty to choose from, with the contents of the enormous mansion to dispose of rapidly. Even the rugs she brought were the right size for the apartment. She had measured carefully and all of it fit. She had even brought curtains, and had the hall boys hang them, which really finished the room. You would never have known you were in a simple building in Chinatown, looking around the apartment. "You're amazing, and I love you," Alex said, putting his arms around her. "Where do we put a baby, when we have one?" Alex asked her gently, holding her.

"By the time we have one, you'll have a better job and we can get a better apartment," she said cheerfully. He loved her optimism and was grateful for her strength. She and her mother had faced their reversals with courage and good humor, which had made it easier for Alex to live with the humiliation he had to tolerate daily from his boss at the bank, who hated him for what he'd come from, even though he'd lost it all. He resented Alex's determination not to be broken by it, which was in great part due to his wife.

When Charles saw what Louise had done with the servants' house and cottage in Tahoe, he was equally impressed. She had turned both houses into a home for them, with beautiful objects and treasures, the furniture that had made their home so distinguished and welcoming. She had put the best paintings in the house they would occupy, and some lovely ones in the cottage for Alex and Eleanor, and she had managed to cram an immense amount of their furniture and favorite belongings into the barn "for better days," as she put it. Charles could no longer imagine "better days" ever coming. But when they did, Louise was prepared for it and could have furnished a whole house with what they'd saved. Charles agreed that they would get next to nothing for it all if they sold it, so he didn't object to her keeping it. She had furnished a lovely home for them with what she'd used, and filled the barn with the rest.

They were ready to vacate the house on Nob Hill in the thirty days they'd been allotted, which seemed remarkable to Charles, but Louise had done it quietly and steadily. She thought the mountain air, and fishing in the lake in the spring would do him good. It had been snowing there for the past two months, but she had bought used snowshoes and cross-country skis and planned to get him out of the house and moving, once they got up there. It wasn't good for him to sit around, mourning their losses and looking back at a time that would probably never come again for anyone in their lifetime. The days of unlimited grandeur were over. Louise was determined to make the best of it, as she had urged Eleanor to do with Alex. She was planning to drag Charles along with her if she had to. It was easier with Alex, at thirty-three. Charles at fifty-two no longer had a career to occupy him, or any hope for the future. Louise was determined to gently pull him into the present at least, and out of the past they had lost. It was undeniably a sudden change. All their lives they had been rich men, until four months before, and now they were paupers and had almost nothing. It was a brutal change in a very short time, and a huge adjustment.

On her last trip to Tahoe before they moved, Louise took some favorite objects out of the main house, and moved them to their new one, and put some more pieces in the barn. The rest of it they were going to sell with the Tahoe property if the buyer wanted it furnished. There had been no interest in it so far. The property was vast and the land too valuable to sell for very little. Charles wanted to hold out for a good price, for as long as he could. And they weren't as desperate for a fast sale, now that they had sold their home in the city.

Eleanor and Alex moved into their new apartment the weekend before her parents were leaving for Tahoe. Leaving the house was painful for all of them, and the house was too quiet once the young people moved out. Eleanor had looked around the house and the ballroom for the last time, remembering her debut there only a year before, and their wedding in the tented garden four months before. It was a time and a lifestyle that they all sensed would never come again.

The hall boys and maids they were no longer paying but were housed for free, had to move out that weekend. They had all found minor jobs as waitresses in restaurants and maids in hotels, truck drivers, and janitors. They were paid poorly and used none of their skills and experience working in a fine home, but they were grateful to find work, and all moved to boardinghouses now that the Deveraux family was finally leaving. There were countless tearful goodbyes among the staff, and with their employers who had always been kind to them, respectful, and fair.

Wilson was leaving for New York the day before Charles and Louise were moving to Lake Tahoe. She had booked passage in third class on a boat to England, and at the last minute Houghton had decided to join her. They planned to try and find a job together in a home in London, as housekeeper and butler or chauffeur. The British economy was suffering too, but not as severely as in the States, or at least not yet. They came to say goodbye to their employers on Monday morning. Charles and Louise were having breakfast, which Louise had prepared for him. She was getting quite good at it, and had never cooked in her life till then.

"We came to say goodbye," Wilson said, already overcome with emotion, and Houghton looked equally moved. They had both worked for them for almost thirty years, their whole adult lives. It broke their hearts to leave them, but there was no place for them in Lake Tahoe, nor money to pay them, and they both needed jobs. "And we have something to tell you," Wilson said as she choked back tears. "We got married on Friday," she said as she reached out to hug Louise, and Houghton shook hands with Charles.

"You did? Why didn't you tell us? We would have celebrated," Charles said immediately. It hadn't seemed right to them to expect the Deveraux family to celebrate anything, when they were facing such severe losses. The newlywed couple had gone out for a quiet dinner on their own.

"We thought that if we were going to try and find a job together, we might as well be married and be a proper couple." Wilson smiled through her tears and Houghton beamed.

"We really hope you find a good job in London," Charles said. He had written a glowing reference for each of them, and given them each a generous check to thank them for their years of service. The kind of jobs they wanted and were so well trained for still existed in England to some degree.

"Please write to us," Louise said, hugging her

again. They had been through so much together, Louise's marriage to Charles, the birth of her two children, the death of one of them, Eleanor's debut and marriage more recently, and her own debut in Boston when Wilson first came to work for Louise's parents. They had shared an entire lifetime, and now they were all leaving. It was the end of an era.

Charles and Louise stood on the front steps and waved to them as they drove away in a cab with their valises with all their belongings packed up to take with them.

They walked back into their home after that, for their last day and night there. The house was silent and dark except for the few rooms they were occupying. They were sleeping on an old bed from one of the servants' rooms, and leaving it behind. The rest was gone. The next morning when Charles packed their last bags into his last remaining car, they drove away from Nob Hill, and Louise looked back at the house for an instant, as tears streamed down her cheeks. Charles gently touched her cheek with one hand as he drove.

"We'll be fine," Charles said, not sounding convinced, and Louise wiped the tears from her cheeks.

"Yes, we will," she said firmly, and smiled at her husband. "I know we will." And whatever it took, she was determined to make it the truth. They had lost an entire world, but they had each other and a place to go, which was more than many people had these days. She had packed away all her fancy evening clothes, and Eleanor's wedding dress, and debut dress. They were all in the barn too. An entire life was packed in the barn, waiting for them in Tahoe, as the Deveraux mansion faded from view.

Chapter 7

In the spring of 1930, the Tahoe property, with the exclusion of the small slice Charles kept, which was only twenty acres as compared to the rest, sold in an arrangement that was unexpected and worked well for them.

It was purchased by an English lord, an earl, who had visited Lake Tahoe several years before and had fallen in love with it. He had heard about the sale of the enormous Deveraux property in Tahoe by sheer coincidence from a friend. He had always said that he would buy land there one day, and hoped to retire there, which at forty-seven was still a long way away. He had other property in England, but he wanted to keep the Tahoe property for his old age, and the price was so reasonable for their many thousand acres that he could afford it, and knew it was a rare opportunity he couldn't pass up. He understood what it took to run a property well. As an absentee landowner, he wanted someone he could trust to keep an eye on it for him. He offered Charles a very comfortable annual amount to watch over it, hire gardeners and groundskeepers, keep the houses in good repair, especially since they were never used. Charles managed it exactly as he had when he owned it, but without the army of domestic help which the new owner didn't need since he had no plans to stay there or visit. He simply wanted to own it.

Charles hired two women from the nearest village to come and clean the house every week, and he oversaw the rest himself. The earl asked Charles to buy back two of the boats he had sold, if that was possible. He did, and he kept on one of the boatmen. There were no horses there anymore, so Charles bought one, so he could check out the parts of the property that weren't accessible any other way. Charles still had the pleasure of living there and enjoying the land and the lake, and was paid handsomely to live there and care for the property, by an owner he had never met and never seen and who had no intention of coming over any time soon. Charles sent him a concise, intelligent written report once a month, and their dealings were pleasant. The sale of the property had been at a decent price. The new owner hadn't been unreasonable and hadn't driven a hard bargain, and he was satisfied just knowing that he owned the land and the main house and some outbuildings, and would retire there one day. It was a little eccentric, but the arrangement was tailor made for Charles, who was content now, living in the servants' house, prettily decorated by Louise. The barn bulged with everything else they'd brought with them and didn't use, and Louise still said she was saving it all for better days.

With the sale of the house in the city, and the Tahoe property, Charles had a reasonable amount saved to ensure their future on the scale they were living now, and the amount paid to him by the new owner to oversee the property was a salary they could live on comfortably. They had few expenses living in Tahoe, and no help, other than a cleaning girl from town. Their life had moved into a whole new phase. Louise loved gardening, and pushed Charles to help her with it. He was surprised to find he enjoyed it. Somehow, it still stunned him, but they had survived the reversals which had shattered their world. And as time went on, he invested the relatively small amount he had left, and hung on to his few remaining investments. What he had grew slowly but it was safe. And the Great Depression continued with little relief for many people. Charles and Louise were better off than most.

The years slipped by, with little change in the economy for a decade. It was the longest economic depression the world had ever seen, and a dark time for the country. Their peaceful life in Tahoe spared them from the rigors of people living in shanties and abysmal conditions of poverty in the cities.

Eleanor and Alex came for a weekend from time

to time, and two or three weeks in the summer for their vacations, and stayed in the cottage that her mother had set up for them. They had remained in the same jobs, and Alex had crawled his way up to a medium position at the same bank that had hired him. His unpleasant superior had quit, but by 1939, almost ten years after the crash, Alex was forty-three years old, and not likely to reach the top again, but he was grateful for the job. Unemployment had remained rampant and the economy had stayed at its lowest ebb for ten years. At twenty-nine, Eleanor was still working at Miss Benson's, and was teaching Latin as well as French and art. The school hadn't changed much in the years since she'd been a student there herself, and the concept of a finishing school of sorts for young ladies was somewhat archaic, but the atmosphere was genteel and Eleanor liked her job.

The only great sorrow in her life with Alex was that they hadn't succeeded in having a baby. She had been pregnant five times, and miscarried every time. One had been a stillbirth at eight months, which had been traumatic for her, and a source of immeasurable grief to both of them. Alex had assured her the last two times that he didn't care if they never had children, he loved her deeply and he didn't want her to go through the same agony again, it was just too hard on her. They were almost resigned to their childlessness by then, although it saddened Eleanor more than she admitted, which Alex knew well. Even

Eleanor's mother had tried to convince her to give up. She had a wonderful husband, and a good marriage, sometimes that was enough. Louise was fifty-six by then, and Charles was sixty-two. He was in good health from his outdoor life at the lake, but there was an undeniable sadness about him ever since the crash. The losses they had sustained had demoralized him, despite Louise's constant efforts to engage him and cheer him up. Supervising the property kept him busy enough, but the changes had been too hard on him. It always saddened Eleanor to see it, but there was nothing anyone could do about it. Their old way of life would never be restored. The depression in the economy had gone on for ten years, and his own along with it. They were much better off than many of their old friends who were leading hard lives, had moved away, or had died in the meantime, unable to cope with a changing world.

Alex and Eleanor were still living in the same apartment in Chinatown. The apartment was comfortable and bright and beautifully furnished with their old things. They had come to like Chinatown, and the rent was ridiculously cheap. Neither of them made big salaries and it was easy for them. Without children, they had no need for a bigger place.

Her parents loved it when Alex and Eleanor came to visit. Louise loved seeing her daughter, and Charles enjoyed male company with Alex. They went fishing together, and drove the boats on the lake. They came up every few months. Charles and Louise hadn't been back to the city in ten years. He said he wasn't interested, and Louise knew it would be too painful for him to visit his lost world as an outsider. He had no desire to see the few old friends who were left, most of whom were depressed. Most of his generation had not fared well, those who were even alive. Alex hadn't seen his brothers either since they left San Francisco, which he regretted, but he had no opportunity or desire to travel East, and his brothers had no intention of coming West again, even to see their older brother. They had drifted too far apart by then, and felt disconnected, although they stayed in touch by writing to each other. Both of Alex's brothers had married, and had children whom Alex had never met. Phillip was in charge of a stable of racehorses in Kentucky, and Harry had married a girl with some money in North Carolina, and was leading the life of a Southern gentleman, with a wife who was willing to indulge him. She had inherited a successful textile mill from her father. Alex's younger brothers had lost their connection to each other as well, and only saw each other once every few years. Alex was part of a lost life to them. The Depression had not only destroyed fortunes, but families as well. Alex had no idea when he'd see them again, if ever, and it didn't seem likely. He hadn't traveled anywhere in ten years since the crash, and their honeymoon in Italy. He couldn't afford to. He was careful with the money he had left, invested it wisely, and they lived on their meager salaries and had no extravagant needs. Considering how they had both grown up, they had limited themselves severely for the past ten years, but weren't unhappy. When they needed a change of scene, they went to Tahoe to see her parents. Being in the outdoors for a short time always cheered them.

Several times when they'd been there, Eleanor had tried to convince her mother to empty the barn and sell what was there. They were never going to furnish a large home again, and she and Alex didn't need it. It seemed silly to hang on to their old furniture and paintings, and there was so much of it. Eleanor wondered if they might fetch better prices at auction now, ten years later, but Louise always insisted she was saving it all "for better days," which Eleanor doubted would ever come again, and surely not to the degree they knew before.

When they came up to the lake for a weekend in September, Alex and Charles had much to talk about. War had just been declared in Europe, and as disturbing as it was, Charles believed, as he had for years, that factories brought back into service for products needed to supply a war would create jobs and help the world and national economy and positively affect the stock market along with it. The increased productivity would eventually boost the economy and reduce unemployment.

They discussed the likelihood of the United States getting into the war, which Charles thought was unlikely, but Alex wasn't so sure. They both enjoyed talking about it, and each other's company.

Despite the talk of war between the two men, they enjoyed other more pleasant conversations, and beautiful weather. Alex and Eleanor managed some private romantic moments in the cottage when her parents were busy. The romance hadn't gone out of their marriage in ten years. They loved each other as passionately as ever. They had passed the honeymoon phase, particularly with all that had happened to them, but they shared a deep love, which nourished both of them. They were always in good spirits when they went home to the city. It reminded Eleanor of the days when they had their own train when she was younger. It was strange sometimes to think of the extreme luxury she had grown up in, and now they lived in a tiny apartment in Chinatown, and were dependent on their jobs. The old days seemed light-years away now to both of them.

They were buying groceries in one of the Chinese markets several weeks later, with all the pungent smells of Chinese spices, and ducks hanging by their feet above them, when Alex saw Eleanor go pale, and look suddenly ill. She seemed as though she was about to faint.

"Are you all right?" He was instantly worried and she recovered quickly and said she was fine. "What happened?"

"I don't know, I looked up and saw all those dead ducks dangling above me and it made me feel sick."

"You're pregnant," he pronounced immediately.

"No, I'm not, don't be silly."

"Yes, you are, it was the weekend in Tahoe," he said with a mischievous look and she laughed. "I don't know why, but I had a feeling you'd get pregnant."

"Why?" He had an uncanny sense of things sometimes, and even though he was in his forties now, there was still something boyish about him, and he was very handsome.

"It was a full moon, and I'm madly in love with you," he said as they walked back to the apartment.

But it happened again a few days later, when she poured his morning coffee before they left for work, and he could see that she felt ill from the smell.

"You are pregnant, I know it," he insisted. "Go to the doctor."

"I'm not pregnant." She didn't want to believe she was and get her hopes up again for nothing. She had given up, or wanted to believe she had. It was just too disappointing when it didn't work out.

"How do you know you're not?"

"I just know," she said quietly, refusing to believe it and have their hopes dashed again.

But he found her asleep a few days later when he came home from work. There were a stack of papers to correct next to her on the bed, and it was another sign. When she was first pregnant, she always slept a lot. After five pregnancies, he knew all the signs. He didn't press her about it for another week or two, until she rushed away from the breakfast table and threw up. He was waiting outside the bathroom with a stern expression when she came out.

"Will you go to the doctor or do I have to drag you?"

"Let me think about that and I'll get back to you," she said with a weak grin, but she knew he was right. She just didn't want to start the whole process again, of hoping, dreaming, and having her heart broken again halfway through the pregnancy. She'd rather pretend it wasn't happening, and see where it went.

He kissed her when he left for work, and gave her the look he always did when she was pregnant, full of unspoken dreams they didn't even dare voice anymore. She didn't want to disappoint him again either.

For the next several weeks, he didn't say anything, and she seemed to feel fine, although she slept more than usual. He could tell that her breasts were fuller than they had been, and it was almost Thanksgiving when he could feel the roundness of her belly as they lay in bed, and she still hadn't been to the doctor yet. He couldn't ignore it anymore, even though she wanted to.

"Are we just going to pretend it isn't happening this time, or are you going to go to the doctor before you give birth here and I have to deliver the baby while you claim you're not pregnant?" She smiled at him and then sighed.

"I just don't want to get our hopes up again, and then have everything go wrong." He nodded, and understood it, since the last one had been heart-breaking. They had come so close, and had been so sure it would be fine that time, and then the baby strangled on the cord a month before the due date. It had been devastating for both of them, and the baby had looked so beautiful and perfect when he was born. The memory of it was still too vivid for her, and it had been almost two years since it happened.

"I know this sounds crazy, given our history, but I have a weird feeling that everything will be fine this time," Alex said quietly.

She didn't answer him for a long time, and then she nodded.

"I don't know why, but so do I." She hadn't felt that way before, except the last time, and then the baby had stopped moving, and she knew. "What if we wait awhile? The doctor won't do anything anyway. I feel fine."

"You look fine to me too," he said gently cupping her suddenly fuller breasts, and she laughed. "But I'd feel better if you see the doctor, just to make sure everything is okay," he said, serious again, she rolled over and thought about it and then nodded.

She went a few days later, and the pregnancy was confirmed. She was two months pregnant, and the baby was due in June.

"You were right," she told him that night. "It must

have happened in Tahoe. And everything's fine," she reassured him.

They told her parents when they went to Tahoe for Thanksgiving, and they were cautiously enthusiastic. She hated to get their hopes up too, but it was inevitable. A baby was such a sign of hope, for all of them.

Despite the good news, Alex and her father discussed the war for most of the time they were there. The economy had experienced a marked upswing, just as Charles had predicted. The Depression was finally coming to an end with increased production of material goods for the war in Europe.

By Christmas, she was three and a half months pregnant, and in January, she felt it move for the first time. There had been no problems, and even the timing was perfect. With the baby due in June, she would have the summer off, and could go back to her job at the school in September.

The heartbeat was clear and strong, and in March she was six months pregnant, and had a full round belly.

The war had taken off in a major way by then, and almost all the countries in Europe were involved. Hitler was trying to take over the world, and the American public was being told that the United States would not enter the war and had no role in it. But increased production was helping the economy.

Eleanor was less and less interested in the war as

her baby grew inside her. They went to Tahoe for the last time in April. She was seven months pregnant, and the doctor didn't want her traveling after that, especially with her history. Her mother asked if they were going to move, and Eleanor said they had no need to. Their bedroom was big enough to have a crib in it, and she didn't want to make any dramatic changes for a baby that might never arrive. But this one seemed normal and strong. It kicked constantly, and was bigger than the last one. Alex laughed when he saw her belly move, and he could feel the kicks when he lay next to her at night. The constant movement and pounding reassured them both that this one was healthy. She'd had no problems with the pregnancy, and then suddenly on a sunny Saturday in mid-May, everything stopped as it had before. Alex came back from doing some errands and found Eleanor sobbing in the kitchen.

"What happened? What's wrong?"

"It's not moving." She cried and held her arms out to him, and he held her and cried too.

"Let's go to the hospital," he said quietly. "I'll call the doctor. Get your things." He called and the doctor promised to meet them at Children's Hospital immediately. Eleanor was dreading the same result as before, and a heartbreak for them. It was all Eleanor could think about. She was silent in the cab on the way to the hospital, crying quietly, as Alex kept an arm around her and held her close. "Whatever happens, we can get through this," he told her quietly, trying to will his strength into her, to endure another tragedy, if it happened. They were braced for the worst as they walked through the emergency room, and took the elevator up to the maternity floor, which they were all too familiar with, but never with a happy result. The doctor was already there. He looked serious as they walked into an exam room, and Eleanor lay down on the exam table, clutching Alex's hand. His eyes were bright with unshed tears, but he locked his eyes with his wife's, and tried to think positively about the baby they both wanted so much.

"How long's it been since you felt anything?" the doctor asked, as he adjusted his stethoscope to listen for a heartbeat he hoped would be there, and feared might not be, again.

"I don't know, about two hours. I had a big breakfast, and then everything kind of stopped. I poked it a little but nothing happened." The doctor nodded with a concerned expression, put the stethoscope in his ears, and placed the round listening device on the other end where he thought he'd hear the heartbeat if there was one. And as he pressed down on Eleanor's hugely round belly, the baby kicked so hard that all three of them could see it, and it almost knocked the listening device out of the doctor's hand. The heartbeat was strong, and the baby continued to kick vehemently for several minutes as all three of them laughed.

"Well, I don't think there's any doubt about that."

The doctor smiled at both of them. "I think the baby may have been asleep. Your big breakfast may have knocked him or her out." The baby hadn't stopped kicking for five minutes and seemed furious, and various pointed appendages were sticking out almost like a cartoon. "I think he or she may be running out of room too, we have a nice big baby in there." That worried Eleanor a little, she was aware of it too. It was considerably bigger than the last one, but she didn't care what she had to go through as long as it was healthy and alive when it was born. She swung her legs off the table feeling sheepish, and the doctor reassured them that given what had happened last time, they were right to come in and check if they had any concerns, and he didn't mind at all. He lived nearby.

"I'm sorry," Eleanor said to Alex in the cab on the way home. "I feel stupid. But it wasn't moving at all."

"It is now." He smiled at her. "I'd say he or she is seriously pissed. That's no little milquetoast you have in there." They laughed about it, but from that day on, it was as though the baby had declared war on her. It pushed and shoved, pounded and kicked. She could feel elbows and legs, feet and knees, it pressed down against her pelvis with its head. It was as though it was trying to make room in a space it had outgrown, and it seemed to be growing noticeably every day.

She could hardly finish the last month of school, but managed to, and by the time her due date came,

Eleanor was exhausted. She'd been taking a beating for the last month, her belly looked like she was having twins, but the doctor insisted she wasn't, it was just a very big baby, and an exceptionally active one. The constant movement and kicking set off contractions that the doctor said weren't serious ones, but they were uncomfortable. Several times, Eleanor thought she was in labor, but then it stopped instead of continuing. She was two weeks late and miserable by the third week of June. When Eleanor saw the doctor, he said they might have to perform a Caesarean section if the baby didn't come on its own in the next week or two. They couldn't let it go any longer than that, and the baby was just getting too big. The prospect of a Caesarean frightened Eleanor. She looked worn out when Alex came home from work. He felt sorry for her, she looked miserable and she could hardly sleep at night. The baby was kicking and pounding her night and day, and the constant mild contractions she had now made it all seem worse. They were painful but never led to active labor.

"What did the doctor say?"

"That it's a baby elephant, and I'm going to be pregnant for two years." He laughed. Everything was ready in their bedroom, all the little shirts and nightgowns, the diapers and sweaters, and little caps. And her hospital bag had been packed for weeks and was waiting at the front door. All they needed was for her to go into labor now. But the doctor had confirmed again that afternoon that nothing was happening yet. Her mother called her constantly. She wanted to be there for her, but didn't want to leave Charles alone, and Eleanor wanted to be on her own with Alex, in case it all went wrong again.

"He said the baby is getting too big, and I may have to have a Caesarean section if it gets much bigger," she told Alex. He was worried about it too. The baby looked huge, and he couldn't imagine how someone as slim and narrow as Eleanor could give birth to it, and surely not easily.

"Maybe that's a good idea," he said, concerned, and lay down on their bed next to her. They both wanted it to be over now and for the baby to be delivered safely. She looked like a mountain lying beside him and he could see the baby kick frantically under her dress. "Settle down in there," he spoke to her belly, and it stopped for a minute and then started again, and Eleanor laughed.

"I think the baby heard you."

"Come out soon," he said then, "we're tired of waiting for you." It stopped and started again, and then Eleanor had a contraction that was stronger than the others had been. The doctor had said that the internal exam that afternoon might get things started, but this was the first real pain she'd had. "Anything happening?" he asked Eleanor hopefully, and she shook her head.

"Probably not." She went to take a shower, her back was hurting from the weight of the baby. She let the hot water pelt down on her belly and her back and it felt great. She stayed in the shower for a long time, and didn't notice the water pouring down her legs in the shower, until she got out, and it continued, and she was standing in a pool of water with a look of surprise, when Alex walked in to check on her.

"You okay?"

She nodded, looking startled. "I think my water just broke." The pool of water at her feet continued to spread, and she wrapped herself in a towel, and got back in the shower until it stopped, and she had several big contractions then, and could feel the weight of the baby bearing down with considerable force. "Something may be happening." She looked at him with a broad smile. The moment had finally come. They were about to be parents, after ten and a half years of marriage. As she thought about it, she had a hard contraction, and had to sit down, and breathe through the pain. "I think I'll lie down for a few minutes," she said, and he looked panicked.

"No, no. Not here. We're going to the hospital. You're having a baby, and I am not going to deliver it."

"Don't be silly. First babies take a long time."

"Great. This is your sixth. And even if miscarriages don't count, the last one does. Let's get you dressed and to the hospital." She had two big pains then, and he brought her clothes in to her, and she was laughing at him.

"I promise, I won't have it here."

"I don't believe you," he said as she tried awkwardly to dress and the pains continued. She could hardly walk down the stairs by the time they left, with her bag in hand, and Alex hailed a cab and gave the driver the address of the hospital. They had called the doctor before they left the apartment, and he promised to meet them there.

By the time they got to the hospital, labor had begun in earnest. A nurse and the doctor helped Eleanor onto the exam table, and when the doctor checked her, they told her she was almost there.

"This baby is in a hurry to meet you." He smiled as Eleanor groaned with another pain. "Would you like your husband to leave now?" he asked her.

"No!" Eleanor said through clenched teeth. "No . . . I want him to stay." It was unusual but after their last bad experience, the doctor was willing to do what they preferred.

"I'll stay," Alex said quietly and took his wife's hand in his. "We're almost there." Mother Nature and the baby took over then. It was one long push and howl from Eleanor as she clutched Alex's hand, and the baby pushed its way into the world, crying loudly as it came out, and both parents watched in wonder as their baby girl was born. She almost did it herself, with very little help from Eleanor. It was all over ten minutes after they got to the hospital, and the baby weighed nine pounds, ten ounces. The moment she heard their voices, she stopped crying. She was beautiful and looked just like Eleanor, but with fair hair. She had perfect features and a little rosebud mouth. She looked at her parents with interest as they stared at her in wonder, the doctor cut the cord, and then the baby closed her eyes and went to sleep, as Alex kissed his wife.

"You are amazing and I love you." It occurred to him that if he hadn't rushed her out the door, he would have had to deliver the baby himself. It had all happened so fast, and despite the baby's size, she had been born with ease.

A nurse took her away then to clean her and wrap her in a blanket, and Alex kissed Eleanor again as she smiled at him, and cried tears of joy. They had finally done it. They had a little girl.

They called her parents a few minutes later, and they were immensely relieved that everything had gone well. Eleanor promised to bring her to Tahoe to meet them soon. And by then the baby was nursing peacefully at her mother's breast.

"What's her name?" the doctor asked after checking Eleanor again. Everything was fine, and it had been an easy birth.

"Camille," Eleanor said softly with a glance at Alex and he nodded. They both liked the name.

"She's a beautiful little girl," the doctor said, "congratulations!" They had earned it. It had taken ten years, but their dearest wish had finally come true. They had so much to look forward to. As Eleanor held the baby, Alex kissed his wife, and she was the happiest woman on earth as she smiled at him. He had given her the greatest gift of her life. Camille was their long awaited miracle child, and had been well worth the wait.

Chapter 8

After a relatively easy first year as parents, they celebrated Camille's first birthday over a weekend in Tahoe with Eleanor's parents, who adored her. She had added immeasurable joy to their lives too. Charles had cheered up noticeably, and was far more optimistic than he had been for years. Louise had bought a cake and put two candles in it, one for her age and one to grow on, and showed her how to blow them out.

Camille was an easy, happy baby. Eleanor took her to a woman she knew who babysat three children in her home for working parents. She had previously been a teacher at Miss Benson's until she had a baby of her own. Eleanor took Camille there every day and picked her up after school. Camille fit right into their life. She slept in her crib in their bedroom. They ate their meals with her. Eleanor had stopped nursing her at six months. They were with her constantly when they weren't working. She was either in her mother's arms or her father's. She was the light of their life, and the center of their universe. She was their dream come true at last.

She loved visiting with her grandparents in Tahoe, and playing outside with them. Charles loved tossing her in the air, and having fun with her. She added a whole new dimension to their lives, and had given them all hope, that if you believed in something long enough, it finally happened and turned out right. In another lifetime, she would have been whisked away by nannies, and been kept in a nursery on an upper floor of the house, and brought to them once a day for a few minutes, all dressed up. Instead, she was part of everything her parents did, and spent time with her grandparents frequently too. Her upbringing was very different than her parents' had been, with hands-on parents who took care of her themselves.

Meanwhile, the war in Europe was continuing, as the European Allies tried to stop Hitler from taking over Europe, and couldn't. The Germans had occupied France a few days before Camille was born, and on her first birthday in June of 1941, most of Europe was in Hitler's clutches. He was trying to conquer and occupy England, but hadn't succeeded so far. By the summer of 1941, there had been considerable loss of life on both sides. America was still sitting out the war, observing keenly, but not involved.

Eleanor would have loved to get pregnant again

by then, but it hadn't happened. She was thirty-one years old. She wondered sometimes if Camille would be their only child. She wanted more, but Camille was so adorable that if they never had another baby, she knew she could be satisfied with just one. Camille was so perfect and such a sweet little girl.

They were in Tahoe for the weekend, the first weekend in December. Eleanor was chatting with her mother on Sunday morning, and her father had the radio on, when they heard a news bulletin come on. Pearl Harbor in Hawaii had just been attacked and bombed by Japanese forces. It had just happened. The news was chaotic and confused, and Eleanor and her parents were staring at each other, as the baby chortled happily, and Alex came in from outside. He had come from the cottage and saw on their faces that something serious had occurred. They were listening intently to the radio, and he heard the same news reports they did. He and Charles exchanged a long glance and then Alex looked at his wife. It had been a surprise attack and a brutal one, and would force America's hand to join the Allied forces in the war. When the final reports came in, three hundred and fifty Japanese planes had executed the attack not only on Pearl Harbor, but five other air stations as well. Two thousand four hundred and three people had been killed, one thousand one hundred and seventy-eight injured, three ships had been destroyed, sixteen damaged, and a hundred and fifty-nine aircraft damaged.

On December 8, the following day, President Franklin Roosevelt asked Congress for a declaration of war on Japan. The U.S. Congress declared war on Japan and the president signed the resolution. America was finally in the war at last, while Europe had been fighting for more than two years by then.

They left Tahoe early because the question in everyone's mind was if the Japanese were going to attack the mainland next, the West Coast specifically. And Alex wanted to get back to the city, although Charles had suggested they stay in Tahoe with them, but Alex and Eleanor both had to work the next day.

Alex was quiet on the drive home, and said very little when they got back to the apartment. He waited until Eleanor had put the baby to bed. He was waiting for her at the kitchen table, and she had a bad feeling from the look on his face. She had not seen him look quite that serious since the news of Black Tuesday had reached them in Italy on their honeymoon. He didn't look panicked this time, or scared. But he was certain of what he wanted to do, and that it was the right thing.

"I'm going to enlist," he said quietly, with a look of determination.

"That's ridiculous. You're forty-five years old. You don't have to. And you already served in one war. Why do you need to go this time?" Eleanor looked frightened the moment he said it, as he knew she would.

"They won't put me in the front lines. You're right,

I'm too old," he said with a small, wintry smile. "But I'm an officer. I can volunteer. They can put me in a finance office somewhere, and relieve someone else for active duty. I wouldn't feel right just staying at home." He spoke calmly and quietly, sure of what he was doing.

"What about us? What are we supposed to do now?"

"What do you want to do? Do you want to stay with your parents in Tahoe?" She shook her head.

"No, I'd feel trapped there with just the two of them." They led a quiet life, and despite his delight over the baby, her father was still depressed. He had never been quite the same after they lost everything. Her mother worked hard to buoy his spirits and distract him, but sometimes even she couldn't. He still had some very dark moments remembering the past and their enormous losses. And no longer working at a relatively young age hadn't been good for him. Eleanor knew she needed her own life away from them, or she'd wind up depressed too. Ten years of a bad economy had taken a toll on everyone. "I don't want to give up my job, I want to stay in the city. I'd rather wait for you here. But I don't understand why you feel you have to go. I don't think they'll draft men your age."

"They might, I'm not as over the hill as you seem to think." He looked faintly insulted, but they both had bigger things to think about, like their daughter, and their future, and the risks for him.

"What if something happens to you? What happens to us then?" Eleanor asked with tears in her eyes.

"Nothing will happen to me," he said confidently. "I was in the infantry last time, but they're not going to do that with guys my age. I can serve some useful purpose in the military in an office, and support my country, more so than working a menial job at the bank every day. I'm just passing time there. I need to do this, Eleanor. It's something a man has to do. We're at war, and I want to defend my country. In a way, I'll be protecting you and Camille, and everything we believe in and this country stands for." He sounded so sure about it, and in a way she envied him the ability to act on his beliefs. She couldn't do that. She had a child to take care of. She couldn't just march off to war and leave him with an eighteen-month-old baby. But he could, and would be considered a hero for it. In some ways, it didn't seem fair, not that she wanted to go to war or enlist. And in his shoes, at his age, she wouldn't have gone off to war, and left a wife and baby at home, so he could be a hero. And she was almost sure that he probably could have avoided the army if he wanted to, but he didn't. She could see that he couldn't wait to sign up. In some ways, it seemed selfish to her. The war was the most exciting thing that had happened to him in years and she could see it. His eyes were alive and he was glowing.

"When do you want to enlist?" she asked him in a dead voice, trying to imagine what her life would be like once he left. It would be complicated and lonely, alone with Camille, with no one to help her, worrying about his safety, praying he was alive, and waiting for him to come home. And what if they didn't assign him to an office and sent him to the front instead? It sounded like a grim future to her. He had had the whole day to think about it, and she was sure he had a plan. But she didn't expect the answer he gave her.

"I'm going to sign up tomorrow," he said quietly. She was shocked.

"Why so soon?" It was almost as though he had been waiting for this, some way out of his dreary job with no future, and now his chance had come.

"I don't want to wait. They need men to enlist now, right away. I want to be one of them. And it sets a good example to others."

"Even though you know our lives will be ruined forever if something happens to you? Camille deserves to know her father and grow up with you," Eleanor said passionately. She was angry at him for wanting to enlist, but she could already tell it was an argument she wouldn't win. His manhood and love of country had kicked in, and he wanted to serve his country and help win the war against the Japanese. The president had called it a day of infamy, and Eleanor didn't deny that, but she didn't want to sacrifice her husband to win the war. She and Camille needed him more than they did.

They went to bed that night and didn't speak to each other. They were both thinking about what he wanted to do. She didn't think she could dissuade him. His sense of duty was too strong for him to pay any attention to what she said. And his mind and heart were set on going.

She cried after he fell asleep that night. She was up and dressed when he got up in the morning. She had hardly slept all night, worried about him. They had waited so long for the baby they had wanted so badly. And now he was going to risk everything and go to war. She didn't want to lose him.

Alex kissed her before he left for the office, with the same determined look as the night before. When he got home that night, he sat down at the kitchen table and looked at her seriously. "I volunteered today." She should have expected it, but she felt as though he had punched her in the stomach. She wanted to feel proud of him, but she didn't, just angry at his deserting her and Camille.

"So you did it." She tried not to look as shocked as she felt. "When do you leave?"

"I report to Fort Ord in Monterey in three weeks for boot camp for six weeks, and an officers' training class after that." They were letting him stay home for Christmas.

"And then what?"

"I don't know yet. They'll probably send me to

Washington, or some other benign place, while someone else gets freed up to go to war."

"And if they send you to a combat zone?"

"They won't," he said confidently. "That would be ridiculous at my age." So was enlisting, in her opinion, but there was no one else to reason with him, and he had already signed up anyway, and who knew how long the war would last. He could be gone for years. And as an officer, she wasn't as sure as he was that they wouldn't send him into combat. What if they did? There was no telling now what could happen.

The three weeks before Alex had to report to Fort Ord felt surreal to Eleanor. He was still part of their everyday life, but in some ways he wasn't. He was so preoccupied with everything he needed to do, that in Alex's mind he was already gone. And then there were tender nights when he made love to her, and it had the bittersweet flavor of farewell, and the terror of the unknown and what lay ahead, for both of them.

Christmas at the lake was somber, with news of the war, and knowing he was leaving. They spent their last weekend together at Lake Tahoe with her parents. Alex and Charles went for a long walk, where they went over details of Alex's investments, in case something happened to him. They had lived very frugally for the last ten years, and he had saved as much as he could of the money he had gotten for his parents' house. It was infinitely less than it should have been, but there was still quite a bit left. He had invested it very conservatively, and he had a life insurance policy to benefit his wife and daughter. It was for a small amount, but they would need it all if anything happened.

"None of this will be necessary," he reassured his father-in-law, "they won't send me to the front anywhere, but crazy things happen in wartime. Eleanor is upset with me for enlisting."

"There are some things a man has to do," Charles said sympathetically. "That's hard for a woman to understand. I was forty-one in '17 when we entered the last war. I volunteered and they kept me at a desk job in the Presidio, but I couldn't not serve. We'll get Eleanor to come up to the lake and stay with us on weekends, as often as she can. She can always live with us here if she wants to. We'd love to have them." He smiled at his son-in-law, proud of him for what he was doing.

It was a tearful moment when they said goodbye to him at the end of the weekend. Louise gave him a warm hug and told him to be careful and promised they would take care of his girls.

"I'm only going to Monterey, Mother Deveraux." He smiled at her. He was more formal with her out of respect, and called Charles by his first name. "I won't be far away." She wiped her eyes and hugged him again.

Alex had already left the bank by then, and his colleagues had shaken his hand and wished him

well. Several of the younger men had already enlisted. One of them would be going to Fort Ord when
he was. On their last night together, Eleanor never
slept. She lay watching him all night, praying nothing bad would happen to him. He was going to have
six weeks of boot camp and four of officers' combat
training which had just been reduced from twelve
after Pearl Harbor, which Alex said was just routine.
He said it was only a refresher course to remind him
how to shoot a gun. It had been twenty-three years
since he had been in the Great War. In some ways, it
made him feel young again to be re-entering the military, with men half his age.

Eleanor saw him off at the train station the next
morning. It was the first of January, a cold wintry
day, and she had Camille in her arms. She wanted to
be with him until the last minute.

"Take care of yourself," he said as he kissed her
and Camille patted his face and squealed with glee.

"Dada," she said over and over again as Alex and
Eleanor kissed.

"I'll call you when I can," he promised, but didn't
know when that would be, or how soon. He knew
she would be allowed to see him in four weeks, and
again when he finished the total ten weeks of training. She couldn't wait to visit him at the end of January.

The platform was crowded with young men and a
few his age, parents and girlfriends and children

waving to their fathers. They kissed one last time, and Eleanor stood and waved with Camille in her arms until the train was fully out of the station, and then she went home to their apartment in Chinatown, to begin her life without him. They hadn't been apart for a day in the twelve years of their marriage, and Eleanor couldn't imagine what it would be like now.

She put Camille to bed that night, and sat in the living room feeling dazed, and thinking about him.

Four weeks later, Eleanor drove to Monterey, and left Camille with a neighbor she trusted. The family had moved in around the time Camille was born and had a baby the same age.

It took her four hours to get to Monterey from San Francisco, she left her car in the visitors' parking area at Fort Ord, and went to the visitors' center to meet her husband. She almost didn't recognize him. He had lost weight, he looked trimmer and his shoulders were broader, his face was thin, his head was nearly shaved, he looked strong and fit and young, and his eyes were alive when he hugged her, and he was delighted to see her. He said the training was going well, although most of it was unnecessary, but he was in the best shape he'd been in, in years.

They had coffee and sat and talked, as she watched families around them visiting, some with small children. They went for a walk in the sea air, as the seagulls flew overhead. They held hands as they had when they were courting, and two hours later, it was over. He kissed her again. He was coming home for a weekend in six weeks, at the end of his training. She'd had very little to tell him except that she missed him. Her life was the same routine it had been since Camille was born. She left her with the babysitter, worked at the school all day, picked up her daughter, fed her, bathed her, put her to bed, and thought about her husband. It was lonely without him, but she didn't say so. She tried to look happy and strong as she waved goodbye to him, and watched him disappear with the other officers in training, back to their barracks.

Then she drove back to San Francisco. She was exhausted when she got home, after eight hours of driving back and forth to Monterey. But she was glad that she had seen him. He looked handsome in his uniform.

But their lives seemed miles apart now. He was embarking on a whole new adventure, wherever it might lead him, and her job was to keep the home fires burning and take care of their daughter. When the training course was over, she hoped he would be assigned to San Francisco, as he thought he probably would in the Presidio, the army base in the city. At least then she could see more of him.

She went to bed that night and lay awake for hours, thinking about him, wishing that the Japanese hadn't bombed Pearl Harbor and things were different.

At the end of Alex's training course in March he got a three-day leave to come to San Francisco. She was waiting for him at the apartment when he arrived. They had allowed her to take the afternoon off from school, and she had left Camille with the neighbor again.

They dove into bed almost as soon as he came through the door, and their lovemaking was filled with the pent-up passion of two months without him, intense loneliness on her side, and extreme physical exertion and challenges on his. He looked and seemed ten years younger than when he left.

Alex had written to tell his brothers when he enlisted. Harry had asthma and a heart murmur and had been rejected. And Phillip had been drafted and assigned to a desk job in Washington, D.C., through his wife's connections. Both of them had been shocked to learn that Alex had enlisted at his age, but said they admired him for it.

Alex took Eleanor out to dinner that night at one of the Chinese restaurants in the neighborhood. And afterward, they picked Camille up at the neighbor's. Alex carried her sound asleep and deposited her gently in her crib in their bedroom. They closed the door quietly and made love again on the living room couch. They couldn't get enough of each other.

They spent Saturday as a family, and took Camille to the park. Eleanor cooked dinner, and after Alex gave Camille her bath, they put her to bed, and sat talking in the living room. He had to be back in Fort Ord on Sunday night, and they were both luxuriating in the pleasures of a quiet evening at home in their cozy apartment. And as they talked, Eleanor suddenly saw something in his eyes that she hadn't noticed before. She didn't know what it was, but she sensed instantly that he was hiding something from her.

"What are you not telling me?" she asked as her eyes met his, and he turned away and lit a cigarette. He had never smoked before, that was new since his training course. He had picked it up from the other men when they had nothing to do. He didn't want to lie to her now, but he was buying time. And as she watched him, she knew she was right. "Is something wrong?" Suddenly she was afraid there might be another woman. She didn't know what, but there was something. And as he turned back to her, she was sure of it.

"We got our orders on Thursday," he said quietly.

"Orders for what? Where they're sending you now?" He nodded. "Are you coming back to San Francisco?" She was suddenly afraid that they might send him East to Washington, where she couldn't see him. It would be much more complicated, and expensive to visit him there, and they only had her salary now, and their savings.

He shook his head in answer. There was no easy way to tell her. Other officers he had trained with were having to deliver the same news he was, and he wasn't sure how to do it. "I'm shipping out," he said so softly she could hardly hear him as she stared at him.

"What do you mean?" She could hear her heart beating. It was louder than his words.

"I'm being sent overseas, I can't say where. To the Pacific. It's not the way it was last time, in the last war. They're sending officers my age into combat zones. I won't be on the ground, in the heart of the action, we'll be in the command posts, and on ships. It turns out that's what the officers' training was for."

"You lied to me," she shouted at him, and swung at him. He caught her fist just before it hit him. "You said they wouldn't send you into combat or overseas. Why did you have to enlist in this stupid war!" She was sobbing, as he pulled her close to him and held her.

"They might have drafted me anyway before it's over. They need everyone they can get. With all of Europe involved, and now the Pacific, the military needs us." She cried for a long time and then looked up at him.

"When are you leaving?"

"This week. In a few days. They don't tell us exactly when, but very soon. This is my last leave before we ship out," he said, and she had never been as frightened in her life. What if he didn't come back? If she never saw him again. The thought of it was too much to bear. She had been spending her last hours with him before he went to war, and she didn't know it.

"Why didn't you tell me sooner, when you got here?"

"I didn't want to spoil our last few days together." She nodded, but his visit had taken on a whole new flavor, an entirely different mood. She could feel the minutes ticking away, like sand in an hourglass, and in less than twenty-four hours he would leave her, maybe forever.

They sat and talked for a long time, about what to do now. He thought she should move to Lake Tahoe to be with her parents, but she still didn't want to. There would be other women like her, with husbands who had gone to war. She didn't want to give up her job and live like a child with her mother and father. He didn't argue with her, but he worried about her in San Francisco. No one knew if the Japanese would be bold enough to attack the West Coast, and he didn't want her in the city if they did, but she was adamant about it. They went to bed hours later, and lay holding each other in the moonlight, while Camille slept in her crib.

They made love as discreetly as they could without waking her, and lay awake after that, and finally fell asleep when the sun came up. Eleanor couldn't stop thinking that it might be their last night together, forever, or certainly for a long time. Alex had no idea for how long he would be stationed in the Pacific.

Eleanor got up when Camille woke, and Alex stayed in bed a little longer. And then they had breakfast together, and spent the day savoring every moment they had, hugging and kissing each other and playing with their daughter, and at four o'clock Eleanor took him to the train station, with Camille in her arms. There were no words left by then. They had said them all. Tears rolled down their cheeks as they said goodbye, with Camille standing next to them, holding her mother's skirt.

"Take care of yourself . . . please . . ." Eleanor said in a hoarse voice.

"I'll write to you," he whispered.

"I love you," she said, as he grabbed his duffel bag, and hopped on the train. He stood on the steps as they pulled out of the station, and he shouted back to where she stood.

"I love you!" She saw his lips move, but couldn't hear him, and mouthed the same words to him. As Camille waved to her daddy, the train rounded a bend and he disappeared.

Chapter 9

They celebrated Camille's birthday in Tahoe again that year. She was two, and Alex had shipped out to the Pacific three months before. Eleanor had no exact idea where he was. She went to visit her parents at the lake as often as she could. School had just let out for the summer, and she stayed with them until a few days before she had to be back to Miss Benson's to teach in September.

Alex wrote to her whenever he was able to. There would be weeks when she wouldn't hear from him, and then he'd write to her again. He gave her no details about where he was and what they were doing, but he said that he was fine, and he missed her and Camille. He had taken a stack of photographs of them with him when he left. And she sent him photographs of Camille every few weeks. By September, she had changed a lot in six months. Eleanor was living from letter to letter, although the time at the lake over the summer had been good for her. And her parents loved having them around.

Her mother spent hours in her garden, and she'd even gotten Charles working in the garden with her. It seemed to give purpose to their life. She had a gardener to help her with the heavy work, and she had created some beautiful effects around their simple house, which really gave her pleasure.

As Charles had predicted ten years before, the war had infused life back into the economy. Factories were operating at maximum capacity, the country was employed again, unemployment was the lowest it had been in a decade. The Great Depression was over at last. It had been the worst in American history.

Eleanor and Camille spent Thanksgiving and Christmas with them. Her father had cut down their Christmas tree himself, and they decorated it together with ornaments Louise had saved from their home when it sold. It brought back memories for all of them to see the same ornaments so many years later, and reminded them of all their traditions before their lives had changed so radically. Charles had just turned sixty-five, and Louise was fifty-nine. They both looked older than they were. Charles had never fully gotten over the losses they had sustained, and the humiliation of having to close the bank and lose their home. And Tahoe belonged to someone else now. He was only a guardian there, an employee, except for the small home they had kept. But seeing Eleanor and their grandchild always cheered them.

They were sad to see them leave three days after Christmas, but Eleanor wanted to spend some time preparing for the term that was starting in January. She enjoyed her work, and the young girls who came to the school with somewhat less lofty backgrounds now. Some of the Old Guard had disappeared, and people with new money were beginning to take their place. The families that sent their daughters there weren't as elite as in Eleanor's day, but Eleanor enjoyed them and the subjects she taught.

She was at her desk, preparing her French classes, and Camille was asleep the night they got home, when the doorbell rang, and a Western Union messenger handed her a telegram. She hadn't heard from Alex in three weeks, but it had happened before and she knew that eventually his letters would catch up with her again. She just had to hope and assume he was alive in the meantime.

The messenger handed her the telegram quickly, and as she opened it, he was already halfway down the stairs. The telegram was from the U.S. War Department. The words in the telegram leapt off the page in capital letters as she closed the door and read them again and again. "Regret to inform you your husband Lieutenant Alexander William Allen wounded December 4, 1942, due to arrive Port of San Francisco approximately January 12 Hospital

Ship USS *Solace*" and it was signed the adjutant general. That was all it said. It didn't state the nature of his injuries or what had happened. All she knew after she read it was that Alex had been wounded, but he was alive and due to arrive in San Francisco in fifteen days, so he was well enough to travel, and thank God he wasn't dead.

Her heart was pounding as she sat down on the couch with the telegram still in her hand and she read it again. His military serial number was listed on the telegram, but there was no one to call, no one to give her the details, except Alex himself in two weeks. But she was grateful he was coming home. He had been gone for nine months. She just hoped his injury wasn't too serious, but maybe serious enough to keep him out of the war once he got home. It was all she could hope for now. She had been aware that there were military transports arriving, and hospital ships, with their wounded who were being sent home, to be tended in the States at military hospitals. And San Francisco was one of the ports they were using on the West Coast.

She read the telegram again the next morning, and called her parents to tell them. The best news was that the telegram hadn't announced something much worse, and if he was coming home by ship, it seemed to indicate that he was well enough to travel. Her parents were concerned, but were encouraged by the fact that he was alive, and his injury wasn't so severe that he couldn't make the journey.

She informed the school when they reopened in January, and by then she had nine more days to wait to see Alex's situation for herself. She didn't know if he would have to report to a military base, would need to convalesce at a military hospital, or if he could come home to the apartment with her and Camille. The days seemed interminable as she waited for the USS *Solace* to reach San Francisco.

She called the Port of San Francisco on January 5 to ask if they had any word of the ship's progress, and they told her to call back in two or three days, they expected to have news by then. They said the *Solace* hadn't reached Hawaii yet, so it would be at least another week before she reached San Francisco, if not longer. They asked if she had someone on the ship, and she said yes, her husband. The voice at the other end was slightly more sympathetic after she said it.

"Most of them will be going to Letterman Hospital in the Presidio, in case you miss him at the dock. Check with them there. It's always chaotic when they come in. You'll have an easier time finding him at the hospital than here." But there was no way she was going to let Alex return to San Francisco wounded and not do everything in her power to meet him at the dock, and accompany him wherever he was going after that, if they let her.

She called every few days to check. They told her there had been storms in Hawaii and finally on the fourteenth, they told her the ship would dock in two days.

"Is it a big ship?" she asked, nervous after what they'd said before, that she might miss him at the dock.

"We have almost six hundred wounded men coming in on her. She's big enough. Normal capacity is four hundred eighteen," the man said. He said the *Solace* might have to wait in the bay for several hours, before they were ready to receive her in the port. "They usually let them dock around seven or eight in the morning. We try to unload the men in daylight." He made the injured men sound like so much cargo.

The last two days were the longest of all since the telegram had arrived seventeen days before with the cryptic message, and so little information for her to go on. She had thought of nothing else since she got the telegram.

The morning of January 16, Eleanor took an early morning bus to the Embarcadero where the ships docked, so she'd have time to find the right one before he got there. There were laborers, construction workers, and dockworkers on the bus with her, and no one questioned what she was doing there. She was the only woman on the bus. She was a young and attractive woman and obviously had a mission of some kind, or maybe a job. The bus made a stop several blocks from the docks, and she got out and began walking at a brisk pace. It was still dark, and she had left Camille with her neighbor the night before, and explained that her husband was being sent home from the war. Her neighbor's brother was an infantryman in Europe, and her husband had a heart defect and was at home.

She reached the port on foot at six in the morning, and saw a huge red cross painted on a white background to indicate where the hospital ship would come in. There were longshoremen standing around, and military personnel. When she asked, they told her where to go. They said they didn't know what time the *Solace* would dock, but it might not be for a while, although they were expecting her that morning. There was a heavy mist and it was damp. She could hear the foghorns in the distance. She took refuge in a doorway, and by eight o'clock, she saw a long string of military ambulances begin to arrive, and park haphazardly near the docks. In another hour, the area was bustling with activity. There were wagons with red crosses on them, a line of buses, more ambulances, military vehicles. And then in the distance, she saw the ship moving slowly through the bay with her precious cargo.

It was ten before she docked, and by then Eleanor had been there for four hours. She was freezing and her clothes were damp from the mist and a light rain, but she didn't care. Before the ship even docked, suddenly there were a swarm of medics and ambulance drivers, doctors, nurses, a sea of medical and military personnel crowding toward the dock to receive the wounded men. She didn't see how she would get through them to find Alex, but she pushed her way into the crowd, and moved as far forward as she could as the ship approached.

It looked huge to her, and it was nearly eleven before the ship with the enormous red cross painted on its side was securely tied up at the dock, as the medical personnel crowded forward, and half a dozen gangplanks were set up, and a number of the medics went on board carrying stretchers to bring off the most severely injured men first. She could see why they had told her she might miss him at the dock, but she was determined to find him. She prayed he wasn't one of the men being brought off on stretchers. She positioned herself where she could see many of them as they were carried past her, but none of them looked like Alex, although some were so heavily bandaged you couldn't tell. They were covered with army blankets, with their few belongings lying on top of them. There were a number of army and navy nurses in the crowd and men guiding the stretcher bearers toward the ambulances. It was a long time before men on crutches began to file past her, being assisted in many cases, and when she saw them, Eleanor began calling his name, hoping he could hear her in the crowd.

"Alex Allen . . . Alex Allen . . ." There was so much noise she had to shout, and she had brought a photograph of him to show anyone who could help her find him.

There were hundreds of men with bandages and canes and slings pouring out of the ship down all six gangplanks, heading toward the buses and transport trucks, and those who noticed her shook their heads when she asked them if they knew Alex Allen or had seen him, while holding up the photograph. Some of them looked dazed and many didn't speak to her, but others shook their heads and said they hadn't seen him, giving her admiring glances. She was the first civilian American woman they had seen since they'd left the States.

Eleanor continued to thread her way doggedly through the crowd for two hours, wondering if she should give up and go to the hospital in the Presidio to find him. The situation at the dock seemed hopeless, and then she saw a long line of wheelchairs waiting to disembark, as one by one soldiers took them and rolled them carefully down one of the gangplanks, and Eleanor watched them, and then she saw him far back in the line. She waved and he didn't see her, and she pushed her way through the crowd until she reached the foot of the gangplank and waited. She was looking up at him as they rolled him down, and then he saw her, and he started to cry, and so did she. The moment the wheels of his chair touched the dock, she put her arms around him and held him and he sobbed in her arms. The medic pushing him moved him out of the way so they didn't block the others, and as Alex pulled back, she looked into his face. He was desperately thin, with his eyes deep set in his head. He had a bandage on one arm, but he looked uninjured other than the fact that he was in the chair, and he had a blanket over him to keep warm. He was shivering, and she wondered if he was too weak to stand. The medic was wheeling him toward one of the buses that had been fitted to carry the men in wheelchairs.

"Where are you going?" Eleanor asked him in a hurry before they lifted Alex's chair into the bus.

"Letterman Hospital in the Presidio. You can see him there." She nodded and kissed Alex, and he smiled at her as though he had thought he would never see her again, and couldn't believe she was standing in front of him. It seemed unreal to her too. She couldn't believe she had found him. She had been there for eight hours by then, but it was worth it. She had actually found him and been there the moment he came off the ship.

"I'll meet you at the hospital," she said as she kissed him and smiled at him.

"Thank you for being here. I didn't know if you knew when we were coming in."

"I got a telegram almost three weeks ago. I've been calling every day." He squeezed her hand as his eyes filled with tears again, and then he tried to pull himself together. "What happened?"

"They dropped a bomb on a ship we were on. It was being moved to a new location. It was a direct hit. I lost most of my men. Only three of them survived, and so did I." He looked exhausted as he told her, and then two men lifted his chair up, and he waved as they rolled him into the bus. He looked frighteningly thin, but he seemed to have come through it relatively unscathed.

She walked quickly back to the bus stop where she'd gotten off hours before, and got on the bus to take her to the Presidio, and realized how lucky they were that he'd been sent to San Francisco. He could have been sent anywhere. This way she could visit him every day. It took her over an hour to get to the Presidio, and he had just arrived when she did. The hospital was a melée of patients and medical personnel, trying to sort them out, assign them to wards or rooms depending on the severity of the cases, and half an hour later, they directed her to the ward where Alex had been taken. She saw him in his wheelchair, and hurried over to him, as a male nurse helped him into bed. The blanket that had been covering him was cast aside before they moved him, and then she saw why he had come home. He had lost his legs, both of them. His thighs were still heavily bandaged. His legs ended just above his knees. He watched her face as she saw what had happened to him and their eyes met. But from what he had told her, he was lucky to be alive, and she would have been grateful if even less of him had come home, or he'd lost his arms and his legs.

"It's all right," she said softly, and gently touched

his face with her fingers, as he reached for her hand and held it.

"Is it?" he asked her, and there were a million questions in those two words. She nodded in answer.

"Yes, it is. We'll be fine, and so will you." He let himself be lifted into the bed then. He had had internal injuries too, but his legs were the worst of it.

She sat down in a chair next to him, as the new arrivals continued to pour into the ward with assorted injuries. She knew their life was about to change radically again. It reminded her of when they were on their honeymoon and the world they knew had broken into a million pieces and been smashed to smithereens. It had just happened again. But it was different this time. It had happened to him, and to them, not to an entire world. But whatever it took, they were going to face it together. Of that she was sure. They would not be destroyed by this. She wouldn't let it happen. She leaned over and kissed him as he sat in his bed, watching her for her reaction.

"I love you, Alex," she said in a strong voice, as he clung to her. She could feel the bones in his back and shoulders as she held him.

"I love you too," he said with a world of regret in his voice, and a silent apology for how he had come home to her. He felt useless now. She could see it, but Eleanor didn't believe that. She just held him tightly to let her strength and faith in him flow into him like a river of love that nothing could stop or diminish.

"Thank God you're home," she said as he closed his eyes and rested his face against her. They were exactly the words he needed to hear and what she had just said was all he needed to know. That even without legs, she still loved him.

Chapter 10

Alex settled into a routine at the hospital fairly quickly. They wanted him to do physical therapy eventually, but he wasn't ready. His internal injuries were still causing him trouble, and his body was full of shrapnel. They had removed what they could, but enough of it was still there to worry his doctors. He had fevers almost every night, and flare-ups of infections of some of the wounds. Their worst fear was gangrene, which was what had happened to his legs after the explosion.

Eleanor came to see him every day after she finished teaching. She corrected her students' homework sitting next to his bed, while he dozed quietly beside her. She stayed with him until dinner time, and then picked up their daughter from the babysitter and took her home and cared for her.

Her parents had been shocked and deeply saddened to hear about what had happened to Alex, and the loss of his legs. Her father wanted to come to the city for the first time in thirteen years to see him, but Alex wasn't allowed to have visitors. He was still very weak, and they were concerned about the infections that continued to plague him. Eleanor was worried about him too. He wasn't fully out of the woods yet. And if any of the shrapnel in him moved significantly, it could kill him.

The doctors were estimating a five or six month stay in the hospital, and then she would take Alex to Lake Tahoe for the summer with Camille. Eleanor knew she would have to find another apartment for them before he came home. He couldn't manage the stairs in a wheelchair and there was no elevator. He would be trapped in the apartment. She was planning to deal with it over the summer, but she had too much to do in the meantime, visiting him every day, working at Miss Benson's, and taking care of Camille at night. Tahoe was going to be a good rest for both of them, and he was looking forward to it. He couldn't wait to get out of the hospital and see Camille again. He hadn't seen her in over a year, and he doubted that she'd remember him. Eleanor had told her that her daddy would be coming home now.

He was making good progress in April when Eleanor got a call from her mother early one morning as she was getting Camille ready for school. Louise was sobbing almost incoherently. Charles had died in his sleep. His heart had given out. He was only sixty-five, but the hard blows he had lived through had aged him prematurely. He had looked much older in recent years, no matter how bravely he tried to face the changes in his life. He never complained or talked about the past, but he had never been quite the same again.

"Oh my God, Mama, I'm so sorry," she said, crying herself as Camille watched her, shocked to see her mother crying. "I'll come up later today, as soon as I tell Alex and the school. I'll take care of everything." Her mother couldn't stop crying, and Eleanor's mind was racing. She had so much to do now, and she had to get to her mother. It almost obscured her own grief for her father. But she knew he would want her to take care of her mother. This was going to be a crushing loss for her, which could easily kill her too, and Eleanor didn't want that to happen.

After she dropped Camille off at the sitter, she explained at school that she needed the rest of the week off to arrange her father's funeral. At another time, fifteen years before, her father's death would have made her an heiress of vast proportions, now it would barely make a ripple in their lives. As far as she knew, he had very little left, just a few investments he had mentioned to her and her mother over the years, that he would be leaving them one day. She had never allowed her father to tell her about them in any depth, and he didn't insist. She didn't want to talk about what would happen when he died. And now he had, and she knew nothing. Whatever he had managed to save would go to support her mother. And she didn't expect it to be much. It was the least of her problems right now. She had Alex to take care of, and Camille, and her mother now too. Louise had always relied totally on Charles, and her world revolved around him.

Miss Benson told her to take the rest of the week off. After she thanked her, Eleanor went to the military hospital in the Presidio to see Alex. He was surprised and pleased to see her so early in the day, but as he saw her approach, he could see that something was wrong. Eleanor looked devastated. He held his breath, praying that nothing had happened to Camille.

"What is it? Why are you here so early?" he asked, dreading her answer.

"It's my father," she said and dissolved in tears. And this time he comforted her, as she had done so lovingly for him. She had convinced him that they would manage without a problem. She would continue working. He would get a pension and maybe would find some kind of job that suited him. They would save a little money here and there. And the loss of Alex's salary was small. Eleanor refused to be defeated, and she was carrying Alex along, on the strength of her love for him. But now the loss of her father had hit her hard, and it would hit her mother even harder. After leaving Camille with the neighbor again, Eleanor left for Tahoe that night in Alex's car, which was getting old, and she used it sparingly.

She found her mother awake and distraught when she got there. Louise was bereft.

"I don't know how I'm going to go on without him," she said to Eleanor, as they sat and held hands in the living room in the house she had made so pretty for them.

"You have to, Mother. We need you. I need you. And you have a granddaughter who loves you." Louise looked at her as though she were lost in the forest. Eleanor realized now that her father had been her mother's reason for living. She had been the stronger of the two and had kept him going since they'd lost everything fourteen years before. It had taken a toll on her too.

Eleanor made all the arrangements for her the next day, and planned a small simple funeral for her father in the local church. He had become a recluse since they moved there. He had maintained no contact with his old friends. Her mother had been his whole world, just as he was hers. They were so intertwined that Eleanor was seriously worried about her now, but she had Alex to think of too.

Only a few of the people who worked on the estate attended the funeral, and Eleanor and Louise. It was heart-wrenching and dignified. Eleanor supported her mother on their way out of the church, as they followed the casket to the cemetery.

Eleanor went back to the city on Sunday after the service, and promised her mother that they would spend the summer with her, as they always did. And by then, Alex would be able to come home. It dawned on Louise then that there were two floors in the cottage they stayed in, with both bedrooms upstairs, which would be impossible for Alex with the wheelchair, whereas the house which she and Charles lived in was all on one level. She suggested exchanging them over the summer, which made perfect sense, and would give her something to do before they arrived. School would be out in six weeks, and they were hoping Alex could be released by then.

Eleanor drove back to the city, thinking of all she would have to arrange and be responsible for now. Alex, Camille, her mother. She had to find a new apartment for them in the city, so she could keep working. It was overwhelming, and she realized too that her father's death left an enormous hole in her own life. He was a kind, intelligent man, who had always given her wise advice and been good to her. Thinking about him and how much she would miss him made her cry most of the way home. She had so much on her plate now, she had no idea how she would get everything done. They were teaching her at the hospital how to help care for her husband, and she was going to get one of the men on the estate to help. And Alex was determined to be as independent as he could.

Once she got Camille back from the neighbor, she put her to bed and fell into her own bed exhausted. She didn't see Alex until the following afternoon. He was deeply sympathetic to the loss of her father, which was a major loss for him too. And he was worried about Eleanor and all she had on her shoulders. He was anxious to leave the hospital so he could help her, but he was still too weak to be discharged.

The next six weeks flew by, as she finished the term at school, and once he was stronger, Alex was able to leave the hospital, after almost four months. His internal wounds seemed to be healing, and the wounds from his amputations. In mid-June, she picked him up at the hospital, and drove him and Camille to Lake Tahoe. It was the first time he had seen their daughter in sixteen months, and he was stunned by how much she'd grown and how bright and talkative she was for an almost three-year-old.

He looked like a happy man as they drove to Tahoe, and Eleanor began to relax with her husband at her side again. And even with Alex's infirmities, life in partnership was so much easier than life alone. After a few minutes of hesitation, Camille was at ease with him too. She wanted to know where his feet went, and said she wanted to ride around in the wheelchair with him.

When they got to Tahoe, they discovered that Louise had already moved to the cottage, and had the house she normally occupied filled with flowers for them. The one-level house was exactly what Alex needed. There were no stairs anywhere, and one of the handymen on the estate had built some minor accommodations for him, handrails, a special seat in the shower, and a wooden ramp at the front and back doors. He rolled from room to room, beaming at the familiar home after a year and a half away. He had been to hell and back, and it had never dawned on him that he might come back seriously damaged. He had so many things to relearn as a handicapped person. Louise embraced him the moment she saw him, and he told her how sorry he was about Charles, which brought tears to her eyes again, but she didn't give in to them. She wanted to be strong for Eleanor and Alex, and all they had to face.

Their time together that summer was good for all of them. Louise and Eleanor had both been shocked at the reading of Charles's will. He was by no means a rich man compared to what he had been, but he had made sound investments with what he had left, he had saved much of the money from the sale of the Tahoe property, and he spent almost none of what the earl paid him annually to run it. Louise would have no financial worries for the rest of her days, and he had left half of what he had to Eleanor, which would give them a cushion now, if none of them were extravagant.

Alex grew strong and healthy in the mountain air. He even devised a system to take Eleanor boating. He wheeled down to the boathouse with her one day, lifted himself into the driver's seat of their favorite boat, and told his wife to get in, in front of him. He reached around her and held the steering wheel and instructed her to work the pedals, which were similar to those in a car. So together, they drove the boat, with Alex steering, and Eleanor in charge of the gas pedal and the brake. It was a little out of sync at first, but they both got the hang of it quickly, and had a good time running the boat around the lake, while her mother babysat for Camille, and was delighted to do it. She could hear the sound of Alex and Eleanor laughing as Eleanor pushed his chair back up from the lake. It was music to her ears. The agony of war was starting to dim for Alex, despite the horrors he had seen and what it had cost him. He still had nightmares on many nights, but they were fading slowly.

He had written to his brothers and told them about losing his legs. Both of them were desperately sorry to hear it. They couldn't imagine him in a wheelchair for the rest of his life, at his age. But after their initial sympathetic letters, he hadn't heard from them again. In reality, he wasn't part of their lives anymore, and only a distant voice from the past, and he knew it, and expected nothing of them. He kept in touch because they were his brothers, even if only in name. Eleanor and Camille were his life.

On a sunny summer day, Alex and Eleanor were just a happy couple, lying in a hammock and laughing or quietly side by side at night. Eleanor's love and strength was healing him more than the doctors.

While Louise kept busy with her gardening, Eleanor decided to explore the barn one day. She was looking for something of her father's that her mother had put away, a box of rare books that Alex remembered and wanted to see again. It had been years

since Eleanor had looked into the barn with any seriousness, and as she peeked under the dust covers,
some of them custom made, she pushed aside sheets
and drapes and plastic covers and suddenly remembered more of the furniture she had grown up with
in her parents' house and how beautiful it was.

She was surprised by how much her mother had
kept. There was nowhere for her to use it in the small
house and the cottage at Lake Tahoe. There was
enough there to furnish several houses, and it was
sad to see it abandoned and unused, knowing they
would never use it again. And in a stronger economy
now, it was worth a lot of money, far more than when
Louise had put it away. She mentioned it to her
mother that night at dinner.

"Now that you're going through Papa's things,
why don't you send all of that furniture to auction?
You might as well get rid of it, it's been sitting in the
barn for years." Fourteen years to be exact, beautiful
things but that she no longer had any interest in. At
the time, Eleanor had paid no attention to what her
mother put away. It seemed pointless to Eleanor to
keep what was there. She thought they should sell it
now.

Louise didn't answer for a moment.

"I thought maybe we'd use it again one day," she
said sadly. "We would have gotten nothing for it
when we sold the house. Everything was selling for
so little, and no one had any money. So I kept the
best pieces. They're a memory of a happier time," she

said wistfully. Selling the house and everything in it had been so hard. She never talked about it and neither had Charles. And Eleanor didn't want to upset her now. It wasn't hurting anyone in the barn, so she dropped the subject when she saw the pain in her mother's eyes. She wasn't ready to give up the last vestiges of their past, even now. "Your wedding dress is there too. And your debut gown," Louise added, and Eleanor smiled thinking of it, and so did Louise. No one had dresses like that anymore, or weddings like hers. It was part of a lost era, a time that would never come again. Everything had crashed around them, only weeks after their wedding. Their apartment in Chinatown was a sharp contrast to their old way of life, which seemed like a dream now.

They had to decide too, with her father gone, who would oversee the Tahoe estate for the earl. It ran itself with the people Charles had hired, but it needed someone on the spot to keep an eye on things. Alex told Eleanor he'd be happy to do it, when they came up for weekends. And her mother was well aware of how things should look, and loved the gardens. The earl had sent a very kind condolence letter to Louise and hadn't been pressuring them about who would replace Charles. Both women were grateful to Alex for the offer. He couldn't walk, but he could certainly come up and speak to the groundskeepers and the gardeners, the boatmen and the maintenance people, and he needed something to do. He didn't want to sit around and be an invalid for the rest of his life.

It reminded Eleanor of what a blessing it had been that her parents had been able to continue living on the estate, thanks to the absentee owner. They didn't seem to miss the big house they had occupied there before, or at least they never said so. But she wondered about it now, with her mother storing so much in the barn, hoping they would need it again one day. But for what? Their old way of life and the houses that went with it would never return.

It was a difficult summer unexpectedly in the end. In August, a month before Eleanor and Alex were due to return to the city, and she was planning to go back to town to find an apartment that would work for Alex, her mother had a heart attack. The shock of losing her husband had been too much for her. Eleanor and Alex had a serious conversation while Louise was in the hospital. Eleanor didn't want to leave her alone in Tahoe, she was fragile now, and there was no one to look after her. And Alex had thrived in Tahoe over the summer.

"Maybe I should take a leave of absence this year, so I can stay here with her?" Eleanor suggested. They didn't have a place they could live in now in the city anyway. Alex couldn't get up the stairs of the Chinatown apartment in his wheelchair. And she hadn't had time to find another one yet. A year in Tahoe would give Alex time to get stronger, and help manage the estate at close range. And the money her father had left her made her job at the school less of a dire necessity. She could take a year off if she felt she had to, and it looked that way. She hadn't touched her father's money and didn't intend to, and they spent almost nothing in Tahoe. They talked about it for several days, and by the time Louise got out of the hospital, they had made the decision to stay in Tahoe for a year. It seemed to be what they needed to do, and made sense to all of them.

Eleanor didn't feel comfortable leaving her mother alone now, so soon after her father's death, and in ill health. And Alex liked the prospect of staying in Tahoe. He had no idea what he was going to do in the city. He could return to his bank job eventually, losing his legs didn't affect his ability to work, but he hadn't fully recovered yet, and he loved being with Eleanor and Camille all the time now that he had survived the war. His job at the bank had been dreary and he'd hated it for years before he had left. He wasn't looking forward to going back, and his options were limited in a wheelchair although there were many men like him returning from the war who were seeking employment, and many veterans were begging on the streets.

They told Louise when she got home from the hospital, and she insisted she didn't want to be a burden to them, but she liked the idea of their staying too. She said she was comfortable in the cottage, and urged them to stay in the larger house as they had done that summer. The decision was made. They were staying. Eleanor sent a long apologetic letter to Miss Benson, and asked for permission to take a year off, to attend to her convalescing mother and husband. And her response a week later was warm and kind and she agreed to give Eleanor a year's sabbatical for compassionate reasons. It would have been hard not to, and particularly since Eleanor had been a faithful employee of the school for fourteen years.

In September, Eleanor went back to San Francisco to give up their apartment. Because it wasn't accessible for Alex, they couldn't use it. She was sad to let it go. They had been happy there and she liked their neighbors, but another chapter had ended. She sent their furniture to Tahoe to add to what was in the barn, since she had borrowed it from her mother originally. And on a warm Indian summer day, she left their Chinatown apartment for the last time. She walked to where she had parked the car, past all the open markets and the familiar sights and sounds of the neighborhood. She sensed that another door had closed silently behind her, and once again, the future and the mysteries it held were unknown.

Chapter 11

Louise seemed to get some of her strength back in the fall, after her heart attack, and she started spending a lot of time in her garden. It was part of the healing process for her and she said it was good for her soul. She had taken refuge and great comfort in her gardening when they first moved to Tahoe as well.

Eleanor and Alex kept a watchful eye on Louise, and as the winter set in, the colder weather and heavy snows, Louise spent most of her time in her cozy cottage and slept a lot. Without Charles to take care of and fuss over, she seemed to be losing interest in life, and Eleanor was worried about her, and glad they had decided to stay in Tahoe with her.

In contrast, Alex had recovered and was fully engaged with whatever was done on the property. He had his energy back. The only difference was he couldn't walk now. But there was very little he couldn't do. His back had been somewhat damaged in the explosion too, so he couldn't stand well enough to wear prostheses, but he got around everywhere in his wheelchair once the paths were cleared of snow, and he loved being with his family. Eleanor knew they had made the right decision to stay in Tahoe. She and Alex had time together, Camille flourished from having her parents close at hand, and Eleanor could keep an eye on her mother. It was harder and harder to coax her from her cottage. By January, after a quiet Christmas, their first without Eleanor's father, Louise seldom left her cottage for meals now. She was content to stay tucked up with a book, and spent more time asleep than awake.

Eleanor went to check on her one morning when she hadn't heard from her yet, and was shocked but not entirely surprised by what she found when she entered the cottage. Her mother had had another heart attack sometime in the night, and hadn't survived it. The doctors said afterward that she must have died instantly. It saddened Eleanor to have lost both her parents so young, but the traumas they had weathered almost fifteen years earlier had eroded their spirits and their health, and without Charles, Louise had lost her will to live. Even her daughter and her grandchild weren't enough to stem the tides. She had slipped away quietly and had no desire to live without Charles. Eleanor was sad, but had a sense of peace about it. At least their final years had been comfortable ones in a place they loved, and they had each other. And Louise had gone to join him in the end.

The war in Europe was fierce by then and had been for some time, in the spring of 1944. Alex followed it avidly in the newspapers and on the radio. The Allies were fighting hard to defeat Hitler, but victory wasn't assured yet. In spite of that, the Allies had liberated Rome in June of 1944 and at the same time, the Allied invasion of Normandy had begun. And as Charles had predicted for years, it had taken a war to end the Great Depression and turn the economy around. The economy was much stronger due to war production and new fortunes were being made. No one lived the way the very wealthy had when Eleanor and Alex were younger, but the country had money and was gaining strength.

It was in the spring after her mother's death that Eleanor turned her attention to the barn, and decided to go through what was in it, and possibly sell it. She hired two young local boys to help her take everything out in the good weather, and she stood marveling at what they found there, including her wedding and debut dresses, which Louise had had carefully sealed in special boxes to protect them.

The furniture they uncovered consisted of some of the finest pieces that had been in the Deveraux mansion, of museum quality, none of it had suffered from being stored in the barn. It had been carefully covered, and looked as pristine as ever, upholstered in exquisite fabrics. Louise had even saved many of the curtains, some of which were antiques they'd brought back from France along with the furniture.

"What are we going to do with all this?" Alex asked, wheeling his chair around it, admiring the obvious quality that had previously been so familiar to him in his own home too. His old possessions were scattered to the winds now. Eleanor still owned a mountain of fine antiques from the barn, and had no way to use them in their real life. Louise had also saved a number of their very good paintings by well-known artists. They would have gotten nothing for them in 1929 and 1930, when they sold the house for a school.

"We should sell it, I guess," Eleanor said, remembering how everything had looked in their home. Seeing it brought back so many distant happy memories. It was like a trip back in time for her.

They got it back in the barn after she inventoried what was there, and photographed it in order to send a list of the barn's contents to an auction house, possibly Parke-Bernet in New York. Eleanor lay in bed thinking about it that night, all the beautiful things her mother had left her. She'd been right to keep them and not sell them at the time, fifteen years later, they were worth a fortune again, and people could afford to buy them. That night she dreamed about selling all of it. When she woke up in the morning, she went to find Alex in the kitchen, having breakfast with their daughter.

"Alex, I've had an idea," she said, eyes bright with excitement, after she'd kissed them.

"You want to go on a boat ride with me after breakfast?" he said happily, looking at his wife.

"No, I'm serious!"

"So am I," he teased her, and Camille asked if she could come too. Eleanor gave her some paper and crayons to keep her busy so she could talk to Alex. They weren't financially desperate now with what her parents had left her, but the contents of the barn represented a considerable amount of money, or an opportunity. In fact, in the current climate of growing national prosperity, the contents of the barn, and the remaining smaller piece of property in Tahoe Eleanor owned now were worth a small fortune. Not the kind of fortune she'd grown up with, but very solid money, and more than enough to start a business, or buy a larger house if they wanted to. They were cash poor, but had her father's investments, and her parents had lived frugally.

"What if we don't send my parents' things from the barn to auction? What if we sell them ourselves?"

"How? Privately, or take out an ad in a newspaper? 'Fabulous antiques for sale'? It would make a hell of a garage sale." He smiled at her.

"I'm serious," she said again as her eyes lit up with excitement. "What if we open a really high-end antique store?"

"Here?" It was a quiet community, and no one had fancy antiques worthy of Versailles at Lake Tahoe.

"No, in San Francisco. We could rent a shop in the right neighborhood. People have money now, and they're willing to spend it. We have enough in the barn to supply a store for a couple of years."

"And when we run out of your parents' things?" He looked skeptical. It sounded a little crazy to him. Selling them at auction would be simpler.

"Then we go to Europe and buy more. The war will be over by then. I suspect there will be a lot of people there who have lost their fortunes, and will have to sell their chateaux and will want to sell their antiques. People don't live like my parents did anymore. They want smaller homes, simpler things, but there must be a market for beautiful things, for people with money, just not on the grand scale that we grew up with. I don't think any of us realized how remarkable it was. It seemed normal to us then. It was the only life we knew. We were the children of a golden era. I think we could have a very successful business with an antique store," and it was something he could do too. He could help her run the business end, and he didn't have to be able to walk to be an antique dealer. "What do you think?"

"Do you really want to be a merchant?" he asked, looking surprised, and she laughed at him.

"Don't be such a snob. You sound like my father, or my grandparents. Yes, I do. I'm not afraid to be 'engaged in commerce,' as my grandmother would have said. I'd love to try it. We could open a shop instead of my going back to teaching. And if it doesn't work and no one buys anything, we give up the store and send everything to auction. Why not give it a try?" He thought about it and started to be intrigued by the idea. Successful businesses had started in stranger ways, and they certainly had more than enough merchandise to get started.

"You don't mind moving back to the city? I love it here," he said wistfully.

"We can come for weekends and holidays." They had lived there for nine months, and it was beautiful, but very quiet. Eleanor was thirty-four years old, and not ready for a bucolic life yet. She missed seeing people, having a job, and keeping busy. With her mother gone, there wasn't a lot for her to do there. And eventually, she wanted to put Camille in a good private school in the city, although she wasn't four years old yet. Alex would have been content with a quiet country life forever, but Eleanor wasn't there yet.

She suddenly loved the idea of running an antique business and had never thought of it before, and they might meet interesting new people running an antique store.

They talked about it for several days, and she convinced Alex to let her go on a reconnaissance mission to the city, and see what was available in the way of shops to rent. They could make a decision after that, depending on how high the rents were. She didn't want to invest too much in it, and risk what they had or gamble all of it, in case it failed, but they already had a full inventory, so all they needed was a store where they could sell it.

She left three days later, and had already called a commercial real estate agent, to show her some shops to rent in San Francisco.

"Don't go too crazy," Alex warned her when she left, but he was intrigued by the idea too.

It all happened very quickly after that. Eleanor said it was destiny. She saw four shops that afternoon, and one of them was absolutely perfect in an area called Jackson Square. A small brick building was available with two floors they could use to show the antiques, a third floor where they could store them, and a two-bedroom apartment on the top floor. It even had an elevator. It was just what they needed, they could even live there. They could leave some of the extra larger pieces in the barn in Tahoe, where they were safe, and had been for many years. And in what felt like a moment of madness, she convinced Alex to let her rent the house the next day, when she called him. By the time she got back to Tahoe two days later, they had a store in San Francisco, and the start of a business. Eleanor wanted to call it Deveraux-Allen, which sounded very distinguished to both of them. The store itself needed a coat of paint inside, and some spotlights to focus on the best pieces.

Her excitement was contagious, and by mid-April, the store had been painted, the lighting installed, and they were ready to move into the apartment above the store, and open the business.

Two long moving vans came to take a large number of the antiques to San Francisco. Eleanor drove down to meet them, and start furnishing the apartment, and tell them where she wanted the antiques placed in the store. Some of them looked truly magnificent. Her parents had left her a barn full of treasures, and she realized again that her mother had been right to keep them. They were an important inheritance for Eleanor and for their future, although her mother had kept it all out of sentiment.

They opened at the end of April, and the store looked impressive. Eleanor had found the guest list from her wedding in her mother's papers, and sent everyone on it an elegant-looking invitation to come and see the store. She knew that once they did, they would want to buy something, or tell friends who could. She put one of their most beautiful Louis XV commodes in the front window. It had previously been in their drawing room, and was a magnificent piece. It was signed and worthy of a museum, the most elegant drawing room, or a chateau.

They made their first sale four days after they opened, to a woman who had just moved to San Francisco from New York. She asked Eleanor if she would come to her new home to give her advice about what to place where. Her furniture had just arrived from New York.

Eleanor went to her address the following afternoon, she had just bought a beautiful mansion on upper Broadway, not far from Alex's old house, although much less grand. The house had good proportions and pretty rooms, but she had no idea how to decorate them. She explained to Eleanor she wanted to have the most beautiful home in San Francisco, and she wanted Eleanor's help to achieve it. She was a widow and her industrialist husband had left her a great deal of money, and she wasn't sure how to spend it.

Eleanor spent two hours with her, making suggestions, and the woman bought three more pieces from them the next day. Eleanor's goal was to fill the rooms with beautiful furniture and objects that the woman loved and help her to establish the elegant home she wanted. Eleanor was happy to introduce her to other dealers too, although she didn't know many, and what Eleanor's mother had left her was prettier than anything else in town, in any other store.

Business was excellent in May and June. Some of her parents' friends showed up and it was nice to catch up with them. They came out of nostalgia and were sad to learn of her parents' deaths. Many had had severe reversals and had never recovered and had come to the shop out of curiosity. Others still had some money left and bought a piece or two of the

Deveraux furniture they had always admired. And there were total strangers who came, had money to burn, and Eleanor was happy to help them do it. Most of them relied on Eleanor's taste, and loved what they bought from her.

By July, they had a thriving business on their hands, and Alex and Eleanor were enjoying it thoroughly. Eleanor's idea had been brilliant, and the experiment had worked. Alex and Eleanor were ecstatic. Alex said it was much more fun than working in a bank and a lot more lucrative. And she was enjoying it more than she had teaching although she'd been grateful for the job.

The best news of all was that Deveraux-Allen was a resounding success, and Alex and Eleanor could work on it together. Decidedly, their new chapter had begun with a bang.

Chapter 12

Deveraux-Allen rapidly became the most respected antique shop in San Francisco, almost from the time they opened it, given the high quality of what they had to sell. Eleanor was knowledgeable about the periods the pieces had been made in, had researched their provenance carefully, and their makers, and even found some of her mother's records on it. And Alex was interested in learning more about it. He loved the history of what they sold and who had owned it, or which French and British royals and aristocrats it had been made for, at what time.

They added a decorating component to the business, based on Eleanor's excellent taste. Their lucrative venture allowed Eleanor to stop teaching. It only took a few large purchases to get them going, and everything they sold was of high quality and value. And their success allowed Alex not to return to the bank. He regained his strength steadily after his war injuries, and owning the shop gave him the leeway to make his own hours and work at his own pace. He tired easily at first but got steadily stronger. He continued to run the Tahoe estate from a distance for the English lord who owned it. Alex spent a few days there twice a month, which was enough to make sure that everything was running smoothly, and they stayed there as a family during holidays and long weekends.

Camille was four when they started the business, and as soon as they were able to, which happened quickly, Eleanor hired a young girl to help her with Camille. They took on a young man, Tim Avery, to help with moving some of the heavy furniture at the shop. He was almost like a son to Alex. He had been injured in the war himself, and he drove Alex anywhere he needed to go. He was devoted to them. And Camille loved Annie, her babysitter, who reminded Eleanor a little bit of Wilson. Annie was Irish too, and very loving. She sang to Camille to calm her down, and Camille easily imitated her pretty voice, singing Irish ballads. The child seemed to have a real talent for music, which neither Alex nor Eleanor could lay claim to.

Eleanor had stayed in touch with Wilson after they left and she became Mrs. Houghton. They had given up their jobs in London once the bombing of London started, and had retired to Ireland, and were saddened to hear of the deaths of Eleanor's parents and impressed by the antique business they had started and sorry not to be there. The Houghtons had fared well, saved their money, and been married for fifteen years by then, and still cherished their memories of their years with the Deveraux.

Alex and Eleanor's first year in business was the last of the war in Europe. The news was alarming at times, but the Allies pressed on to victory. They liberated Paris in August.

Alex had sacrificed his legs for his country, but they had a good life, and with Alex running their finances, and Eleanor's hard work, they were able to buy the building where the shop was and they lived. They had a simple life, based on their diligence, good management, and their stable marriage. Camille remained the joy of their life.

By the time Deveraux-Allen had been open for two years, in 1946, the war was over at last and they had sold almost all of her parents' furniture, and the barn was empty in Tahoe.

"We need new merchandise," Eleanor told Alex one afternoon when they were going over the books. She still couldn't believe how well they had done with the business. They had clients coming from other cities now, from word of mouth, and her decorating was much in demand in San Francisco. The country was flourishing and they had caught the wave at the right time. "There's nothing to buy here," she said. "Wilson says that half the castles in Ireland are up for sale, and there are some beautiful antiques there." She still called her Wilson, and couldn't imagine calling her by her first name, Fiona, or even Mrs. Houghton. "And the French are selling everything too."

A year after the war, Europe was still ravaged, and its people starving. But in recent months, travel had become easier. Alex and Eleanor hadn't gone anywhere since their lost days of grandeur, except to Lake Tahoe, but if they were to keep their shop doors open, they needed something to sell, and all the fine pieces in San Francisco had been sold during the Depression, and taken elsewhere. They both still grew nostalgic when they drove past their old homes. Alex refused to enter the hotel his family home had been turned into. He couldn't bring himself to do it. He hadn't seen his brothers in seventeen years by then, since they left San Francisco, but were still in touch with occasional correspondence. They seemed like strangers to him now and the life they had once shared a distant dream that had no reality to it. He had never met their wives or children and didn't know if he ever would.

The school that had been established in the Deveraux mansion, the Hamilton School, was still there, and Eleanor pointed to the house whenever she and Camille drove past it, and she told her that it was where her mama had grown up, which didn't interest Camille particularly when her mother said they couldn't move back there. It was just a big house to Camille. It was a time and a home that had no bearing on their present-day life. It was merely history, and beloved memories to Eleanor and Alex. The gardens had been sold off by the school as a separate lot, and another wealthy family, with new riches, had built a rambling modern house there. Their old home still made Eleanor's heart ache a little when she drove past it.

Alex booked passage for them on the RMS *Aquitania* again sailing from New York in June of 1946. She was still in "austerity service," with valuable art removed, and was still painted gray after serving as a troopship during the war. They had fond memories of her from their honeymoon, even if she was less luxurious now. Alex insisted that they travel in first class, which Eleanor thought was extravagant, but he said they could afford it. Annie agreed to stay with Camille, and Tim Avery was excited about running the shop in their absence, and he could reach them by telegram if he had to. He had learned a great deal about the antiques they sold in the two years that he had worked for them. He was young, bright, conscientious, and proud to be part of a successful enterprise, with kind employers.

They knew that the stewards on the ship would assist Alex with his personal needs, and Eleanor could help him too. He managed extremely well on his own, and they were planning to hire someone in Europe to travel with them during their trip. They had plans to be in France, England, and Ireland for a

month, and already had a long list of towns and chateaux where they thought they would find new merchandise to bring home. Boarding the *Aquitania* in
New York brought back vivid tender memories for
Eleanor, of her trips with her mother to buy her debutante gown and her wedding dress, as well as their
honeymoon on the same ship. She had read that
Jeanne Lanvin was not well, and her daughter,
Marie-Blanche de Polignac, was running the famous
couture house. The House of Worth was still functioning, still run by Charles Worth's great-grandson
Jean-Charles. Chanel was closed after the war, since
Gabrielle Chanel had fled to Switzerland, after col-
laborating with the Germans during the war. Their
earlier crossing to Europe, and hers with her mother
on the SS *Paris,* seemed so long ago, and was part of
another life. Eleanor didn't mourn it, or even miss it
anymore. It felt like someone else's life, and she was
happy with Alex. She was thirty-six years old and he
had just turned fifty. His mind and spirit were young,
Eleanor had infused new life into him with their
growing business, but his war injuries had taken a
toll on him and he looked older than his years. More
than once, people inquired if he was her father,
which shocked her. She never thought about the age
difference between them, and they were closer than
ever.

They stayed at the Ritz, as she had before, which
had been restored to civilian use after the war, after

housing the officers of the German High Command during the Occupation. And as evidence of her collaboration with the Germans, Gabrielle Chanel had been its only civilian resident during the war.

Eleanor couldn't resist a little shopping to check on Paris fashions, but they left the city quickly, with a young *chasseur* from the hotel they hired to help Alex, to begin their driving trip through the countryside to discover treasures to sell in San Francisco. They found them easily. Impoverished aristocrats were selling their ancestral homes, and their contents. The country was still badly scarred by the Occupation, and the advance of Allied troops across France during the Liberation. The stories they heard were tragic, of husbands sent to work camps never to return, their homes occupied by the Germans, the rape of women and young girls by German soldiers, and the deaths of sons and daughters in the Resistance. The people they met were strong and determined, but in dire need of money to survive. Some were still trying to save their homes, but selling everything in them, others were selling their chateaux with their contents. Again and again, Alex and Eleanor found beautiful antiques and purchased them for the low prices their owners were asking for them. They felt bad at times paying as little as the owners requested. Almost every chateau was up for sale, and many were badly damaged, or in serious disrepair. They went to a few country auctions and *brocantes,* which were like yard sales, and found treasures there.

What they found in England was similar, although the British were trying to hold on and rebuild their lost world, with considerable difficulty. Many were living in poverty and had sold their land to preserve their home. They were running enormous estates and castles with only a handful of people to help them. They were selling their possessions, but unwilling to relinquish a way of life that had existed for centuries and was foundering in the modern world. It tore at Alex's and Eleanor's heartstrings, reminded them of their own losses years before, and they were frequently invited to dinner by the people who were selling the contents of their homes. France had seemed more shell shocked after the Occupation, but England was just as poor. They had protected the country from invasion, but their old way of life was impossible to maintain. Life in the States seemed more secure, but the country hadn't been invaded or occupied, and had greater resources to fall back on, and the post-war industrial boom was breathing new life into the economy and filling the nation's coffers, and creating a whole class of the newly rich.

They found equally beautiful things in the castles in Ireland, and Eleanor had the thrill of seeing the Houghtons in Dublin. Wilson and Eleanor flew into each other's arms like long-lost relatives, as Houghton smiled at them benignly with damp eyes. They had aged considerably since Eleanor had last seen them in 1930, but they were healthy and in their seventies now. They both said that they missed California and their life in the States, but had a small tidy cottage and a good life in Ireland. They were living on their careful savings, and hadn't tried to find work since the war, and there was little to be had anyway. London was still severely damaged by the bombings, although Alex and Eleanor had seen construction going on everywhere. Britain was determined to recover.

By the time they got back to Cherbourg to board the ship again, they had filled three large trucks with priceless antiques to send back to San Francisco. In a month or so, their shop would be full of pieces to sell that were as beautiful as the antiques of the Deveraux, which they had been selling for two years. The trip had been a great success, although it had been poignant and humbling to see firsthand the suffering that Europe had experienced during the war.

It was a peaceful trip home on the familiar ship. The crossing was smooth. They were both tired after moving from place to place constantly for a month, examining the contents of castles in England and Ireland and chateaux in France. And for each piece they bought, they knew they would remember the stories that went with it, and the owners who had touched them with their courage and their losses. It had been a trip that they knew neither of them would ever forget. And Deveraux-Allen had a store full of new merchandise to sell.

When Alex and Eleanor got back to San Francisco, Camille looked to them as though she had grown a foot. She was six now, and she had learned new songs from Annie while they were gone. The child's singing talent was undeniable, and she was as sunny and happy as she had been for all six years of her life so far. Eleanor had bought her some pretty little dresses in Paris, and a new doll, which she loved. And she told them solemnly that they were never to go away without her again.

They closed the shop in August for a month's vacation at Lake Tahoe, and when they got home, everything they had bought in Europe had arrived. It took them and Tim Avery days to unpack it all, and place it advantageously in the shop. Their storeroom on the third floor was full again, and they had to send some of the larger pieces to the barn in Tahoe, until they sold some of the new pieces in the shop.

Their regular customers leapt on the beautiful new things they'd brought back, and the business continued to thrive.

They hardly saw the time passing for the next dozen years. They made several more successful buying trips to Europe. The economies had improved there, although more slowly than in the States. But Europe proved to be their best resource for antiques, as one by one the great estates disappeared, and noble families gave up their homes, and Americans bought them and their contents and had the money to do so.

Alex and Eleanor no longer traveled by ship for their buying trips, but flew to save time. They had taken Camille with them on two occasions, once she was in her teens, but she had complained and been bored the entire time. She had no interest in her parents' business, and thought it was depressing the way they sold relics from the past, and lived on the remnants of past grandeur. Her previously easy nature changed when she was about fifteen. She hated the schools they put her in, ridiculed their traditions, and was rebellious at every opportunity. They wanted her to attend college, and she flatly refused to consider it and said she had no interest in anything they would teach there. They had a major showdown with her when Eleanor talked to her about making her debut at the San Francisco Cotillion Debutante Ball when she turned eighteen. The grand balls of the past no longer existed in 1958, few people could afford them, nor had the homes for them, but a joint ball, the cotillion, had been established where roughly twenty young ladies of good families with aristocratic lineage were invited to "come out" and be presented to society, as had been the tradition in the past. Camille was outraged by the very idea, and tore up the letter inviting her to be one of them when it arrived.

"That's the most disgusting thing I've ever seen," she shouted at her mother. She was as beautiful as ever, tall and blond with blue eyes and a striking figure, but headstrong and difficult, and had been for the past three years. Her whole personality had changed, as both Alex and Eleanor struggled with her. She was due to graduate from high school in June, and was in her third school in four years. She was determined to be a rebel. Her teen years had been trying for Eleanor, although Alex had more patience with her, though not always better results. She was determined to reject everything they stood for, and thought they were dinosaurs left over from an antiquated world that was no longer relevant and was on its way out. She opposed everything that reeked of tradition, and making her debut was top of that list.

"There are no people of color at the cotillion, no Italians or Jews or anyone except people like you. Did you ever think of that?" she said with a look of disgust. And her father conceded that she had a point, but that might change one day, and he knew that although Camille's motives in not making her debut sounded noble, mostly she just didn't want to do what was expected of her, or anything that would please her parents. Her rejection of them was painful. She was in full rebellion, and her sweetness as a young child had disappeared. They had expected her teenage years to be challenging, but Camille was extreme.

Eleanor had lovingly shown Camille her own debut dress, carefully packed away thirty years before, and Camille ridiculed it.

"I'd look like a freak in that, you probably did too," she said disparagingly of the beautiful gown by the House of Worth that Eleanor had been thrilled to wear. "Everything you and Dad do is so old fashioned. It's all so yesterday. You're living in the past," she said cruelly, which wasn't true either. They respected the traditions they had grown up with, but had struggled to move forward despite the blows in their lives, which their daughter had no concept of, nor did she care. She thought they were fossils, who understood nothing of the modern world. "The cotillion is a cattle market, Mom, and I don't want to be one of the cows. They're all looking for husbands, which is why they go to college too, and the minute they get engaged, they drop out. Or they get pregnant, and *have* to get married. I don't want to get married, and I'm not going to let you show me off at the cotillion and marry me off to some snob."

"What *do* you want?" her father asked her shortly before her eighteenth birthday. She had refused to apply to college, her grades were terrible, she barely studied, and flatly turned down the opportunity to be a debutante in the coming winter season, even to please her parents. Camille did what she wanted. She had racy friends who weren't going to college either, and a weakness for all the handsome bad boys around town. James Dean, as the original angry young man, had been her hero, and she mourned his death for months when she was fifteen, which had been a turning point toward a darker side.

They worried about her constantly, and had for several years. She exasperated Eleanor, and Alex was always seeking a compromise and trying to reason with her, which seldom worked. They were both afraid she'd fall in with bad company and come to a bad end. It had happened to others. And she clearly had no intention of following her parents' path. She insisted that a new day had dawned and the old traditions meant nothing to her.

Camille was startled when her father asked her what she wanted. She insisted they had never asked her that before, and just tried to impose their wishes on her. Alex decided to try a new tack. She had threatened to run away several times, but never had. But he saw it as a possible outcome if they were too strict with her, and wanted to avoid that at all costs. She hated living over their store, no matter how elegant it was, or how profitable. She thought everything they sold was like old bones in a cemetery. It took all of Eleanor's self-control not to take the bait of her insults and get drawn into arguments with her. Alex had stronger nerves. She was their only child and he didn't want to lose her, neither did Eleanor, but she and Camille argued constantly, and were at odds.

"I want to sing," Camille said simply. It had been her passion all her life. Her voice was untrained but as beautiful as it always had been. And she was a gorgeous young woman, and looked older than her years. "I want to sing with a band, and make albums with them." It had been her dream since her early teens.

Several well-known bands had gotten their start in San Francisco, and Alex knew there were a number of small music producers in town, but he had no idea who they were.

"How would you make that happen?" he asked, curious about what she'd say, as her mother cringed. The kind of people she'd meet in show business seriously worried her, and would only make things worse. Alex wanted to negotiate a truce with her if he could.

"I know a couple of boys in bands. One of them said I could go to Vegas with them sometime and audition there." Las Vegas was becoming a mecca of showgirls and musicians, but also Sodom and Gomorrah in their minds. A lot of the big stars from Hollywood went there, like Frank Sinatra and his crowd, and Eleanor didn't want her falling into their hands. Prostitution was also rampant there, which drew a dangerous element for young girls. Alex didn't like it any more than his wife did, but he thought that if they let Camille get a taste of the music world, she'd tire of it quickly and come home to settle down. Maybe not to be a debutante, they had given up on that, but to get an education, and a respectable job. They thought she should work, as they did, and wanted her to lead a wholesome life, anathema to Camille.

"I don't think Las Vegas is a good idea," he said quietly, "but maybe you can sing with a local band, and see where that leads." She had a pretty voice, but he didn't think she would wind up a big star, and she might get discouraged quickly. It was his fondest hope.

"Thank you, Dad," she said, with an evil look at her mother, who understood nothing in her opinion, and she left the house shortly after to meet up with friends. None of the people she hung out with were interested in an education, they had big dreams that her parents thought weren't likely to go anywhere, nor would Camille's. What she really needed to do was stop dreaming of a career in show business, and grow up, but there was no sign of that yet.

"I think you're making a huge mistake encouraging her," Eleanor said unhappily, but she understood why he wanted to try.

"What choice do we have? Imagine if she runs away. She's a stubborn girl."

Eleanor didn't know what else to say. They were at their wits' end. Discipline didn't work with her, cajoling, compromising, making deals, threatening her. Camille was determined to do what she wanted, and cared nothing for her parents' wishes or concerns. In her mind, they were her enemies.

She managed to graduate from high school a few weeks later, by the skin of her teeth, tossed her di-

ploma in the garbage immediately after the ceremony, and sang with a band she had known for a few
weeks in a sleazy bar downtown, and a friend of the
lead singer came by and heard her, and needed a girl
to fill in in the chorus of his band. They were going
to Vegas in a week's time to open for a bigger band.
It was the opportunity Camille had been waiting for,
and the one her parents had dreaded. She told them
the next day. They hated the idea, but she didn't ask
their permission. She told them what she was going
to do, and the singer who had hired her for his band
said they were going to make an album and were
negotiating for a tour. If they kept her on, she'd be
traveling around the country with them for three
months if she was any good and they got the tour.

Eleanor felt sick thinking about it, but they reluctantly agreed. They told her they wanted to hear
from her regularly, and reminded her that they hadn't
agreed to the tour, only to a brief stint in Las Vegas.
She laughed at them. As far as she was concerned
she was on her way. They were going to be cutting an
album in Vegas while they were there, and she hoped
to be on it. It was everything she had dreamed of for
years.

She left two days later and drove to Las Vegas
with the band. Alex and Eleanor had their hearts in
their mouths when she left. The lead singer picked
her up at the house. He was cocky and arrogant and
good looking, in jeans, a T-shirt, and a black leather
vest. He carried Camille's bag to the car, and said

nothing to her parents, as though they didn't exist. Camille reluctantly hugged her parents before she got in the car, and thanked her father for letting her go. The singer, named Flash Storm, laughed when she said it.

"What are you? A baby? Your parents *let* you go? You're eighteen, aren't you?" She nodded, and looked like a child again to Alex and Eleanor, she was somewhat cowed by the leader of the band, who looked unsavory to them, with slicked down hair, and a cigarette behind his ear. "I hire women, not children. Remember that," he said and got in the car. She slipped in beside him and they drove off, and as soon as they were out of sight, Eleanor burst into tears.

"He'll ruin her," she said, as Alex pulled her onto his lap in the wheelchair so he could hold her.

"We just have to hope she gets tired of it quickly," he said, praying he had done the right thing.

Chapter 13

They hardly heard from Camille once she left for Las Vegas. She had called to tell them the phone number of the house where she was staying with the band, but when they tried to call her, no one ever answered. Eventually they spoke to a few of the band members, who lived at the house too, and they promised to give her the message, but it was several weeks before they heard from her, although she had promised to call them frequently. She said the band's engagement at the nightclub where they were playing had been extended, and they were working on the album now. She told them she was fine, and didn't mention the tour. They were relieved. All they could do was wait it out, and hope for news.

Camille came back to San Francisco in September. She just appeared one night, in tight blue jeans, a tight white satin top with a plunging neckline, looking sexy and infinitely more grown up than when she'd left. Eleanor noticed that she slurred some of her words and wondered if she was drunk. She stayed with them, in her old room.

She said they had been booked for a tour as the opening band for the group they were working with, and they were leaving in a week. She seemed suddenly more womanly, and not like a young girl anymore. Any semblance of innocence was gone. It was obvious from the way she referred to Flash that they were lovers now. Her parents were sick about it, and her mother asked her point-blank if she was on drugs. Camille laughed, and didn't answer her. Eleanor was almost sure she was.

She slept most of the time, and was euphoric and rambling when she was awake. She talked about what a big star Flash was going to be, and he was going to take her all the way with him. She mentioned several big singers at the time, and said that Flash said they were going to be bigger than they were. She said he was hotter than Elvis Presley and more talented. She had a million dreams and illusions and was on a high. Flash had promised to make a single featuring her which would make her a star in her own right.

Alex and Eleanor could feel her slipping through their fingers whenever they talked to her. They couldn't stop her. Flash was paying her, which gave her some independence, and they knew that if they tried to hold her back now, she'd be gone in an instant. They watched her leave for the tour with tears in their eyes.

"Please take care," Eleanor begged her fervently, and Camille laughed at her.

"I'll call you from the road," she said vaguely and got in the cab. She was meeting Flash at the airport, and they were flying to L.A. to start the tour. They would be heading east from there, into the South, through the Midwest, and end up in New York at the end of the year in December. It sounded grueling, but it was what she wanted desperately, and Flash had become her hero. He had made it all happen for her, or said he would.

They heard from her sporadically after that, sometimes once a week, sometimes not for a few weeks. They were playing almost every night, and driving from one town to the next in a bus with the other band they were opening for. They played a venue in Coney Island, in New York in December for the last night of the tour, and she said she'd be home after that for Christmas, but they didn't hear from her and she didn't show up until New Year's Day. She just walked in, and stood staring at them as they ate dinner in the kitchen. She looked jaded and tired. She was scantily clad, and had dark circles under her eyes. This time, there was no doubt in their minds. She was on drugs. There was no sign of Flash. She said he was visiting his mother in New Jersey.

"We signed up for another tour," she said, "opening for a bigger band. We go back on the road in two weeks." She had signed on for a hard life, and they were frightened by the destruction they were afraid Flash was leading her to. But she was on an express train they couldn't stop. They tried talking to her about it while she was there, but she had no interest in what they said, and she was an adult and they couldn't lock her up. She was gone in a few days, and they didn't hear from her for two months after that. Thinking about her was an agony for her parents. They never knew where she was or what she was doing. All they knew was that she was on the road somewhere, with Flash, and on drugs. The child they knew and loved was lost to them.

She turned nineteen in June, and showed up again a few days later. They hadn't seen her in five months. She seemed a little more sober than the last time, but not entirely, and Eleanor could see the minute she walked in that she was pregnant. She was shocked but could no longer be surprised by anything their daughter did. She had taken the road to perdition a year before, and now she was on drugs and pregnant, and the sex slave of a bad guy, all in the name of her music career. It took all of Eleanor's self-restraint not to cry when she was talking to her.

"What are you going to do about the baby?" she asked in a low voice of despair. Alex hadn't seen her yet, and she knew he would be devastated. Their daughter had been ruined by a man called Flash, and what would become of the child?

"I'm going to have it. Why?" Camille looked surprised.

"Are you and Flash going to get married?" Eleanor asked cautiously, afraid to enrage her.

Camille shrugged as though it didn't matter.

"Maybe. Later. I don't know." She didn't look embarrassed, just confused.

"Where are you going to have it?" She wanted her to come home now, for Camille's sake and the child's.

"I can't leave the tour. I'll have it wherever we are. It's not a big deal, Mom. Women have babies all the time, drop them in fields, and keep going."

"Is that what Flash told you?" Eleanor said, wanting to kill him for what he was doing to her. He had brainwashed her, and was keeping her supplied with drugs, Eleanor was sure. He must have found her easier to deal with that way, and it was how he lived too.

"Yeah, one of the girls had a baby last year. She had it at the hotel, and was onstage the next night." She looked unconcerned.

"Camille, you need to come home, so we can take care of you and the baby." She said it as gently as she could and Camille bristled instantly.

"Flash and I can take care of the baby. I don't need you for that."

"You're on drugs." Eleanor decided to be honest with her. "You're going to damage your baby, and yourself. Come home, at least until the baby is born."

"Hell, no!" she said vehemently. "I'm not leaving

Flash. You're just jealous because I have a good life with him and I'm happy."

"I wouldn't call it a good life. You're in a different city every night. God knows what he's giving you. You could lose the baby or die yourself. You need to come home."

"Don't waste your breath," she said angrily, as her father rolled in in his wheelchair and saw the pregnant belly. His eyes flew to her face with a look of shock.

"What's that?"

"Your grandchild, Pops." She grinned at him. She had never called him that before and he wanted to burst into tears but he didn't allow himself to.

"Are you married?" She shook her head and looked disappointed.

"You sound like Mom. I don't need to be married to have a baby."

"It would be preferable," he said in a raw voice, and he could see she was on drugs too. "You need to come home and take care of yourself." She had left a year before, and was on a straight trajectory to her own destruction.

"Flash takes care of me now. He's going to deliver the baby. He did it once before." She sounded blasé about it.

"You need a doctor, a hospital, and us to take care of you. We love you," he pleaded with her and she turned away from him. He was interfering with her life and she would allow nothing to come between her and Flash, surely not her parents. Flash had warned her that they would try to do that and told her to resist. He'd been right, and she followed his advice.

She spent two days with them, while they argued constantly, and on the third day, when they woke up, she was gone, back to Flash again. They didn't even know how pregnant she was and neither did she. She looked four or five months pregnant to Eleanor, but there was no way to be sure. The situation was heart-breaking and there was nothing they could do.

They hardly heard from her after that and worried about her constantly, and the baby. It ravaged Alex noticeably. His only child was in the clutches of a terrible man. Eleanor was just as devastated, but worried about Alex, which gave her something else to think about. He was sixty-three and his war injuries, age, and the stress Camille was putting them through aged him overnight. Eleanor was forty-nine, and hardier than he was. She was younger and in better health. But it was taking a toll on her too. Worrying about their daughter was always at the back of their minds, whatever they were doing. And they talked about her constantly, wondering how and where she was.

They got a collect call from a number in New Jersey on the first of December. They accepted the call immediately. It was Camille. She sounded almost too weak to talk. She was in a hospital in Newark.

"I had the baby last night. It's a girl. I think she was early, she's kind of small. She weighs four pounds. I had her when I came offstage. I didn't know it was happening, so we went back to the hotel, and did some . . ." There was a silence while they filled in the blanks, they had done drugs, which may have been why they didn't know she was in labor, or didn't care. "Flash delivered her. It wasn't too bad, but I bled a lot. They said something was wrong with the placenta. Someone called an ambulance, and they gave me a transfusion. I'm okay. Just tired. I can leave in a few days, but she has to stay in the hospital for a while until she gets bigger, and can breathe better." Camille sounded drugged out, but they couldn't tell if they had given her something at the hospital, or if she was still high from whatever they had taken the night before. Either one was possible, and they could both envision a seriously damaged infant, who might not even survive, or might be mentally or physically disabled if she did, from her mother's drug use. "She's cute. She looks like you, Mom," Camille said weakly, "except she has red hair."

Both of her parents were crying openly at the situation both their daughter and grandchild were in. "I'm going to leave her with Flash's mom when she can leave the hospital. We have to finish the tour and I can't take her with me. She's too small."

"We'll come and get her," Eleanor said, sounding desperate.

"No, that's fine. Flash's mom said she'd keep her till we can come back to get her in a few months."

"I want to come and get your daughter," Alex said suddenly in a booming voice. They had been through enough and so had the baby, only hours after its birth. He and Eleanor remembered only too well what a miracle Camille had been to them when she was born nineteen and a half years before. This was a nightmare, and if they couldn't save their daughter just yet, at least they could save her child.

"I don't want you to, Dad," Camille said in a thin voice. "Flash wouldn't like it. She's his baby too. He wants her with his mom. You probably wouldn't give her back, and you'd make her do all those things you tried to make me do, like be a debutante and go to a fancy school." The baby's life was at stake. This was not about fancy schools. The baby had drug addicted, irresponsible parents, and they had no idea if Flash's mother was any better than they were.

"We want to see you," Alex said in a voice choked with tears, "and the baby. Where are you?" She told them the name of the hospital in Newark, and then her voice seemed to fade away, she was too weak to talk to them any longer.

"What's the baby's name?" Eleanor asked before Camille hung up.

"Ruby Moon," Camille said with a sigh. "There was a beautiful moon last night when I had her. The sky was full of rainbow colors, and the moon was bright red. Ruby Moon Allen." They could easily guess that she'd been on LSD when the baby was born. And then she hung up.

Alex and Eleanor flew to Newark that night, and went straight to the hospital when they arrived in the early morning. They found Camille's room in the maternity ward easily. She was sheet white, with dark circles under her eyes and was getting another transfusion. Her eyes were closed and she opened them as soon as she heard them, and started to cry when she saw them.

"Don't take me home," she pleaded with them. "I want to be with Flash and my baby." She was immediately agitated and her mother tried to calm her down, as Alex turned away so Camille wouldn't see him crying. They couldn't take her home anyway, or the baby. She was legally an adult.

"We want you to come home with us, but we can't force you," Alex said quietly when he turned around and Camille closed her eyes again, reassured that they weren't going to kidnap her and the baby. Flash had said they would try to do that. They were the enemy to Camille now. He had convinced her of it. Alex could see it whenever she spoke to them. She turned to her mother then.

"It hurt more than I thought it would, even though she's so little . . . and there was blood everywhere." Eleanor could imagine it and was grateful she hadn't died. But she looked terrible, and they went to see the baby a few minutes later. She was the smallest infant they had ever seen. She was in an incubator, and they were giving her small puffs of oxygen. Everything about her was tiny. She stared at them through the glass with enormous eyes, and gave a lusty cry when a nurse changed her diaper. She was being bottle fed because Camille was too weak and sick to nurse her.

They went back to see Camille then, and she was asleep. They left and checked into a hotel and for the next two days, they visited Camille. Flash never came to see her. She said he was busy in a recording studio preparing to make the single he had promised her. They tried to convince her to come home with them, but got nowhere. And on the third day when they showed up, Camille was gone and had taken the baby with her. They spoke to the doctors in the nursery who said that being removed at such a low birth weight wouldn't kill her, but would leave her vulnerable to complications which could prove fatal. Alex and Eleanor had no idea where to find her, where they'd gone, if they'd taken the baby with them, or left her with Flash's mother, as they said. They didn't even know Flash Storm's real name, or his mother's, or how to reach the band. They had no phone numbers or names. They tried every avenue they could think of to make contact with Camille, to no avail, and a week later, they went home, without their daughter, or the baby. They were both deeply depressed and worried about the baby, and Camille. They had no choice but to accept their own helplessness. Camille sent them a telegram a week later from a Western Union office in New York. "Ruby and I are fine. I'm with Flash and Ruby is with his mother. Don't worry. I love you." It was small consolation, and Eleanor could hardly think straight when they went back to the shop and put a good face on for their customers. No one knew that their hearts were breaking. But at least they knew that both Camille and the baby were alive when she sent the telegram. They just hoped that it stayed that way.

It was a rugged Christmas, worrying about both of them. They were haunted by the vision of the tiny baby they had seen in the incubator. They were having breakfast on Christmas Day, the shop was closed until after New Year's, and they were planning to go to Lake Tahoe for a few days. The phone rang while Eleanor was clearing away the dishes and Alex answered. Eleanor had a sudden premonition that something was wrong and watched his face. He looked stone faced as he wrote down some information, hung up, and bowed his head, bracing himself before he turned to face his wife. He was fighting tears and couldn't hold them back.

"What is it?" But she knew before she asked him, and took a sharp breath. "Camille?" He nodded.

"It was the Boston police. They played at some bar last night. She and Flash OD'd sometime during the night afterward at their hotel. Their drummer found them this morning. They'd already been dead for several hours. She had us on her ID card in her wallet," he said, sobbing, as they rushed into each other's arms. Their little girl was dead. Flash had killed her. The worst had finally happened, a year and a half after she'd left home with him. And Eleanor suddenly remembered the baby.

"Where's Ruby?"

"They didn't say. Her telegram said she was with Flash's mother." They had no idea where to look for her, or what the woman's name was.

Alex called the Boston police back a few minutes later. The sergeant who had called them before said that their drummer had identified the bodies, so the Boston coroner could release Camille's body to be sent home. Alex asked about the baby, and if they knew anything about the whereabouts of Flash's mother.

"You mean Herbert Goobleman?" he asked in an angry tone. He hated stories like this one. The girl was just a kid. Goobleman was thirty-six years old, and had tracks all over his arms and legs. He had obviously been doing hard drugs for years, and he had a police record for possession and sales. "That's Flash Storm's real name. We have a next of kin listed on his driver's license. Florence Goobleman. We just called her. We couldn't reach her, her boyfriend said she's in jail. We checked. Passing bad checks, posses-sion of a firearm, and some minor drug charges. She has a record an arm long, and some old prostitution charges," the sergeant said disapprovingly.

"My daughter left her baby with her," Alex said, sounding panicked. "The baby is three weeks old."

"I'll look into it," the sergeant said sympathetically. Alex reported what he'd said as they waited. The phone rang half an hour later.

"The infant is in Child Protective Services, in foster care in Newark, New Jersey. They took her when Mrs. Goobleman was arrested a week ago. She has no formal custody arrangement. They were trying to track down the parents, but Goobleman wouldn't give them any information, she probably didn't know."

"We'll be there as soon as we can get there," Alex said, sounding frantic. Camille was dead. Her baby was in foster care somewhere in New Jersey. Their whole world was upside down and had fallen apart. He explained the situation to Eleanor as they rushed to pack.

They were on a flight to Newark that night, and they went straight to Child Protective Services from the airport in the morning after they landed. The case worker was extremely helpful, and they met with a judge of the family court later that morning. The circumstances were clear, as was their right to custody. The foster mother who had been assigned temporarily brought the baby to court, she was a kind, sympathetic woman. The baby was still tiny, and the foster mother said she'd been malnourished when she got her but was eating well now. She handed the baby over. Alex and Eleanor signed all the documents, and the judge extended his condolences over the death of their daughter, whose body was on its way to San Francisco for burial. He wished them luck with the baby. A doctor at Child Protective Services cleared her to fly to California with them. They gave them enough formula, diapers, and clothing to get her home, and last them for a day or two.

By that night, they were on a plane to San Francisco with Ruby in Eleanor's arms. She slept peacefully, as they cried over their daughter, and gazed in wonder at the gift she had left them. They prayed that they could do a better job with her than they had been able to do with Camille. Ruby Moon was theirs to love now. It was the only thing left they could do for their daughter. And on a lonely flight from Boston, Camille was on her way home in a casket.

Chapter 14

When Ruby came to live with her grandparents, it rejuvenated them in some ways, and exhausted them in others. It cast them backward in time to when Camille was a baby, and they loved Ruby as much as if she had been their own. As she grew up, they took her to school, and to Tahoe with them for holidays and vacations. They attended school plays and all her sports events and ballet classes. Eleanor hired a young girl to help her when Ruby was an infant, but as much as possible, with their successful business, they took care of her themselves, sharing their life with her.

They never pretended to be anything other than her grandparents, and as she got older, they showed her photographs of her mother, and shared their happy memories with her and some sad ones. When she was old enough, they told her the circumstances of her mother's death, and hid nothing from her. Remarkably, despite Camille's drug use when she was pregnant, Ruby had suffered no ill effects from it. And although they did nothing different with Ruby than they had with Camille, all the things that had angered Camille about her parents were comfortable for Ruby, and she embraced them. She had no rebellious side, even in her teens, and was very conservative by nature, fascinated by their family's history, and she enjoyed their traditions. She looked remarkably like Camille, and bore a strong resemblance to Eleanor as well, since mother and daughter had looked similar, except that Eleanor had dark hair and Camille was blond. Ruby had their features and their body shape, the same blue eyes, and her hair was red. Ruby was a beautiful child and grew into a very beautiful young woman.

Unlike her mother, she was an excellent student. She was accepted at Stanford, and her passion was computer sciences. She spent hours explaining computers to her grandfather, and Eleanor always laughed and said she didn't understand a word and didn't want to. Ruby preferred studying to social life, and she was shy about making friends, and often preferred to spend time with her grandparents to people her own age. She loved working in their shop during the summers. When the letter came that summer inviting Ruby to be presented at the cotillion and be a debutante, Eleanor was sure she wouldn't want to, and would think it frivolous or old fashioned. A decade of girls before her had boycotted it, in the sixties and the days of "flower power," not long after Camille had refused to do it. But by 1977, when Ruby received the invitation to be a debutante, she pounced on it and waved it at her grandmother.

"Can I do it, Grandma? Can I?" She was starting her freshman year at Stanford in September, but she loved the idea of being a debutante in December, right before Christmas, just as her grandmother had done, almost fifty years before. She said she had always thought it sounded like being Cinderella or a fairy princess for a night and Eleanor grinned when she said it, and was pleased. Life had a way of coming full circle.

"Of course you can. I was afraid you'd think it silly."

"I think it sounds exciting. You made your debut. I want to too." Eleanor smiled at the memory and Ruby's reaction to it, the opposite of Camille's vehemently negative response nearly twenty years before.

"It was different when I came out," Eleanor said with a sigh. "People gave their own balls, they didn't come out together the way they do now. I met your grandfather the night of my debut. He looked like Prince Charming to me." Just for the sake of history, she showed Ruby her debut dress by Worth, still carefully preserved, and told her about going to Paris to have it designed for her. It looked old fashioned now, and very much of its era in 1928. She and Ruby went to Saks and picked out a beautiful white or-

ganza gown that floated around her and showed off
her figure and tiny waist, and she invited a boy she'd
gone to school with to be her escort. They were just
friends and he was as crazy about computers as she
was. She had had no serious romances yet and didn't
seem to care. But she could hardly wait for the big
event in December.

Alex and Eleanor watched her come down the steps
at the Sheraton-Palace Hotel on the arm of her escort
in the beautiful white dress, with her flaming hair
falling in waves down her back, and they smiled at
each other. It was what they had wanted for Camille,
and had been such a battle. And nineteen years later,
Ruby was thrilled. She had loved looking at the
photographs of Eleanor as a debutante, those of her
grandfather at the same time, and the photographs
of their wedding a year later. Eleanor had shown
Ruby her wedding dress, and it didn't look outdated.
Ruby said it was the most beautiful thing she'd ever
seen.

Ruby thoroughly enjoyed her presentation at the
cotillion. Her escort had been the right choice, as just
a friend. He was at Harvard, and they spent the
whole night talking computers. And it was a fun opportunity for them to see the young people they had
gone to school with, since several of the girls being
presented at the cotillion had been her classmates.
To Ruby and her grandparents, the evening was a

great success. It wasn't marked by the vast opulence of Eleanor's debut forty-nine years before, but it was appropriate for the era, and a lovely party, filled with young people and their parents and grandparents in evening clothes. It was everything Camille would have hated, and that Ruby loved.

She had more in common with the grandparents who had raised her than she would have had with her mother, who was such a rebel. Ruby was never rebellious at any age. If anything, she studied too hard and they had to remind her to take a break and play. She thought studying was fun.

In her sophomore year at Stanford, she was studying in the library one weekend, when a senior sat across the desk from her, seemed fascinated by her, and stared at her red hair. They left the library at the same time, and he explained that he was working on his senior project. He said he'd had a summer job at Xerox's Palo Alto Research Center the previous summer, where he said he got interested in GUIs. He explained that they were graphical user interfaces, which allowed a person to interact with a computer through graphics. He made it sound fascinating. His senior project was to devise some applications for GUIs to make using a computer easier for a home user. His name was Zack Katz, and she understood what he was talking about immediately and thought it was brilliant. He grinned when she told him that and they became fast friends from that moment on. He shared his progress on his project with her, and they studied for exams together. He had grown up in Palo Alto with his father, who worked for Hewlett-Packard. He said his parents had been divorced since he was eleven, and hated each other, and now he rarely saw either of them, and had no home life, and never had. They had gotten married because his mother was pregnant with him. He was an only child like Ruby. His mother had remarried and lived in Texas and his stepfather was a jerk. He hated visiting them so he no longer did. His father hadn't remarried but had a constantly changing slew of very young girlfriends. "My family defines dysfunctional," was how Zack summed it up. It sounded sad to Ruby. She told him about her parents OD'ing when she was three weeks old, and being raised by her grandparents, whom she said were fantastic and she adored. She seemed happy, normal, and well balanced, and they liked each other immediately and rapidly became best friends and constant companions.

Zack was what other students called a geek, and during school holidays and weekends when she was there, he dropped in to see Ruby at her grandparents' shop in the city. He enjoyed lengthy conversations with her grandfather, and thought that he and Ruby's grandmother were "cool." He liked being around them, unlike his own family. He hung out as long as Ruby's family would let him.

"He's so smart, isn't he, Grampa?" Ruby said admiringly, and Alex laughed.

"He certainly is. I have no idea what he's talking

about most of the time." But he liked him and he was a good friend for Ruby, and a very decent boy. Alex felt sorry for his disrupted home life too.

"Really?" She seemed surprised at her grandfather's comment that Zack's theories were beyond him.

"He makes everything so simple to understand," she said easily and Alex shook his head.

"For you maybe." Her grandfather smiled at her. "For us mere mortals, he's speaking Chinese."

Zack invited Ruby to his Stanford graduation. She had met his father by then. His mother hadn't come, and his father brought a cheesy girlfriend who wore a tight dress with a plunging neckline, and was younger than Zack, and Zack's father flirted with Ruby during the ceremony. Zack was mortified by him. He invited Ruby to join them for lunch at a restaurant in Palo Alto. It was awkward but she stayed.

Two weeks later the applications he had designed for GUIs as a senior project and the new software he had written sold to a high-tech company for two hundred million dollars. He was interviewed in *Time* magazine and had dazzled the company that bought his software. Zack treated it as an ordinary occurrence, and went to work immediately on more complicated ideas for networking to connect researchers all over the world. He took Ruby out to dinner to tell her about it.

"Wait a minute, hold on here. You just sold your senior project for two hundred million dollars? That's a *huge* deal, Zack." She tried to get him to focus on it and he looked embarrassed. He had picked her up for dinner wearing cutoff jeans, a faded T-shirt, and old high-top Converse with holes in them, and she was wearing shorts and flip-flops and a Stanford T-shirt. They were an even match.

"My next one will be better. That was just the rough model. I don't know why they bought it." He looked puzzled.

"Oh my God. You're crazy. You're rich now. You're a huge success. You're going to be famous in computer circles." He already was but was paying no attention to it. The newspapers had been full of the story for two days. He had made history.

"My dad's going to invest the money for me." He didn't like his father but thought he was smart in business. Zack was twenty-two and looked like an overgrown kid and acted like one. They had burgers for dinner at Jack in the Box, and then walked back to the building where she still lived with her grandparents, above the shop, when she wasn't at school. It never occurred to Zack to take her to a better restaurant after his win, and neither of them considered it a date. They were just friends. "I'm going to Europe on a graduation trip with my dad. He's bringing one of his girlfriends." He rolled his eyes when he said it. "What are you doing?"

"Just going to Tahoe as usual. It's nice there. You should come up when you get back." He nodded and liked the idea, gave her a hug and left her at her front door, and she ran into her grandparents when she got home.

"That's quite a deal your friend Zack made," Alex commented and she nodded. He'd been reading about it in the papers. It was all over the press.

"He's already working on other concepts." It was becoming clear that he was something of a genius in the high-tech world, the money didn't mean anything to him, the challenge and the fun did, and she loved that about him. She hated show-offs. Zack was anything but that. He was the perfect geek, and her closest friend.

He drove up to Lake Tahoe for a weekend in his battered Toyota when he got back from Europe, and visited Ruby regularly at Stanford that winter whenever he had time. He had kept his abysmally ugly student apartment just off the Stanford campus, where he still lived. He didn't care how it looked. The project he was working on was intricate and intense and took up all his attention. He explained it to her carefully, and she had a relatively good grasp of the theory, and loved talking to him about it. She was studying computer sciences too, but she was nowhere near his league. She felt earthbound compared to him while he was out in the stratosphere somewhere. All she wanted was a good job with a great high-tech outfit of some kind, when she graduated. He said he'd help her find one. She still had another year at Stanford to get through. There were never any romantic overtones between them. He dated occasionally, but usually scared the girls off after the first date. He was painfully awkward or stood them up when he forgot about the date and kept working. Ruby told him to set an alarm clock, but his dating skills were embarrassingly poor, and he didn't seem to care. He had other pursuits that interested him more, like work. Most girls bored him to extinction and if so, halfway through dinner, he said so, despite Ruby's coaching. She called him a Space Age Neanderthal in the dating world.

She had dated a few people too, but by the time she graduated, she had never been in love. She had loved her years at Stanford and graduated with honors, but the nerdy boys she met were always too boring, and looked like unmade beds, as her grandmother said. The ultra smart ones who were more worldly and hell-bent on success were too full of themselves, and too superficial, to interest Ruby, and the pretty boys were too narcissistic. She wanted to fall in love with a real person, like her grandfather.

She admired the relationship her grandparents had after fifty-two years together. Her grandmother was seventy-one, and her grandfather eighty-five, but still going strong. They had withstood the test of time and everything that had happened to them. She didn't want anything less than they had and had never met anyone like them. Most of her friends' parents were divorced, and her own mother had been a disaster. Ruby wasn't worried about meeting someone, when she graduated, all she wanted was a good job that used the skills she had learned, and her innate talent with computers.

A month after she graduated, she was sending out applications, when Zack called her and told her he had made another deal for his concept for a new operating system. He told her it was a much bigger deal than the first one and far more complicated. He sounded a little dazed when he called her. He told her about a menu bar and controls for windows he had incorporated into his entirely new operating system, and computer animated films.

"Fantastic!" She congratulated him. "How much did you get this time?" she asked him casually. "Jack in the Box tonight to celebrate?"

"Yeah, sure," he said just as casually, and then in an undervoice, "A billion."

"A billion what?"

"I sold it for a billion dollars," he said. "It's kind of embarrassing. It's too much money. They overpaid me."

"Holy shit! Are you serious?" she screamed at him. "A *billion* dollars? What are you going to do with that?"

"I don't know. I need new Converse. Do you want to go shopping with me tomorrow?"

"Zack, will you stop for a minute. This is a *huge* achievement. Can you please enjoy it for a minute? You can do anything you want. You're a super important person, and very rich now," at twenty-four. He couldn't get his mind around it yet, and was trying to ignore it.

"Yeah . . . maybe . . . I don't know . . . I never think about that."

They had dinner at Jack in the Box that night, and shopped for Converse the next day. She talked him into buying two pairs, a low-top black pair he said he would use on dress occasions, and high-top white ones. He wasn't cheap. He just didn't care about material things for himself. He loved creating things that involved computers. The money was less important to him. He was twenty-four years old and a billionaire. It was beyond his ability to comprehend. Ruby knew that people would try to take advantage of him now. They had been since the first win, and Zack knew it too. She felt sorry for him sometimes. It was hard for him to know who his friends were. But he always knew who she was. She was a constant for him. They were still best friends, and always would be. He knew he could count on her.

"Don't forget, I need you to help me find a job," she reminded him. "Maybe your dad can get me an interview with Hewlett-Packard." He had a very senior position, although Zack didn't talk to him often, and was happier when he didn't.

"I'll ask him but you don't need his help with that. You're the smartest girl I know," Zack said, smiling at her. He could talk to her about anything, his computer inventions, or other things like sports or books or people or movies, or abstract concepts.

He thought about it that night when he went home. He had messages from *The New York Times* and *The Wall Street Journal* wanting interviews, and some foreign newspapers, and *Time* magazine and he erased them. He had nothing to say to the press. He wasn't interested in talking to them. And he knew Ruby agreed with him. She thought they would exploit him, and had warned him of that.

He thought about the job she wanted him to help her find, and then he realized he knew exactly the right one. He called her in the morning and woke her up.

"Why are you still asleep?" He sounded annoyed.

"Because it's seven o'clock on a Saturday morning and I stayed up late, watching a movie on TV last night," she grumbled at him. "You're supposed to wait till nine o'clock to call people on a weekday, ten o'clock on weekends. My grandma told me so."

"That's regular people, not you. I thought of the perfect job for you."

"Did you talk to your dad?" She sounded hopeful as she sat up in bed. It was a foggy San Francisco summer day, and she had promised her grandparents she would help them in the shop. She'd been doing that a lot since she'd finished school a few weeks before.

"No, this was my idea," Zack said about the job he had in mind for her. "I'll come over and tell you about it later."

"I'm working in the shop today."

"I have to get something and then I'll come over."

"I'm not going anywhere," she said, and then they hung up, and she got up a little while later. They didn't open the shop until eleven, and she was going to work with Tim Avery and a young woman who worked for them now too, and helped her grandmother with her decorating business. Her grandparents were taking the day off. They were going to a museum exhibit that her grandmother wanted to see.

Ruby was helping a customer who was interested in an English partner's desk when Zack came in just before lunchtime. He sprawled in a chair and smiled at her, while she gave the customer all the details, and a photograph of the desk to think about and show her husband. She left and Ruby came over to talk to him. He was wearing a pair of ancient shorts and his new white high-top Converse. He looked excited, and she smiled at him.

"So what's the job for me?"

"Easy. I should have thought of it before, but you had to graduate anyway."

"Big company or start-up?" She looked intrigued.

"More the latter. You're perfect for it. You're brilliant, Ruby Moon. You can do anything. You understand everything I talk to you about." He was smiling at her, and as he said it, he slipped down on one knee in his shorts and new high-top white Converse that made him look like a little kid, which he almost was anyway. He was twenty-four years old and looked about fifteen. "Will you marry me, Ruby?" he asked her, with a hopeful look as she stared at him in disbelief, looking irritated.

"Will you stop making fun of me. I thought you had a real job for me. That's not funny. I need a job. I can't live off my grandparents forever."

"I'm serious," he said, remaining on one knee in front of her, as Tim and his assistant watched them with interest, wondering what he was doing. Tim had been reading about Zack's new windfall. The whole world had been. As he spoke, Zack pulled something out of the pocket of his baggy shorts that had had too many washings and were clean but faded and torn. He pulled out a small gray leather box with a white satin ribbon around it and handed it to her.

"What's that?" She looked confused as she took it from him.

"It's for you. Open it." She pulled off the ribbon cautiously and opened the box, and an enormous round object sparkled at her with such vehemence that it almost blinded her.

"Holy crap, Zack, what is that?" He stood up then, took it out of the box, and put it on her finger.

"It's an engagement ring, you dummy. Haven't you ever seen one before?"

"Not like *that*." She looked at him then and could see that he was serious, and her eyes opened even wider.

"I realized last night that I love you. You're the

most fantastic woman I've ever met, and I want to marry you. That's the job I meant. I want you to be my wife. It's full-time." He grinned at her and she laughed. "And the ring is thirty carats by the way. It was the biggest one they had in the store. I thought bigger might be too showy, but they can get a bigger one if you want." He talked about it like a skateboard, or a television he had bought for her. But he looked pleased when he saw it on her finger. She was staring at it. It looked like a headlight from someone's car. She was wearing a denim skirt and a sweater, and he looked like he was going to the park to walk his dog. They looked like kids, as she stared at the incredible stone on her hand.

"Aren't we too young to get married? I'm twenty-two and you're twenty-four."

"I love you, Ruby," he said simply, and then he kissed her for the first time, as the two shopkeepers smiled, and Ruby smiled when he stopped.

"I love you too. I've always loved you, Zack. I thought we were just friends."

"We are friends, that's the best part. We each get to be married to our best friend. Besides, it would be nice to have kids one day. Do you want kids?" She nodded. It was all happening so fast, just like his enormous success. Zack was someone who moved at full speed and didn't like to waste time. But she did love him, and she liked the idea of being married to him. She'd never even had a serious boyfriend before. Maybe she had been in love with him all along. She wasn't sure. But she was now. She looked at the ring then, and then back at him.

"You don't have to give me a big ring like that," she said softly. "I would marry you with nothing."

"That's why I love you," he said, and kissed her again.

Her grandparents stopped by the shop then to see how things were going, although they knew Ruby was always conscientious when she was there. They smiled when they saw Zack.

"Are you buying antiques now, Zack?" Alex teased him as he rolled his chair in. Eleanor was right behind him and suddenly stared at her granddaughter's left hand.

"Good heavens, what's that?"

"It's a diamond," Zack said matter-of-factly. "I just asked Ruby to marry me." He smiled and Ruby looked suddenly shy.

"Did you now," Alex said. "And what did she say?" Zack frowned then and looked puzzled as he turned to Ruby, no longer sure.

"What did you say?" Zack asked her and she grinned and leaned over to kiss him on the cheek.

"I said yes . . . or I was going to . . ."

Zack beamed at her and turned to her grandfather. "She said yes." Alex smiled at them, and Eleanor laughed as she shook her head.

"Congratulations," Alex said and shook his future

grandson-in-law's hand, while Eleanor took Ruby in her arms and hugged her.

"And now we have a wedding to plan," she said with delight. They were young, and Zack was a little odd, but it seemed right for them. And Ruby would be good for him, and he would be for her.

Chapter 15

Once she had gotten used to the idea, Ruby loved being engaged to Zack. She couldn't think of anything better than being married to her best friend. She could say anything to him, she knew him better than anyone, they understood each other, and once they were engaged, Zack blossomed, and all he wanted to do was spoil her and make her happy. The engagement ring that looked like a headlight was only the beginning. He brought her presents constantly, talked about trips they would take, houses they would buy, things they were going to do. His genius had brought them an incredible fortune, which he couldn't even fathom yet, and all he wanted to do was lavish it on her. The fact that Ruby didn't expect it, or even want it, made it all the more fun. She was an unassuming, undemanding woman, which he loved about her. It made him want to spoil her even more.

He assumed she'd move into his ugly student apartment with him until her grandmother gently suggested it might be too small, and Zack realized she was right. Besides, he had gotten his furniture at secondhand stores, and it embarrassed him to have Ruby live there. They realized that they needed a house or an apartment, but they couldn't decide where. Zack wasn't sure if he wanted to live in Palo Alto where he grew up, or San Francisco where she had. Ruby said they could always live with her grandparents for a while, in her room, until they figured it out. Zack liked that idea because he liked them so much and they were so nice to him. So once they figured that out, there was no rush to find a place to live and could focus on the wedding, which seemed more pressing to Zack.

The wedding was likely to be awkward on his side. His parents didn't speak to each other and refused to be in the same room, and he assumed his mother wouldn't come. She never did. He had grown up with his dad, after the divorce. And his father didn't have a house where they could get married. They consulted Ruby's grandparents, who knew the finest homes in the city and had furnished many of them. They thought a hotel would be too commercial. Alex's old home wasn't an option. The hotel that it had been turned into had changed hands several times and had supposedly gone to rack and ruin, and was seedy now, and the furniture had been sold years before. The most recent owners were thinking of tearing it down. He'd never been inside it since he'd sold it, and didn't want to see it again. He said it would make him too sad remembering what it had once been. But Eleanor cautiously suggested the Hamilton School which was what the Deveraux mansion had become. She hadn't been back either, but she'd been told by several of her decorating clients that the school rented out for weddings, and with enough flowers and a good event decorator, it could look very pretty for an event. Seeing it again gave her some qualms, but at least the location had some meaning for them, especially since she and Alex had been married there. Ruby said she loved the idea. Zack was game for whatever they found. Neither he nor Ruby had an enormous number of friends, and they thought they would have about a hundred and fifty guests, maybe two hundred. The school appealed to both of them, for its historical ties to Ruby's family.

"Shall I make an appointment to see it?" Eleanor asked Zack and Ruby one night when they had dinner with them, and Ruby said she'd love to. They wanted to get married in the fall, and were thinking October, which was when her grandparents had gotten married, too. Working out the wedding plans had suddenly superseded her search for a job, and she had decided to wait until the first of the year, after their honeymoon and the holidays before she got back to serious job hunting. They wanted to find a place they both loved for the wedding first.

Eleanor was surprised by how easy it was when she called the school. She thought she'd have to explain who she was, and what they had in mind. They had an events coordinator who handled the frequent rentals. The woman told her it had become a very popular venue for weddings, and they even had a brochure, which they sent her in the mail. It listed the prices, the packages, the available spaces, and the rules. When Eleanor studied it, she saw that the ballroom was almost unchanged. They used it for all school assemblies, the brochure said. Weddings were confined to the reception floors. The upstairs bedrooms were all classrooms now, and didn't lend themselves to parties. But the grand staircase could be used for the bride to make an entrance if they wished. It was strange for Eleanor to read the brochure, and bittersweet when she saw the historical photos on one page, showing one of the grand parties of the past, which Eleanor recognized instantly as her coming out ball, with all the footmen standing at attention in the front hall, holding trays of champagne as the guests arrived. It gave her a pang of nostalgia to see it.

"Will it be too hard for you if they have the wedding there?" Alex asked her afterward, with a tender look.

"I don't think so. Bittersweet perhaps, and nostalgic certainly. But I think it would mean a lot to Ruby. She is fascinated by our history." His wife smiled at him. "And I like the idea of her getting married in the same house we did, even if everything is changed, and it doesn't belong to us anymore." But many things were still the same. "It's funny, isn't it? Camille had no interest in any of it, and Ruby does and is very attached to our family history. Maybe that kind of thing skips a generation," she mused.

"They're very different women," Alex said quietly. "Ruby is much more like you. Camille wanted to forge her own path, and it led her to disaster."

"I think Ruby has always been afraid she'd be like her mother. She said that to me once. But she's nothing like her. Ruby is as conservative as we are, and she loves all our old traditions." Their daughter had been gone for twenty-two years, and losing her still made them sad. Ruby had been an enormous consolation to them, and a lovely, easy child. They had never had any problems with her. She had never rebelled against them, and had always been close to her grandparents.

The day Eleanor and Ruby went to see the house, Zack decided to come with them. He was in awe of the beauty of the house the moment they walked in. So was Ruby. They held hands and gazed up at the high ceilings, the beautiful moldings, the wood paneling, the chandeliers, the grand staircase. It took Eleanor's breath away for a moment too. It was a trip back in time for her. She hadn't been there for fifty-one years, since she and Alex and her parents left it in 1930, when her parents moved to Lake Tahoe, and she and Alex to the little apartment in Chinatown. So much had happened since then.

The event coordinator took them around and explained how the rooms could be set up, and Eleanor smiled as she explained. "We had dinner guests seated here," Eleanor said dreamily, "and in an enormous tent outside. We tented the whole square," she explained, and the woman smiled.

"Have you rented here before? I've only worked here for four years."

"I used to live here," Eleanor said quietly. "I grew up in this house. It was my family home. My husband and I were married here." The event coordinator looked vastly impressed.

"Then you know much more about the house than I do. We can set up the ballroom for dinner guests too. And of course you know we can't use the original gardens. They were sold many years ago and there's a home in that space now. But we have some pleasant paths where people can walk around on a warm night."

They walked through all of the reception rooms and Eleanor had to resist being flooded by memories in every room—her parents, Alex, Christmas dinners they had given, balls, her debut, her wedding. The rooms were filled with ghosts for her, but they were happy memories, and Ruby and Zack were deeply moved when they left.

"Oh, Grandma, I love the house so much. Would it upset you too much if we rent it for the wedding?"

She was concerned, and Zack was still floating from the beauty of visiting the Deveraux home.

"No, I'd love it," Eleanor said generously. "Your grandfather and I would be delighted if you get married where we did. I wish we still owned the house so we could really do it the way we used to. I noticed that the school requires you to end an event at midnight. Our wedding, and my debut, went on until breakfast the next morning."

"That sounds like fun." Zack grinned. "Egg Mc-Muffins for everyone!"

"More like blinis and caviar." Eleanor smiled at him.

"Wow!"

"I think you two can really have a fabulous wedding there," Eleanor said, looking as excited as they were. In a way, it felt like going home. "Shall we do it?" Both young people nodded, and she told Alex all about it that night. She told him what had changed and what hadn't. She had wanted to explore the upstairs but it wasn't allowed. They had made changes, in order to institutionalize it a little for the school, but the alterations weren't too extreme. She hadn't been shocked by it, only touched by her flood of memories, mostly happy ones of the good years, not the end.

She confirmed it with the event coordinator the next day, and Alex wrote a check for the deposit. Tim dropped it off at the Hamilton School on the way home. Zack and Ruby had chosen Saturday, October third, as their wedding day, two days before her grandparents' anniversary. They had four months to plan the wedding, and Eleanor got busy with it. She had to call the florist, a caterer, look for a band the young people would want to dance to, a wedding cake baker. There were myriad details to attend to, and it was a happy task. Eleanor had everything organized by the time they left for Lake Tahoe at the end of July.

Before they left, Ruby came home one afternoon to meet with her grandmother. The enormous box was waiting in her bedroom. The exquisite Jeanne Lanvin wedding dress was still in its original box, with all the accessories that went with it. Eleanor had promised to show it to Ruby so she could decide if she wanted to wear it, or get another dress. She hadn't made her mind up yet whether she wanted to wear a new dress or an old one. She wasn't sure her grandmother's dress would fit, or would look too dated. The dress was fifty-two years old, but the design that Eleanor and her mother had chosen had been timeless. She removed all the tissue paper around it and lifted it carefully out of the box, as Ruby stared at it, and then gasped as her grandmother held it up. She had never seen anything so beautiful in her life. Then she took out the veil, which looked as lovely as the day they had put it away. Wilson had packed it up the day Eleanor and Alex left on their honeymoon. She was glad now that they had not sold it when they sold everything else, including most of her mother's fur coats and some evening gowns, in 1929. They had sold everything for almost nothing.

Eleanor carefully undid the buttons and Ruby took her skirt and top off. Eleanor slipped the dress on her effortlessly. The dress was heavy, with the embroidery and the pearls, but it went on easily and was perfectly balanced so the person wearing it didn't feel the weight. She fastened all the tiny buttons, and then Ruby turned to look at herself in the mirror and gasped again. The most beautiful bride she'd ever seen was staring at her in the mirror. Even the length was perfect, the arms, the tiny waist. Eleanor gently put the veil on her head and adjusted it, and told her she had kept the tiara that she had worn with it. It was one of the few pieces of jewelry she had left, but she hadn't been able to part with it.

"Oh, Grandma, can I wear it?" Ruby asked breathlessly, and Eleanor could almost imagine Madame Lanvin smiling at her, and her own mother, and Wilson discreetly in the background. Eleanor knew that Wilson was still alive in Ireland at ninety-eight, and Houghton had passed on several years before.

"Of course, you can wear it, my darling. Nothing would make me happier than to see you in that dress." She hugged her granddaughter, wishing that things had been different, that Camille were still alive, and she had worn it too, instead of the way her life had turned out and ended so tragically. But things happened for a reason, and Ruby had been the greatest gift in her life and in Alex's. Now she would be starting her life with Zack, in Eleanor's wedding dress.

She helped Ruby take the dress and veil off, and they folded it away carefully in its box. She was going to hang it and air it, when they got back from Lake Tahoe, but in the meantime, it was safely put away, waiting for the Big Day.

When they left Eleanor's room, it was as though they shared a special secret. Eleanor couldn't wait to see Ruby in it on her wedding day, and Zack's and Alex's faces when she wore it.

Ruby had to struggle not to tell Zack about the dress when she saw him an hour later. She wanted to keep it a secret until he saw it on their wedding day. He didn't even know the dress existed. She hadn't said anything since she didn't know how it would work out or if she would want to wear it.

They had been engaged for a month and after trying on the dress, Ruby really felt like a bride now. The wedding was falling into place. Everything had happened so quickly that the reality hadn't sunk in yet. They had been friends until now, and they were getting married in three months. They hadn't even slept with each other. It was hard to find the opportunity. She lived with her grandparents and he lived in an abysmal apartment an hour away in Palo Alto. He didn't want the first time he made love to her to be among the secondhand remnants of his college life. And they hadn't even looked for a place to live yet, since they were planning to stay at her grandparents' for a while.

Zack didn't really care where he lived. They had talked about going away for a romantic weekend, but hadn't had time to. Her grandmother had said he could stay in the cottage with Ruby in Tahoe. They were surprisingly modern about things like that. After all, they were engaged and the subject had never come up before. She'd never brought a boyfriend home, had never been in love before, and had only had sex twice in her life, with a boy she wasn't in love with, when she had too much to drink at a party in college. But she and Zack were excited and feeling shy about making love for the first time.

She had promised to help him try to sort out his apartment that night. He said he wanted to throw most of his stuff away, and Ruby had said she'd do it with him. He said he'd provide the pizza and garbage bags if she'd do the packing with him. The only thing worth keeping was his computer, in his opinion.

She drove to Palo Alto after trying on the wedding dress and felt like she was in a dream all the way there, and kissed him tenderly when she arrived with a mysterious smile, thinking of the dress.

"That was nice," he said, grinning at her and kissed her again. They had spent so little time alone since they'd been engaged that it was nice to have the time, even in his dump of an apartment, which had been adequate as a student, but no longer appropriate given his massive success, but he didn't care. He hadn't moved after he graduated.

She looked around and cringed. She'd been there before when they were in college, but it seemed to have gotten worse.

"When did you last clean this place?" she asked, trying to make room to sit down among the books and newspapers on the battered couch.

"I don't know . . . Christmas? Last summer? Why?"

"I think most of it needs to go in a dumpster, not a garbage bag," she said honestly.

"That bad, huh?"

She nodded. "Why don't we just pack the books, and I'll get rid of everything else," she suggested.

"That'll work." He had gotten some cartons and she put the books in them while he sliced the pizza and poured them some wine in the only two glasses he had. He was staring at her as she bent over to pack the books, and she glanced at him to see what he was doing. He was mesmerized by her, as though seeing her for the first time.

"What? Do I look weird or something?"

"No, you're so beautiful, Ruby. I can't keep my eyes off you."

She blushed as he said it, and he walked over and kissed her and slid his hands under her T-shirt. He was breathless and gently pulled her T-shirt off and

tossed it behind him, and kissed her again as he un-
hooked her bra, and then bent to kiss her breasts.

"I thought we were supposed to be packing," she
said in a hoarse voice as she unzipped his shorts, and
they fell to the floor, and he stood there in his underwear and she topless, and the rest happened effortlessly. He carried her to his bed, and took the rest of
her clothes off and his. They lay naked together, exploring each other's bodies for the first time, and discovered the passion they had for each other and never
knew. He was a passionate, energetic lover and tender
at the same time and she blossomed at his touch and
suddenly felt like a woman with him, not just a girl.

They lay breathless afterward and he was smiling
and she laughed. She was happy and she loved him.

"I should have brought you here to pack before,"
he said, admiring her body as she lay next to him.

"You should burn this place down." She grinned
at him.

"I think we just did," he said, kissing her, and got
up to get the wine and handed her a glass. "I love
you, Ruby Moon."

"I love you too, Zack."

"I'm going to love being married to you," he said
happily. They took a sip of the wine, and then they
set their glasses down and did it again.

Eleanor used the time in Tahoe that summer to rest
before she came back to the city to plan the wedding

in earnest, and attend to all the details. She spent hours in her garden, and got Alex to help her with it. It was always a peaceful time there. They went out on the boat, Alex went fishing. And Zack came up with Ruby and spent a week with them. They stayed in the cottage, and loved making love all night and waking up together. They were both thrilled with their engagement, and were busy making plans of their own. Zack had rented a yacht for them in the Caribbean for their honeymoon, and it sounded incredibly luxurious to Ruby.

The only disagreement they had was about what to put on the invitation, about the attire for the guests. Zack wanted it to say "casual," which Ruby objected to, before her grandmother ordered the invitations.

"If you say that, all your techie friends will show up in Converse and shorts," Ruby complained.

"What's wrong with that?" Zack asked, surprised, and Alex and Eleanor exchanged a look of amusement, and knew that Ruby was right. Zack always looked like he'd dressed in clothes he'd picked up from the floor.

"I want everyone to look nice at the wedding," Ruby insisted. Especially if she wore her grandmother's exquisite dress, she wanted Zack in a real suit. "It won't kill them to look like grown-ups for a change." Zack grumbled about it but finally conceded. Ruby told her grandmother that she didn't want to wear her fabulous wedding dress surrounded by a sea of guys looking like they were on their way to the beach or to play basketball. And Eleanor agreed. They put "coat and tie and cocktail attire" on the invitation, to dress them up a little.

Ruby took Zack to buy a suit in San Francisco, since he said he didn't own one. He was one of the richest men in America and he didn't own proper clothes.

When they got back from Lake Tahoe at the end of August, Eleanor got busy with all the details for the wedding. The flowers, the food, the cake, she checked the tablecloths at the Hamilton School and asked them to order new ones. She met with the florist several times at the school, and tried to re-create the same atmosphere and look of her own wedding, without going to the extremes her parents had fifty years before. There had been garlands over every doorway, then. Eleanor managed with just two. The dinner tables were set up in the ballroom, and there was still enough room for the band, and the guests to dance.

Eleanor found the time to pick out a dress for herself. It was navy blue lace with a matching coat. The wedding dress was hanging and ready in the guest room, with the shoes Ruby had chosen to go with it. She and her grandmother were the same height, but the shoes Eleanor had worn were tiny. She still had small, narrow, elegant feet. Modern women had bigger feet.

Since Zack's parents weren't on good terms after

the divorce, they decided not to give a rehearsal dinner, which upset Zack at first and Ruby convinced him was okay, but he hated the fact that they couldn't make the effort for him to be civil for one evening. His mother was bringing her jerk of a husband to the wedding, according to Zack, and his father was bringing his current girlfriend who was a year older than Ruby. They had met through a dating service and Zack was annoyed. Zack and Ruby were going to go out for dinner with her grandparents the night before the wedding.

Zack was already working on new concepts for networking that were more intricate than the concept he'd sold for a billion dollars. He had only just begun his meteoric climb in the high-tech world. He loved what he was doing, and he couldn't wait to be married to Ruby. When he left her the night before the wedding, he kissed her and they lingered at the front door for a few minutes.

"I can't wait till tomorrow," he whispered.

"Me too." She smiled. They were perfectly suited to each other.

She lay awake in her bed for hours that night, thinking about him, and the dress she was going to wear the next day. She couldn't wait for Zack to see it.

Chapter 16

It was a golden October morning when Ruby woke up on the day of her wedding. Her grandmother came to give her a hug, and was busy all morning after that, checking on the last details.

The ceremony was going to be at six o'clock at Grace Cathedral, on Nob Hill, which was newly built with its spectacular bronze doors since Eleanor and Alex's wedding. The guests would then wander across the street to the Hamilton School, the old Deveraux mansion, where the reception was being held.

Alex kept busy and stayed out of the women's path all day. The hairdresser came at two and did Ruby's hair in a simple chignon, similar to the style Eleanor had worn but without the finger waves to frame her face. She attached the tiara to Ruby's head securely, and at five o'clock Eleanor helped her put on the dress that Ruby had been dreaming about since she'd seen it in July. Then they settled the veil over her tiara. It was the thinnest layer of white tulle, the merest illusion, and as soon as it was in place, Eleanor stood back with tears in her eyes as she admired her granddaughter in the mirror. Ruby looked serious and innocent, and spectacular in the dress that had survived more than half a century since her grandmother wore it.

"Darling, you look incredible," her grandmother whispered and Ruby faced her in the mirror, and for the first time in a long time, thought about her mother.

"She really missed the boat on everything, Grandma, didn't she?" Eleanor knew who she meant and nodded with a sigh. She meant Camille. She had left Ruby motherless three weeks after she was born, and broken her parents' hearts. It was a long time ago now, but still a dull ache for Eleanor and Alex whenever they thought about her.

"I'm sure she would have wanted to be here," Eleanor said sadly. She didn't speak of Camille often. It was still painful, twenty-two years after her death. "She followed the wrong path, and got lost along the way." But she and Alex had been there for Ruby, and she had never lacked for love or attention and was grateful to them for it. Now she and Zack would have a family of their own. But she still wished at times that she had known her mother. It made her want to be the best mother in the world to her children one day. The way her grandmother had been to her.

Camille had also had a wild streak, which Ruby

never did. Eleanor couldn't imagine Camille wearing the wedding dress that Ruby had on, under any conditions. She had done everything to reject her parents' values and fight tradition, whereas Ruby embraced it. Ruby had wanted everything to be as close as possible to her grandmother's wedding, and had carefully studied the wedding albums. She was even carrying an identical bouquet of tiny phalaenopsis orchids and lily of the valley.

Eleanor carried Ruby's train down the stairs for her, as Wilson had done for her, and Alex stared at his granddaughter when he saw her. He felt as though he had been cast backward fifty-two years. Except for the red hair, Ruby looked just like her grandmother. And now that he saw it again, he remembered the dress perfectly. It was just as beautiful on Ruby as it had been on Eleanor.

The three of them rode to the church together, in the car they had hired with a driver. It was a vintage Rolls-Royce. Alex waited for the chauffeur to set up his wheelchair for him when they reached the church, and he got into it smoothly, and then Eleanor helped Ruby out. Alex was going to roll down the aisle next to her. They entered the cathedral through the rectory, and waited for the music to start as their cue, and then Ruby walked slowly down the aisle, next to her grandfather, with her eyes on Zack waiting for her at the altar, as their friends stared at her in her grandmother's exquisite wedding dress. She looked like a vision from the past, but there was something timeless about it. Zack looked totally bowled over by her when she stood next to him, and Alex rolled himself next to the first pew to take his place next to Eleanor.

"I feel like I'm watching you at our wedding," he whispered to her and took her hand. Except that the church had been a temporary one, and the park outside had been tented.

Zack and Ruby had decided on traditional vows, and exchanged simple gold wedding rings, while Eleanor and Alex cried unabashedly, and when the minister declared them man and wife, Zack kissed her so hard she was breathless and everyone laughed and applauded, and then they went back down the aisle, beaming at their friends.

When the wedding guests arrived at the house, Alex looked at them in amusement. Some of the richest men in America were there, and they looked more like boys going to summer camp than business moguls. About half of them had worn suits that looked brand new and in which they appeared supremely uncomfortable, and as though they'd never worn a suit or tie before in their lives. The other half of the men had come in jeans and had worn jackets with them, a few had worn shorts in spite of what the invitation had said. Some of the boys in suits were wearing T-shirts and sneakers with them. There were more high-top sneakers in the room than proper shoes. And all of the men there were considerably under thirty. They looked like children to Alex, and yet most of them had already made astounding fortunes in high-tech.

"All that brain power and not one of them knows how to wear a tie," Alex said, smiling at his wife. "You look beautiful," he complimented her. He felt as though there were two of her there that night, the woman he was married to now, and the vision of her as a young girl in the wedding dress. It had been the happiest night of his life, and he remembered every minute of it distinctly. Zack looked just as happy now, and when Ruby and Zack danced their first dance, Eleanor and Alex felt as though they were having an out-of-body experience watching them. The house looked wonderful, with all the touches that Eleanor had remembered to add to replicate their wedding, just as Ruby wanted. The floral centerpieces on the tables were the same, and copied from old photographs.

When the guests sat down to dinner in the ballroom, everyone started dancing, and Alex looked at his wife wistfully, wishing that he could dance with her again. She guessed what he was thinking, kissed him, and whispered to him.

"You danced with me so much that night that it has lasted me a lifetime." He kissed her then, and she disappeared for a while to check on the guests. They had seated Zack's parents at opposite ends of the room. And Zack was pleased that they both came, a first since the divorce. Neither of them wanted to miss his wedding, which Eleanor was pleased to see, for his sake. From what he had said, he had had so little family support as he grew up, while his parents waged war on each other.

The cake was an exact replica of the one she and Alex had had. Eleanor noticed that the female guests looked more respectable than the men, with most of them in very pretty cocktail dresses. But Ruby was the most beautiful of all. Zack had been gazing at her all night, and danced with her again and again. He very politely asked Eleanor to dance too, and danced once with his mother, who was being infinitely nicer to him since his recent deal, and invited him to Texas with Ruby while they danced. His father's girlfriend looked predictably unsuitable, but no one cared, not even Zack.

They had paid the school an extra fee to allow the party to go on until one A.M. It was a far cry from her grandparents' all-night wedding, but no one gave parties like that anymore. Ruby's wedding was particularly glamorous, with the unforgettable wedding dress, the garlands and the flowers, and the tablecloths the school had ordered and Eleanor had placed white lace over them. The tiara gave Ruby a regal look. It was incredible to Alex that the awkward-looking young boys around the room had made unimaginable fortunes. You would never have guessed it from their age or the look of them. But a new era had dawned, the country was thriving as never before with the high-tech era, and the crash that Alex's generation had lived through was only distant history now. The young people of Ruby and Zack's generation had no idea of what that had been like or the lives it had destroyed. Now no one remembered, except those who had lived through it.

At the end of the evening, Ruby tossed her bouquet and a friend from Stanford caught it. It was a special "throwing bouquet" so she could keep and preserve her real one. They were going to spend the night across the street at the Fairmont hotel, and then leave for the Caribbean by private plane the next morning. Zack was becoming familiar with the conveniences of his new status quickly and sharing them gladly with Ruby.

They were just about to leave the house after thanking her grandparents, when Zack turned to smile at his bride.

"You're the most beautiful bride I've ever seen, and it was a fantastic wedding. We'll have to give another big party for the housewarming."

"What housewarming?" Ruby looked at him blankly.

"I know how much this house means to you and your grandmother," he said in a low husky voice that no one else could hear. "The school was looking for bigger quarters. They said that they've outgrown this house and have been looking for a while. I bought it for you," he said quietly and Ruby stared at her husband.

"You did what?"

"I bought the house from the school. It's my wedding present to you. It's yours, Ruby. I put it in your name. You and your grandmother can have fun now restoring it to how it used to be." He looked innocent and ingenuous when he said it, as though it was a perfectly normal thing to do, which to him it was. He thought it had cost him very little money.

"Oh my God, Zack, you're crazy, but what an incredibly wonderful thing for you to do. I have to tell my grandmother." She found her in the ballroom, sitting quietly with Alex, enjoying a last glass of champagne. She sat down next to her and told her. And Eleanor looked as though she thought it was a joke, and then she realized that Ruby meant it, and so did Alex.

"He bought the house?" Eleanor stared at her. "You own it now?" The house had been out of their hands for fifty-one years, and now it was back. Alex looked thunderstruck, and then she hurried off to thank Zack. There were no words to tell him what it meant to her, but he could see it in her eyes, and his wife's, and he was glad he had done it. It seemed like a small thing to him now, but it was huge to Ruby and her grandmother.

The bridal couple left a moment later, and Eleanor went back to where Alex was still sitting, talking to one of Zack's friends. The young man left a few minutes later, and Alex looked at Eleanor with a peaceful expression.

"I never thought this house would be back in our family again," Eleanor said, still shaken by Ruby's revelation. She couldn't believe it. The home of her childhood had been returned to them.

Alex wouldn't have wanted to have his back. It was too far in the past now, but he liked the idea of owning and living in the Deveraux house. Somehow it seemed fitting to have it back in family hands again, thanks to Zack. The project of restoring it to what it had been would keep Ruby and her grandmother busy for a long time. He smiled at his wife then as she sat next to him.

"It was a spectacular wedding." He beamed at her.

"Theirs or ours?" she teased him. "I don't recall any men in shorts at ours." They both laughed at the vision, and as they looked around the ballroom, Alex could remember perfectly the exquisite sensation and the thrill of dancing with her. He kissed her, and the memory of their wedding night was just as vivid and alive as it had been then.

Zack and Ruby's honeymoon on the yacht he had chartered for them was as romantic as he had wanted it to be. They lay on the deck in the sun, being waited on by a crew of twenty. They sailed into ports, went shopping, had dinner ashore sometimes, or stayed on the boat just outside the ports, swimming at midnight, and making love all night long.

Ruby felt as though she lived in a constant haze of happiness now. And when they got back to San Francisco, she went through the house with her grand-mother, making lists of everything they needed to restore. The school had promised to be out by February since they had found a temporary location for the next few years. Zack had hired an architect to help Ruby and Eleanor with the restoration.

Four weeks after their wedding, Ruby realized she was pregnant. Zack was ecstatic. The baby was due in July, and they hoped to be in the house by then. It changed Ruby's mind about looking for a job. There didn't seem to be much point to it, with the house to work on, and a baby coming, and Zack didn't want her to work anyway. He felt she just didn't need to.

It took some getting used to, for Ruby to adjust to Zack's constant flow of generosity, and it was even harder to realize that he could afford anything he wanted now. They still ate dinner at Jack in the Box occasionally, but suddenly her best friend through most of her college years that she had shared cheap wine and pizza with, could buy anything that caught his fancy.

He bought a plane in February, and they had liked the boat so much on their honeymoon that he bought a yacht and called it the *Ruby Moon*, which seemed like the height of luxury to Ruby.

"Shouldn't we be saving all this money?" she asked him from time to time, looking worried. Her family's history of losing everything in the Crash of 1929 had always marked her and she didn't want the same thing to happen to him if things went awry.

"If I lose it, I can always make more." He had total confidence in his limitless earning power, and he didn't seem to be wrong. When he turned twenty-five, six months after they were married, his net worth was estimated at four billion. With his first remarkable deal, he had planned to seek his father's investment advice, but by the second deal, his fortune became so vast that he had hired high-powered money managers to advise him. And in the meantime, there seemed to be nothing he couldn't buy. He was like the proverbial kid in a candy store multiplied by four billion. Ruby couldn't even conceive of it. But despite the vast fortune he had made, he still enjoyed the simple pleasures, weekends in Tahoe at the cottage, fishing with her grandfather, going to the beach, hiking in the mountains. And at the same time, he denied her nothing. Anything she wanted for their new house was fine with him. He didn't even expect her to ask, and gave her carte blanche. He couldn't wait to spend time on the yacht with her after the baby came. The boat was currently in the Mediterranean, and he was planning to leave her there through the summer.

One thing he and Ruby both noticed was that with his sudden immense fortune, women and men threw themselves at him. Women wanted to seduce him, regardless of the fact that he was married, men wanted to do business with him. Even his own mother and stepfather, who had been inattentive and uninterested in him for the last fourteen years and

had told people openly that he was weird, suddenly
wanted to court him, spend time with him, and invite him to come and visit. But Zack was no one's
fool, and those who hadn't been there for him before
were of no interest to him now, even his own mother.
The only person in his life that he truly trusted was
Ruby. She had loved him and been a faithful friend
before he made his fortune, and she was just as devoted now. He knew she would have loved him if he
had nothing. Ruby was above all real, and always
had been. And she was deeply grateful for the family
house he had restored to her, and how happy he had
made her grandparents by doing so.

Zack thought the women who threw themselves
at him now were pathetic and desperate and he ignored them. They were flattering, but none of them
were as bright and exciting as Ruby, and he couldn't
wait for the baby to arrive. In less than a year he had
become an adult and an important man. He was determined not to let it turn his head, and so far it
hadn't. Ruby hoped it never would. She loved his
honesty and innocence, which was almost childlike,
in contrast to his genius with computers.

Ruby and her grandmother were poring over auction catalogues looking for furniture that closely re-
sembled what had been in the house originally. Since
they had sold most of it, or a great deal of it, through
their own antique store, she had photographs of
whatever they had sold, which made it easier to replace whenever fine antiques came up for auction.

Ruby and Zack took their last weekend trip to Lake Tahoe in May, and in June they moved into the Deveraux mansion, a month before the baby was due. Many rooms were still being worked on, but the reception rooms were coming along well, the master suite with both dressing rooms was finished, as was the nursery, which looked exactly as it had when Eleanor was a child. She still remembered it perfectly.

Zack had already bought a miniature Bugatti for the baby, with a proper engine, assuming it was going to be a boy. But he said it didn't matter, as long as the baby was healthy. He said he wanted at least a dozen more children with Ruby anyway. The life they were leading was heady stuff for Ruby, and finally, when they moved in, their life slowed down for a while. Zack was still working on his latest research projects. He had dreams of connecting the world through computers, and was determined to find a way to do it. He had a computer lab and an office in the house.

Eleanor was still looking high and low for furniture for them, and Alex spent some time in Tahoe with Eleanor while she worked on her gardens, to get away from the city. He felt as though they hadn't stopped since the wedding, and he was tired. He had just turned eighty-six, and was slowing down a little. Ruby had noticed it and so had Eleanor. Their life had been moving at a fast pace ever since Ruby had married Zack, people even approached them now to be introduced to their grandson-in-law. Eleanor was slightly worried about Ruby too. She remembered all too well the problems Camille had experienced when she gave birth to Ruby, although her lifestyle had been unhealthy. Eleanor wanted everything to go smoothly for Ruby, and Alex said he was sure it would. Ruby was the picture of health and a happy woman. She was positively glowing. She looked radiant whenever they saw her, and she dropped by the store frequently, and talked to her grandmother on the phone several times a day about their special projects, the nursery, the house, and the baby.

Zack wanted to be at the delivery and they were taking Lamaze classes together, anonymously. By her due date in July, Ruby was staying home, folding tiny undershirts and putting the very last finishing touches on the nursery. Eleanor had painted a mural for the nursery herself, an old talent she had revived. She had painted a circus, with clowns and animals all the way around the room, with a girl dancing on the high wire in a sequined tutu. And she had faux painted the circus train along one wall. Zack and Ruby loved it.

They had hired a baby nurse to help them for the first few months, but after that, Ruby said she wanted to take care of the baby herself. She wanted to be the exact opposite of the kind of mother her own mother had been, and Eleanor had no doubt she would be. Alex was disappointed that she didn't want to use her education to get a high-paying job, but with the kind of fortune Zack had made in a short time, it didn't seem to make sense for Ruby to be working.

She'd rather stay home and take care of their children, which was what Zack wanted her to do anyway.

He had an office in Palo Alto, and called her several times a day to make sure nothing was happening. And when things finally got started, she was picking curtain fabrics for the ballroom with her grandmother. Eleanor called Zack and he drove back to town immediately, and once Zack got there, Eleanor went home to tell Alex the baby was coming. Ruby promised to let them know as soon as she and Zack went to the hospital. They spent the afternoon at home, timing contractions and watching movies on TV. They were planning to go to the new birthing center at the hospital, and when they left for the hospital at six o'clock, Ruby was still smiling. Once they got there it seemed to be taking forever, but the nurses told her that first babies were always slow.

When the contractions began in earnest, Zack did everything he'd been taught to help her. They were so young and earnest, and so much in love that the nurses were touched when they were in the room with them. Ruby wanted a natural delivery, and when she finally started to push at midnight, the baby came easily and quickly. With three enormous pushes, Zack and Ruby saw their daughter born. Everything had gone easily. The doctor cut the cord and lay the baby on Ruby's stomach, and she and Zack were laughing and crying as they looked at her. One of the nurses commented that they made it look easy.

At twelve-thirty, they called her grandparents and told them that Kendall Eleanor Katz had arrived and how easy it had been.

"Thank God," Eleanor said as she nodded and smiled at Alex and gave him a thumbs-up. They had been worried sick about her all night while they waited for news of the arrival of their great-grandchild.

"She's beautiful, Grandma," Ruby said, sounding elated. Zack got on the phone with them a minute later and told them what a miracle the birth had been, and he was thrilled to have a daughter. Eleanor and Alex promised to come and see her in the morning.

He called his parents after that. His mother's phone went to the answering machine and he left her a message. His father answered and congratulated them. The call was brief and to the point, unlike their conversation with Ruby's grandparents who wanted all the details and to know who she looked like. They were much warmer people.

Everything had gone smoothly, which was so different from Ruby's birth twenty-two years before. Zack and Ruby were living proof that dreams came true, and love prevailed in the end. And none of them doubted for a minute that Kendall Eleanor Katz would be a special person and a golden child.

Chapter 17

Ruby had never been happier in her life than when she was taking care of her baby. And the baby was so easy they let the baby nurse go after a month. Ruby was a natural mother. She was constantly nursing her and fussing over her, changing her, or dressing her. She brought Kendall to visit her great-grandparents at the shop almost every day. They loved seeing her. And Zack was crazy about Kendall too.

"She has to be the most loved child on the planet," Eleanor commented to Alex, and she was pleased. Ruby's husband and child meant everything to her. Two months later, mistakenly thinking she couldn't get pregnant while she was nursing, she got pregnant again. Zack was startled by the news, but as soon as he adjusted to the idea, he was thrilled. The baby was due in June. Kendall would be eleven months old when her brother or sister was born. Irish twins.

Ruby and her grandmother were almost finished restoring the house by then, and it looked remarkably like it once had, except for some things that were missing, like the large adjoining garden, which had been sold by the school. There was a small garden now where they could eat lunch at a table on sunny days. They'd been living in the house since right before Kendall was born, and were continuing their restoration work while living there. It would have been too disruptive to bring a baby home to her grandparents' small house, so they had moved into the house on Nob Hill while it was a work in progress. Ruby loved living there, and Eleanor loved visiting and helping her to restore it. The house was so full of memories for her. It was the greatest gift Zack could have given them.

By Christmas, so soon after the last baby, the pregnancy showed. Ruby loved being pregnant, and taking care of Kendall. She had never realized she'd enjoy motherhood so much, but since she wasn't working, she had nothing else to do. And Zack was busier than he ever had been as his empire grew. He had turned into an adult, a husband, a father, and a business mogul overnight, and one of the new breed of high-tech billionaires at an absurdly young age.

They spent Christmas with her grandparents, and for New Year's, Zack had their new yacht brought to the Caribbean. Ruby hadn't seen it yet, she'd been too busy with the baby to join Zack on it. For New Year's, they left Kendall with a babysitter they trusted, and boarded the boat in Saint Martin, and headed for Saint Bart, on the incredibly luxurious 286 foot motor yacht Zack had named the *Ruby Moon*. They spent two weeks on it, but Ruby was so miserable without Kendall that all she wanted to do was go home. It wasn't as romantic as their honeymoon on the boat they'd chartered fifteen months before. She missed Kendall so much, called the babysitter on the Satcom every few hours, and Zack could tell her heart was with the baby at home. It brought the point home to him that he wasn't the only love in her life anymore. The baby was just as important to her as he was, maybe more so, which was a shock for him. In the end, they left four days early to go back to New York. The boat was beautiful but Ruby wasn't ready to go so far from Kendall, and they didn't want to bring the baby.

Zack knew Ruby wouldn't be able to travel after late March, with a baby due in June. So when they left, he had the boat sent back to Europe. He planned to use it the following summer with friends in the Mediterranean, and he suspected now that Ruby wouldn't leave the new baby until the fall, so she wouldn't be on it with him.

Things were subtly different between them after the boat trip. It had shocked Zack to realize that Ruby would rather be with the baby than with him. He was chilly for a few weeks and she didn't notice. She was just so happy to be home.

In April, Ruby commented to her grandmother

that Zack was working till all hours every night at the office, and coming home as late as midnight sometimes. She didn't seem concerned about it, and said he always worked around the clock when he had a new idea, he was clearly a genius, but Eleanor couldn't recall his doing that before. She said something about it to Alex at dinner and he looked at his wife with a serious expression.

"Ruby better be careful. She has a young husband. He's barely more than a boy, and he's a very, very rich man. He's easy prey for some greedy woman. Ruby is so crazy about her baby, and she's been pregnant since they've been married. She needs to pay more attention to Zack. It's not a good sign when men start staying late at the office and coming home at midnight. She'd better watch out." Eleanor wondered if that was an old-fashioned point of view, or if he might be right. Their situation had been very different. They'd been alone for ten years, and tried desperately to have a child. And then he'd gone off to war and been wounded, and after that she had spent years worrying about him. They'd been inseparable. And then they'd started a business and worked together. All those things had brought them closer. And Alex had been older and mature when they married. In many ways, Zack was still a boy. But she thought it was premature to get worried, and once the new baby was born, Ruby could turn her full attention back to Zack again. And Alex was right. She had been pregnant so far for their entire marriage.

A few weeks later, Ruby mentioned it to Eleanor again, and she said that Zack was so intense about his work that sometimes he spent the night at his office and didn't come home. That time, Eleanor's alarm bells sounded too. She didn't know what to say to Ruby, who was eight months pregnant by then, uncomfortable, and focused on the delivery in a few weeks. It didn't seem fair to worry her so late in her pregnancy. The next time Eleanor saw her, Ruby was driving a convertible Rolls. Eleanor thought it was too showy, but Alex was impressed.

"That's quite a car," he commented and Ruby laughed. It was bright red, and she had Kendall's car seat in the backseat.

"I feel a bit like a drug dealer driving it," Ruby admitted. "Zack gave it to me last week."

"For a special occasion?" Eleanor asked casually. "A baby present?" She hoped it was that.

"No, just for fun." When Kendall was born, Zack had given her an incredibly beautiful ruby and diamond bracelet. But there was no apparent reason for the fancy new car. After she left, Eleanor looked at Alex and voiced her concerns.

"Do you think Zack is having an affair?"

"No. Why?" He looked surprised. He had forgotten their earlier conversation about Zack's working late at night.

"She says sometimes he doesn't come home at night now, and sleeps at the office. And now, that very expensive car he gave her for no reason." Alex frowned.

"I hope he isn't," he said seriously. "Zack loves extravagant gifts and spends a fortune, since he has one. Like the houses, the plane, the boat, the new Rolls. They're all toys to him. But if he is having an affair and she finds out, it's going to blow them right out of the water. They're too young for him to be fooling around. They should be madly in love, and totally faithful. They're laying down the foundation of their marriage. She should get a sitter, leave the baby, and go out with him more often, and have some fun. But she's ready to give birth again. Maybe he's tired of that." Alex believed in fidelity, but they both knew that sometimes people got bored and played around, especially after long years of marriage. Twenty months into their marriage, an affair would be disastrous, but she'd been pregnant for eighteen of those twenty months and he was a twenty-five-year-old boy with a mountain of money and racy women were bound to chase him.

"I hope there's nothing going on," Eleanor said, and Alex nodded. He didn't want to interfere and say anything to him if they were wrong. And Ruby hadn't expressed any concern to them, just benign comments that he was working late, and slept at the office from time to time. Neither of Ruby's grandparents wanted to frighten her or put ideas in her head, if their worries were unfounded. It didn't seem fair to upset her so close to when their second baby was about to be born. The new baby was all she could think about now, and Kendall. And the time she spent with Zack was more limited every day as she slowed down. Zack felt as though she was either in the nursery folding baby clothes or on their bed, resting. And she wasn't in the mood to go out anymore. She felt like a whale.

Eleanor invited them over to dinner, and they seemed fine. Zack was very attentive to her, and Eleanor and Alex decided that their fears were a product of their own imaginations. He was a computer genius after all, so maybe he really was working late.

The baby was overdue this time. Ruby was two weeks past her due date. The baby nurse had arrived, and was taking care of Kendall before the new baby came, so Ruby had more free time while she waited for labor to start. She was restless, excited, and bored, with free time on her hands.

She decided to surprise Zack at the office, and have lunch with him. So she got in her red Rolls, put the top down, and drove to Palo Alto. She was wearing a white tent dress and sandals. She looked huge, but very pretty and very pregnant, when she walked into his office complex, and walked down the hall without having the receptionist announce her. She didn't knock on his office door, which was closed. She opened it, and hopped in, looking like a giant marshmallow, or a white cupcake, and saw a young blonde in a tight skirt sitting on the corner of his desk. They were laughing, and Ruby could see that he had a hand on her thigh, as she sat high on his desk turned slightly toward her. She was a very pretty girl, and they both looked shocked when they saw Ruby standing in the middle of the room. The girl didn't move and Zack stood up, as Ruby stared at them both, too paralyzed to move. She wanted an explanation, but couldn't say the words. It was so totally unlike him. He had never been a womanizer before.

"I'm sorry . . . I thought . . . I came down to have lunch with you." Her eyes filled with tears and she started to back out. The girl got off the corner of his desk, but took her time about it, and looked as though Ruby was the interloper and at fault for showing up, not guilty that she had had Ruby's husband's hand on her thigh, and shouldn't have. The girl didn't look guilty, she looked annoyed.

"Bethany, this is my wife, Ruby," Zack said awkwardly, and the girl nodded at Ruby and left. She was bold about it. Ruby followed her immediately and Zack rushed after her.

"Ruby, it's not what it looks like . . . she's an intern . . . nothing's happening. Let's have lunch." She didn't answer him as he ran after her, and she turned with a look of devastation in her eyes.

"You're a son of a bitch. I trusted you. I'm about to have your baby, and you're screwing interns."

"No, I'm not. I don't know why I did it. I had my hand on her leg . . . that's all it was . . . she just hopped up on my desk before I could stop her."

"I don't **believe** you. You haven't been coming home at night. Is this what it's going to be like being married to you now?" she said as she left and he followed her out to the parking lot. She hated him at that moment and she hated the fact that she loved him, and he could hurt her as badly as he just had. She knew she wouldn't ever trust him again.

"Ruby, I swear, nothing happened. We were talking. Come on, Ruby, you've been pregnant since the day we got married. Can't I even talk to a woman anymore?" He looked desperate and he could see hatred and heartbreak in her eyes.

"You can do whatever you want," she said angrily and then looked at him intently. "Where are you when you don't come home at night? With her? You're a cheater, Zack. Don't be a liar too." She got in the car then and slammed the door, while he stood there, looking stupid, and feeling like the heel he was. A second later, she put the car in gear and drove off. She drove back to the city at full speed, and was shaking when she got to her grandparents' shop. Her grandfather was out, and her grandmother was in her office, going over some paperwork on recent pieces she'd sold. She looked up and saw Ruby's tearstained face.

"What happened?" She was on her feet immediately, and gave her a hug.

"I think Zack is cheating on me. I just went to his office to surprise him for lunch, there was a hot blonde sitting on his desk and he had a hand on her thigh." Eleanor winced. It was what she had been afraid of. But it was one thing guessing or suspecting, and another thing seeing it happen. She could see how upset Ruby was. She was shaking.

"What did he say?" Eleanor asked and handed her a glass of water from the pitcher on her desk.

"That it wasn't what it looked like. All the crap you'd expect him to say. I know what I saw. And the girl didn't even get off his desk once I was there. She acted like it was her turf and not mine."

"He may just have been stupid and was flirting with her. You didn't catch them in bed," her grandmother said sensibly, hoping it was true. Men were stupid sometimes, especially if tired of having a pregnant wife. And he was young and very rich and had opportunities galore.

"He stays out all night a couple of nights a week now. I think they're having an affair. She's a gorgeous girl."

"So are you," her grandmother reminded her, and Ruby started to sob.

"I look like an elephant."

Eleanor smiled. "No, you don't. You look like you're going to have a baby any minute."

"How do I trust him after this?"

"You probably don't for a while. And hopefully, he'll behave."

Eleanor offered to take her to lunch, but Ruby said she was too upset to eat, and she wanted to go home and lie down. Her heart had been pounding since she'd walked into Zack's office. She left the shop a few minutes later, and Zack called as soon as she got home. The baby nurse said he had already called three times.

"Are you all right?" she asked Ruby. "You look pale."

"I'm fine," she said and answered the phone. "What do you want?" she asked Zack.

"Ruby, I'm sorry. It wasn't what it looked like. I know it looked bad. She's kind of a cheeky girl. She flirts with everyone."

"That's her business. You had your hand on her. If I'd come five minutes later, maybe you'd have had your dick up her skirt." She was furious, terrified, and very hurt.

"I swear, I haven't done anything with her."

"Your hand on her thigh is bad enough. You looked like you were about to climb into bed with her. And I don't believe a word you're saying."

"This isn't good for you or the baby. Please calm down. I'll come home early tonight. I have a one-thirty meeting or I'd come home now. I love you. That girl means nothing to me."

"Did you sleep with her?"

"Of course not." He sounded shocked.

"Then where have you been sleeping when you don't come home?"

"At the office. We have a room in the back for cra-zies like me, when we're too exhausted to go home.

All the techies do it. A lot of them sleep here when they work late."

"Does she?"

"She's an intern, not a techie."

"And you're a jerk," she said and hung up.

Ruby lay down on their bed and her heart continued to pound. She could feel the baby thrashing around, probably from her own adrenaline rush. She just lay there and stared at the ceiling, hating him for what she'd seen. She kept playing it over and over in her mind, until she fell asleep. He didn't call her back. She was too worked up to listen to reason. And when she woke up two hours later, feeling exhausted and sick, the bed was soaked around her. Her water had broken, and she realized a contraction had woken her. She was in labor and didn't want to be. She didn't want to see Zack, or have the baby right now. She was too upset.

She got up and went to the bathroom and took her dress off, wrapped herself in towels and lay down on his side of the bed where it was dry. She knew she should call the doctor, but she didn't want to do that either. She didn't want to have this baby now. She wanted the contractions to stop.

They got stronger as she lay there, and she could tell they were closer together. When they finally got too strong to ignore, she went to find the baby nurse to tell her, but she was out. She must have taken Kendall to the park. They only had a small staff, and one maid was on her day off. The other one was on vacation. Ruby was alone in the house. She timed two of the contractions, and they were two minutes apart. She had to get to the hospital, and she was going to have to drive herself. She didn't want to worry her grandmother, and Zack was too far away to help. It would take him forty-five minutes or an hour to get home, and she didn't want to see him anyway. She wondered if he was with the pretty blonde.

She got up to get dressed and she couldn't walk during the contractions. They were too close together now for her to dress, leave the house, and drive herself to the hospital. And suddenly she was scared. She thought about calling Zack, but all she could think of was the blonde on his desk.

She picked up the phone to call the hospital, and suddenly she heard someone running up the stairs, and a minute later, he was in her room. It was Zack. They looked equally surprised to see each other.

"What are you doing here?" she asked him between pains.

"I live here. I came to talk to you."

"I'm in labor." She grimaced as she said it. The pain was already unbearable, worse than she remembered. How could she have forgotten this?

"Why didn't you call me? Why aren't you at the hospital?" He was panicking.

"Because you're a shit and I hate you," she said and then couldn't talk again. He grabbed the phone, and dialed 911.

"What are you doing?" She looked frightened.

"I think you're having the baby. I think you waited too long." She thought so too. But everything was wrong this time. She heard him tell the operator that his wife was having a baby, and gave their address, and then he ran to the bathroom, and came back with a stack of towels, and he looked her in the eye.

"Whatever happened, whatever you saw today, whatever you think, this is our baby, and I love you. Can we just forget about that whole mess long enough for you to have this baby? I love you, Ruby. I won't be a jerk anymore." She didn't answer him, she was in too much pain, and it felt like the baby was forcing its way out and there was no way to stop it. It had all gone so smoothly last time, and this time it was as wrong as their marriage was, and as painful as what she'd seen that morning, and getting rapidly worse.

"I think I'm having the baby," she said, and started to cry. The doorbell rang, and Zack left her, as she lay in misery and sobbed. A moment later, there were firemen, and a paramedic and a policeman in the room. The paramedic stood over her and spoke to her gently. He took off the towels she was wrapped in, and Zack's face was next to hers and she didn't know if she hated him or loved him. The room swam around her and she felt like she was drowning. She heard someone scream, and then she heard a baby crying from the deep blackness where the pain had pushed her, and then the paramedic was holding the baby, and he said it was a boy, and Zack was crying and telling her he loved her, and for a minute she believed him, and then she remembered, and she cried too.

"We have a boy," Zack kept saying to her, and someone put an oxygen mask on her. They had opted not to know the baby's sex so it would be a surprise, only now the blonde in his office was the surprise. They cut the cord and lifted her onto a gurney, while the policeman held the baby, wrapped in a blanket.

"We're going to take you to the hospital," the fireman said to her and she nodded. The pain had stopped, but she couldn't stop crying, and they laid the baby next to her, and covered them both with a blanket.

"He's beautiful," Zack said to her as they carried her out. "And I love you. Everything is going to be okay." She nodded even though she didn't believe him. She saw the baby nurse and Kendall on the way out, and heard Zack telling her what had happened, but he didn't tell her why it had happened that way. She hated him for that too. He had ruined everything with that girl on his desk and all the nights he hadn't come home. She had been such a fool to believe him. She wondered how long it had been going on. She had no proof that he was sleeping with her, but deep in her gut now, she knew he was.

They were in the ambulance then and she looked down at the baby in her arms. He looked so innocent and so sweet and then she had terrible pains again, and Zack held the baby, while the paramedic delivered the placenta, while they raced to the hospital, with the siren shrieking. They were there ten minutes later, and they carried her into the hospital, while Zack followed with the baby. The nurses took over then, and a doctor came to examine her. She thanked the paramedics when they left. She was shaking, and she felt sick. Then they cleaned her up and checked the baby, and the doctor came a little while later and told her everything was fine. But it wasn't fine. She knew it every time she looked at Zack. It would never be fine again. She wondered now how long he had been cheating on her. Since the beginning? Only recently? For all of her second pregnancy? And the first one too?

"I guess you missed the train this time," her doctor said, joking with her a little. "You were ready to pop. It went pretty fast. We'll have to get you in at the first sign of labor next time. The fast ones always get faster. I have one patient who hasn't made it to the hospital yet with three kids. But everything looks good. The baby weighs eight pounds two ounces, by the way. He's perfect. Your husband is in the nursery with him now. He'll bring him back in a few minutes. You can go home tomorrow if you like, or stay a few days. It's up to you." Ruby nodded and listened to him, but everything had gone so fast, she felt like she was still in shock, from the morning, the baby, and the fast delivery which had been intense. And knowing that her marriage, and her feelings for Zack, would never be the same again.

Zack came back pushing the baby in a bassinet a little while later, and they had given her something for the cramps she was having from her uterus contracting. She was dozing, and she woke up and looked at Zack as he handed the baby to her. They had agreed to name him Nicholas if he was a boy.

"Do you want to hold him now?" a nurse asked her, and since Ruby was woozy, she shook her head. She just wanted to be left alone.

"These emergency home deliveries can be pretty rough," the nurse said to Zack, and he agreed. Ruby closed her eyes and went to sleep. All she wanted was for this day to end. And to stop loving Zack as soon as possible.

Chapter 18

Everything was different this time. Even the next day. And the recovery. She had terrible cramps the following day, and they gave her something for the pain. Zack came back in the morning. He hadn't spent the night with her in the hospital as he had the first time when Kendall was born, and she wondered where he'd been. Maybe back in Palo Alto with the blonde. She didn't know what to say to him. It made her sad every time she looked at their son. What a terrible day to be born. And whatever happened, she knew she'd never trust Zack again. That hadn't changed from the day before, and she didn't think it ever would. What was she going to do now? She had two babies with a man she was sure had cheated on her and probably still was, and perhaps had all along. Zack was turning into his father. He had cheated on Zack's mother for their entire marriage, and Zack hated him for it. He had lost all respect for him when he found out. And now Ruby wondered if he was doing the same thing.

As she thought about it, he handed her a familiar little gray box. She knew something was in it that she didn't want. She didn't want gifts from him now. When she opened it, it was the biggest ruby she'd ever seen, a cushion-cut fifty carat pigeon's-blood ruby, the best there was. He was trying to buy her off. The measure of his guilt was in the size of his gifts. She understood that now. She wanted to give it back but she didn't.

When her grandparents came, she couldn't even pretend to be happy. She just cried and clung to her grandmother. Eleanor could see in Ruby's eyes how upset she still was. She knew why she had gone into labor so quickly, and hadn't called anyone, and so did Zack. Eleanor looked at him and he could tell that Ruby had told her. Alex was very quiet too. They admired the baby, talked to Ruby for a little while, and then they left, and Ruby was alone with him.

"You can't let this come between us forever, Ruby. You just can't."

"That's why you gave me the car," she said miserably, and knew she'd never touch it again. It was spoiled for her, just as he was now.

"That's ridiculous. I just thought it was fun," he said, but they both knew it wasn't true. She was onto him. She wondered how long he had been cheating on her. Maybe the whole time. They had two children now, and they needed two parents. She wasn't going to do what her mother had done, and abandon them, or deprive them of Zack. She had to stay with him, for them. Kendall and Nick needed their father, but something in her was so deeply wounded she doubted she could ever forgive him. Their whole marriage seemed like a sham now. She didn't know how long he'd been cheating on her, but she suspected that the blonde in his office was not the first one, and maybe not the only one.

Ruby went home two days after Nicholas was born. The mood was somber as soon as they got home. There was none of the joy that had accompanied Kendall's birth. The baby was healthy, but their marriage no longer was.

Zack set out to prove she was wrong. He was gentle and kind to her and apologetic, wonderful with the baby, thrilled to have a son. He was patient with Ruby, and lavished attention on her. He was home with her every night. Eleanor could see how big an effort he was making, and Ruby made none. She was completely closed off.

It was August and they were in Tahoe when she finally began to soften a little and warmed up to Zack again. They went for long walks, and she didn't say anything, but he could tell she had begun to forgive him. Whatever he had done, Eleanor was well aware that Ruby had made him pay dearly for it, and she felt sorry for both of them.

By the time they got back to the city at the end of August, things were almost back to normal again.

Ruby was more reserved with him than she had been before, and more cautious, but she was inching toward Zack again, and he clung to her like a drowning man. He didn't want to lose her, and he was willing to do anything to restore their marriage to what it had been before, if that was possible. She finally slept with him again in September. It had taken three months after Nicholas was born.

They spent Thanksgiving with Alex and Eleanor, since Zack's parents didn't celebrate holidays with him anymore, and hadn't for years. He had usually spent it with friends until he and Ruby were married. His mother went to her husband's family, and his father went on a trip with his girlfriend of the hour every year. So Zack and Ruby spent all holidays with Ruby's family. They had left the two babies with the baby nurse at home.

Alex went out to the kitchen to carve the turkey, and he took a long time coming back. Eleanor went in to see if he needed help, and she came out a minute later looking sheet white. Zack rushed to the kitchen to see what had happened, with Ruby right behind him. Her grandfather was slumped over in his wheelchair. He must have died in an instant. When Zack checked, he had no pulse. He looked as though he had just gone to sleep. His heart had stopped. He was eighty-seven years old and Eleanor was seventy-three. They had loved each other for fifty-five years. All three of them stood crying as they looked at him. They called 911 and the paramedics came, but there was nothing anyone could do. It was over. And despite his reversals and injuries during the war, Alex had lived a good life.

Eleanor held his funeral the Monday after Thanksgiving, and the church was full, with people he had known in his youth, people he had worked with, clients from the shop, and someone he had served in the army with, whom Eleanor didn't even know. Eleanor looked like she was in shock. Ruby stayed close to her every minute, and suggested she stay with them afterward, but Eleanor wanted to be at home. She closed the shop for a week, and then opened it again, but her heart wasn't in it once Alex was gone.

She made the decision to close the shop in the spring. It had lost its meaning for her. They didn't need the money anymore, and they'd had a good run. They had had it and enjoyed it for forty years. That seemed long enough. In the summer, she decided to rent out the building in the city, and move to Lake Tahoe. She wanted to live in the cottage and work in her garden. The British owner had hired a new overseer by then, shortly after Alex died. The original earl had died last year too, and the earl's son had inherited the estate, although he'd never been there. He was putting off making any decisions about it, until he saw the property himself, and had no plans to come over for the moment. He wasn't well himself.

Ruby worried about her grandmother being in

Tahoe alone once she moved there, but she seemed happy. She spent most of her time outdoors, in her gardens. She had a greenhouse built and grew orchids. It suited her. She wasn't interested in their city life alone. She had kept a few of her decorating clients, but eventually gave them up too. That chapter of her life was closed.

Ruby came up to visit her whenever she could, and brought the children to see her. Things seemed to be back on track with Zack again. It had taken a year after her discovery of the girl on his desk, but Ruby had finally forgiven him, and the atmosphere between them had warmed up at last.

A year after Eleanor had moved to Tahoe, Zack suggested they take her with them on their boat in July. It was a beautiful boat and they didn't use it often enough. It was dangerous for toddlers running loose on the boat, so they never took them, and Ruby hated to leave her children, but she agreed with Zack that it would be good for her grandmother.

Ruby convinced her to go with them in July. Alex had been gone for a year and a half by then, and they were delighted when Eleanor accepted the invitation. They were going to meet the boat in Monaco, and travel into Italy, possibly as far as Sardinia, and spend two weeks on the boat. Eleanor wanted to do some traveling on her own after that, and Zack and Ruby were going to Saint Tropez to meet friends. They were planning to be gone for three weeks in all, and were leaving Kendall and Nick at home. Nick was two and Kendall was three, and it was still too dangerous for them on the boat. They could easily have fallen overboard or gotten hurt. It would be the longest span of time Ruby had ever been away from them.

Ruby was going to fly from San Francisco with her grandmother, and Zack was planning to arrive a day later, after a meeting in London. It would give Ruby and Eleanor a day to shop in Monaco, and relax on the luxurious yacht before Zack arrived. Eleanor was looking forward to the trip, and Ruby to being with her. They left in good spirits. It was a long flight and they arrived in Monaco in the late afternoon. The crew was ready for them and had the cabins all set. Ruby and Eleanor had dinner on deck, in the warm summer night, and went to bed early after the long trip. The next day they set out on their adventure to explore the shops. Zack was due to arrive on a commercial flight at five that afternoon and one of the crew would pick him up.

The two women had just gotten back to the boat after a day of shopping, when the captain came to see Ruby in her cabin to inform her that Mr. Katz had called while she was out. He had missed his flight and would arrive the next day at lunchtime. He was staying at Claridge's. She called to talk to him and find out if everything was all right, but he was out. She called him again that night, and he wasn't back yet, but she didn't think anything of it. She hadn't had a whiff of any misbehavior on his part in two years. His hanky-panky days appeared to be over. She had stopped worrying about it. They had just been in a bad phase, with her pregnant for two years running. They had somehow become disconnected, but were back on track again. It made her loath to have a third child. She didn't want to disrupt their marriage, and Zack needed her full attention. She realized now that he had been so starved for affection growing up that there was a part of him that needed Ruby almost like a mother, and at times he felt in competition with his own children for her love.

Eleanor and Ruby had a lazy morning, and took a long walk along the port. They were back in time for lunch, and Zack was scheduled to arrive by then. Instead, when they got back, the captain had another message. An emergency meeting had been called and Zack was going to be another day late. She called him but he wasn't in his hotel room, and she left him another message. To pass the time, Ruby had the captain take them out on the boat that afternoon. They motored to Cap d'Antibes, got off at the Hotel du Cap and had a look around, and then returned to Monaco. The emergency meeting had apparently extended, and Zack said he would be there in two days. He called her himself before dinner, apologized profusely that his meetings had gotten extended, and suggested that she and Eleanor spend a day in Portofino, which was a charming little port town. He apologized sincerely again and told her he missed her and felt terrible about the delay.

In the end, Zack arrived five days late, flustered and apologetic. Ruby and her grandmother had been taking day trips all week. They were enjoying being together, but it was frustrating waiting for Zack every day. He arrived at last in a flurry of apologies and kissed Ruby passionately and seemed genuinely happy to see her, and her grandmother.

As a peace offering, he brought Eleanor a beautiful Hermès scarf, and an Hermès alligator handbag for Ruby, which she knew cost a fortune. The minute she saw it, her blood ran cold, she knew what had happened and why he had been delayed. The shock of realization was evident on her face, and her grandmother saw it and didn't comment. She didn't want to make the situation worse with her own suspicions and thanked Zack profusely for the scarf.

They set off that night for Sardinia, and enjoyed the rest of the trip. They spent another week on the boat together, he was attentive and loving to Ruby, and she looked distracted. And then Eleanor took off for Lake Como, which she had wanted to see years earlier on her honeymoon, when she and Alex had had to cut their trip short. Then she was going to visit favorite clients of her shop, in Madrid. It was a major adventure for her and she was excited about it. As soon as she left the boat, Ruby descended to their cabin, and the boat took off for Saint Tropez. She didn't emerge until lunchtime and she was icy with Zack when she did. The alligator bag was back in its box by then, and she handed it to him at the lunch table. It had been the tip-off as to what he was doing in London, and why he was five days late when he joined them.

"What's that?" He looked surprised when she handed the orange box to him.

"Don't try to buy me off, Zack. It's not worthy of you. And it gives you away every time." It had a familiar ring to it and dredged up memories she had tried to forget.

"What's that supposed to mean?" He looked innocent and hurt but she knew better.

"You know what it means and so do I. What were you doing in London for five days while my grandmother and I cooled our heels waiting for you?"

"I told you. I was stuck in meetings all week. I would have come sooner if I could. I'm sorry you don't like the bag."

"I love the bag, but I know what it means when you give me presents like that." He had finally sold the Rolls after she had refused to drive it again. He got the point. She didn't say anything to him after that all through lunch, with the crew serving them, and they got to Saint Tropez late that afternoon. There was no room for them in the port, because the boat was so big, so they anchored just outside, and she went into the port with the tender, and walked around town, wondering if she had been unfair to him and overreacted. But she didn't believe his ex-

cuses about London and his five-day delay. Whatever
he'd been doing, he'd been a fool to do it then, while
she and her grandmother waited for him on the boat.
He had a knack for getting caught in his infidelities,
almost as though he couldn't stop himself, and there
was something compulsive about it, even if it meant
getting found out. Somewhere in him there was an
insatiable need for affection, a void he could never
fill because he'd been abandoned by his mother as a
child, no matter how much Ruby loved him. He
needed more, and in his position, it was easy to find.

When she got back to the boat, they had to dress
for dinner. She was trying not to act on her suspicions about him. They were meeting a group of people whom Zack knew and she didn't. It had sounded
like fun when he'd suggested it and organized it for
them. But she wasn't in the mood for it that night.
They were meeting at a popular restaurant, and all
she knew was that there would be eight or ten people who were planning to be in Saint Tropez at the
same time, and all knew each other, and he had insisted she'd enjoy them.

They went back into the port with the tender, and
were the last to arrive at the restaurant. She could
see immediately that they were a fashionable group.
They all looked very chic and the women were wearing good jewelry. Ruby had dressed very simply and
felt instantly out of place when they arrived. Zack
hadn't warned her that they were a jet-set crowd.
When he introduced her, she realized that about half

of the group were British and the others were French, and most of them had houses in the area. The conversation at the table was lively, and Ruby was seated between two Englishmen who were interesting to talk to and very funny. She relaxed as the evening wore on. The others were all couples, except two people who were houseguests of the others. One was a gay man, and the other was a very attractive single British woman named Marlene. She somehow wound up seated next to Zack, and in a lull in the conversation, Ruby heard her say to Zack, "It was fun in London, darling, wasn't it?" He nodded and smiled and said something to her, and didn't realize Ruby was watching them. The woman spotted it immediately. Ruby saw her end the exchange abruptly, and turn to talk to the man on her other side. But several times during dinner, Ruby saw Zack and Marlene exchange glances. Her antennae were up and her instincts alert and she knew instantly that her suspicions had been correct, and obviously the whole evening had been orchestrated so he could see Marlene again. She had just come down from London. Ruby was smarter than Zack gave her credit for, and it explained the alligator handbag from Hermès.

She was quiet for the rest of the evening after that, and when he invited the whole group to the boat the next day for a day sail she didn't comment. But when they got back to the *Ruby Moon,* she turned to him with an icy look.

"Tell me, how does this work, just so I know the

ground rules for tomorrow. You sneak off with Marlene, while I entertain your other guests? Or I turn a blind eye and pretend I don't know what's going on while she hangs all over you in plain sight?" She had watched them lean toward each other at dinner and touch arms several times, sitting close together.

"What are you talking about?" He'd had a lot to drink at dinner, and he wasn't as smooth as he would have liked when he responded.

"You know exactly what I'm talking about." She imitated Marlene's voice perfectly then. "'It was fun in London, darling, wasn't it?' Do you actually think I'm going to sit here and let you make a fool of me while you play out the charade tomorrow? I thought dinner in Saint Tropez was going to be fun. As it turns out, it was carefully planned, and I was the fool there. You're not very subtle, Zack. Or very smart."

"Fine," he said angrily. "Do you want me to call and cancel them for tomorrow? I will if that's what you want." Ruby suspected that he wouldn't deprive himself of the chance to see her. He was still the boy in the candy store, who wanted it all and could afford it, and thought he could pull it off. And he was still so young. Too young to have a wife and two kids and his colossal success. Ruby realized now that she'd been a fool to think all that money wouldn't matter and it wouldn't change him. It had.

"That's up to you," she said, about canceling the guests for the next day, and went downstairs to their cabin.

As it turned out, he didn't cancel, and the whole group turned up at noon, excited to be spending a day on their fabulous yacht. One of the deckhands gave it away, when he said "Nice to see you again, miss" to Marlene as she came on board. Ruby didn't say a word and let the whole scenario play out. Everyone went swimming topless before lunch, and then they sat down to a lively lunch. Marlene just happened to sit next to Zack, again, with Ruby at the other end of the table. Zack offered her a tour of the boat, which he didn't offer the others, and they disappeared for half an hour, and returned looking flushed and a little disheveled. She would have laughed if Zack had his shorts on backward or inside out. He didn't need to. It was obvious what they'd been doing, and he had a small lipstick smudge on his neck, which Ruby spotted immediately and pretended not to notice.

She got through the day somehow, with her heart aching. At six o'clock, they got back to their spot outside the port, and all the guests got in the tender. Marlene had swum topless all afternoon, and Zack could barely contain himself. They both waved as the guests departed back to the port, Zack enthusiastically and Ruby with a sad, defeated look. He had won for the day, but lost so much more in the process.

As soon as they left, Ruby headed downstairs to their cabin and started to pack. Zack followed her a minute later, sensing a showdown in the offing.

"What are you doing?"

"Packing," she said, filling her suitcase as quickly as she could, tossing her shoes in, and the assortment of beach clothes she'd brought with her. She said nothing.

"Why are you doing that?" He tried to look innocent but wasn't convincing.

"You must be joking. Other than Billy the deck-hand telling Marlene that he was happy to see her again, her tits in my face all day, and your giving her a tour of the boat for half an hour, where you both came back hot and sweaty with her lipstick on your neck." She pointed and it was still there when he glanced in the mirror and looked mortified. "I can't imagine why I'd be packing, but maybe you can. Just how dumb do you think I am?"

"You're the smartest woman I know," he said, looking like a beaten child. "She's a very effusive, lonely woman. She's a widow, and she's harmless."

"I'm very sorry to hear it, about her being a widow. Tell me something, is that what you use this boat for? Your little flings while I think you're away on business and you lie to me about where you are? That must be an expensive hobby for you, keeping the boat for that." It cost him a fortune to run it, but he loved it, far more than she did. "If that's the case, I won't be coming back here again. I'm not going to have the whole crew laughing at me behind my back, while you bring your girlfriends here, and then invite them back on the boat when I'm on board. That's a bit much. Don't you think? Or have you lost all sense of decency? Are you so rich and important now that you think you can buy anything, and have anyone you want? Or is that really how it is? And you don't care if you have a wife and kids to come home to, you just want to grab it *all,* the eternal kid in a candy store. The trouble is you're twenty-eight years old, almost twenty-nine, you're at the top of your game, and you can have any woman you want. You never used to care about all that, but you do now. You shouldn't be stuck with me, Zack. That was our big mistake. You were my best friend. But I guess I'm not very interesting compared to the women you meet now. And they all want you. And you need all of us, not just me. You're turning into your father, or you will if you're not careful. He needs a flock of women to feed his ego. You want them to fill the void you can never fill.

"I don't want to be part of a team, Zack. I don't want to share you, or be the home team while you have Marlenes on the road. If that's what you want, you shouldn't be married. Not to me anyway." And the worst of it was she was twenty-six years old, and if she stayed with him, he would break her heart again and again forever. She knew that now, and if she stayed, she couldn't pretend to herself that it would be any different. It wouldn't be, and they both knew it. This was who he had grown up to be. They were kids when they got married. And this was who Zack Katz was turning out to be as a grown-up, a billionaire, and a spoiled brat who wanted his cake and to eat it, and to cheat on his wife. He needed the Marlenes, and whoever the next one would be, and he thought he could get away with it, and he deserved it. She realized now that there would always be another Marlene stashed somewhere. He couldn't help it, and didn't want to stop.

"Are you leaving me?" he asked in a frightened voice.

"Would you care?" she responded in a hard tone.

"Of course I would, I love you," he said with tears in his eyes, and she could see that he probably meant it. His mother had more or less abandoned him when he was eleven, he couldn't bear the thought of losing Ruby too. And he needed all of them to fill that void.

"Maybe you do love me, but you need the others too. That's not what I want. The problem is we have two very young children, a two-year-old and a three-year-old, and I have this pathetic old-fashioned belief that children need a father. A real one. And if I leave you, they get screwed. If I stay, I do. So I haven't decided yet what I'm going to do."

"Why don't you stay and we'll try to work it out. We'll have a good week together somewhere." His tone was pleading. He wasn't a bad man, he just couldn't be faithful to her and never would be. She knew that now.

"And then what? You go back to London for a week of 'emergency meetings' to see Marlene, until the next one comes along that you can't resist. I thought you were over that, but apparently not, and now I get that you never will be. You're always going to need just one more to fill the void in you that you can never fill. You want me and everyone else. And they're all so willing and desperate to have you because of who you are and what you have. I actually loved you for who you really are, or who you used to be. And I don't like playing second fiddle, or tenth fiddle, or whatever fiddle I am in your busy life. So no, I'm not staying, and I need to think about what I'm going to do now. You can give the alligator bag to Marlene. It'll knock her socks off. I assume she'll be back on board as soon as I leave." She closed her bags then, and went to see the captain. She told him she needed a car and driver and a flight out of Nice that evening, most likely to Paris, or any city where she could connect to San Francisco.

"You're leaving us, Madam?"

"I have to get back to my children," she said quietly, and he told her he would get on it immediately. She waited on deck, and he came back to her ten minutes later.

"I'm afraid it's not ideal," he said apologetically. "There's an eleven P.M. flight to Paris, which will get you there an hour later. And an eight A.M. flight from Paris to San Francisco. You'll have an eight hour layover at the Paris airport. And you'll have to leave immediately to get to Nice in time for your flight."

"That's fine. I'm packed."

"I'll have a driver at the dock in five minutes, and

I'll have the boys get the tender ready," he assured her. It was embarrassing talking to him, knowing clearly now that Zack brought his other women on the boat.

She went back downstairs to see Zack, and noticed that he had gotten the lipstick off his neck.

"I'm leaving," she said coldly to mask the overwhelming hurt she felt, and the disappointment.

"You won't stay?" He looked at her mournfully. She shook her head. "Don't leave me, Ruby. I swear, I won't be an idiot again. I get carried away sometimes. You're right. Women throw themselves at me."

"And you catch them." She smiled sadly at him. She got her handbag out of their cabin then. Her suitcase was already gone. She walked down the stairs to where the tender was waiting, got in, and looked up as they pulled away. Zack was standing at the railing, watching her, and she wasn't sure in the twilight, but she thought he was crying. She looked away then, and as they sliced through the water at full speed on their fastest tender, she was sure that Marlene would be back on the boat to console him before she got to Nice. Ruby didn't know if she was going to leave Zack or not, and divorce him, but whether she did or not, whatever she did now, the marriage was over. If she stayed, they would be married in name only. It was a lot for her to give up at twenty-six.

Chapter 19

When Zack came back to San Francisco from the boat, a week later, he checked their bedroom as soon as he arrived, and saw that Ruby wasn't there. It had the orderly look the room had when she was away. He checked her closets, and her clothes were still there. The children's rooms were empty, and he asked the maid if Mrs. Katz was away, and felt foolish doing so. She hadn't called him or left him any messages since she left the boat, and he hadn't the courage to call her.

"I think they're at Lake Tahoe, sir." He didn't call her there either. Ruby had been right of course. He'd had Marlene move onto the boat the night Ruby left. He couldn't help himself. It was always so tempting, and he thought he'd get away with it. And most of the time, he did. He hated being alone. He couldn't stand it. It was agony for him. He needed a woman with him at all times to love him. He knew now that

it had been a mistake marrying Ruby, marrying anyone. He loved her, but he wanted to have fun too,
which to him meant lots of women, not just one. And
the older he got, the more he enjoyed the women
who flocked to him and adored him. Ruby was
wrong. They did fill the void, even if only for a short
time. But he loved their children, and so did she.

Ruby had gone to Tahoe with the children as soon as
she got home. She was there when her grandmother
returned from Europe and she told her what had
happened in Saint Tropez.

"What are you going to do about it?" Eleanor
asked her.

"I don't know," Ruby said honestly. "The children
are too young. I can't deprive them of their father."

"What about you? You can't stay in a loveless
marriage with a man who cheats on you. You deserve
better than that."

"Maybe in a few years . . ." Ruby said, thinking
about it.

She spent the rest of the summer in Tahoe, as they
always did, and Zack didn't come up, or call her. He
was afraid that anything he did would push Ruby
over the edge, and he didn't want to lose her. He
wanted to stay married to her. He didn't want to lose
his kids. And neither did she. And if she divorced
him, she'd take them with her. Or he'd have to leave.

Ruby spent the month of August gardening with

her grandmother, and playing with her children. The gardening they did together made her feel peaceful again. Her grandmother showed her how to do it, and explained that a garden was a living, breathing thing, and it taught you patience and gave you strength.

"My mother taught me that. She learned how to garden after they lost all their money. It helped me when your grandfather was away in the war. It will help you while you make your decision." Ruby found that she was right and it did. She went back to the city at the end of August ready to face the future. She decided to wait a few years before leaving Zack. He was a good father. For her, the marriage had ended in Saint Tropez. She was staying with him for the children, not for him or herself.

Zack didn't ask her what she was going to do after she got home, and she didn't tell him. They continued to live under one roof, as their lives became more divergent year by year. The children were the only thing that kept them together. They hardly spoke anymore. They became strangers to each other. She was sure he had other women, and she didn't want to know. He no longer had her.

Kendall was seven when she saw her mother crying one day. Ruby was thirty and wondering why she stayed with him. She couldn't see any future, except a lonely life with a man who didn't love her anymore, and whom she hadn't loved in four years. The spirit of the marriage was dead.

She visited her grandmother whenever she could and they gardened together. Ruby had gotten good with the orchids and loved working with them. They were so beautiful, and she loved the rare species. She had just come back from Tahoe and the emptiness of her life had hit her again, when Kendall found her crying.

"Why are you sad, Mama?" Kendall asked her, and she couldn't answer her. She was too young and the answer was too big. She was lonely. She and Zack were no longer even friends. Yet, as the children got older, Ruby knew she had done the right thing staying with Zack. Kendall worshipped her father and said she wanted to be like him one day. She loved computers as much as he did. He wanted Nick to come and work with him too. What they saw was an incredibly successful man, a legend in his industry and in the world, a man everyone admired. There was no denying that he was a genius. But he had broken Ruby's heart irreparably, and staying with him was killing her spirit. Part of her was dead inside and she knew it, but she tried not to care.

Her grandmother knew it too and hated to see it. But the decision to leave him had to come from her.

When Kendall was fourteen, she turned on her mother and criticized her constantly. Her father was her hero, and she was more and more like him in obvious ways. Hard, demanding, smart. Despite his success, Kendall was actually tougher than he was in some ways. There was a cold side to her that worried her mother.

Nick was more sensitive, gentler, kinder, warmer, and more like Ruby. He said he was going to work for his father one day. He was thirteen, and he wanted to work in finance or computers.

Four years later, Kendall went to UCLA and loved it, and Nick went to the London School of Economics the following year and said he was happy there, but his mother didn't believe him, until he met Sophie Taylor in his second year there and everything changed. She was a sculptress, and her father was a carpenter, and she taught Nick to make beautiful furniture. He dropped out of school, moved to the Cotswolds with Sophie, and opened a business with her. Ruby loved visiting them, and was proud of what he was doing. Zack constantly criticized him, and Nick stopped talking to his father entirely. He thought his father was toxic. Ruby didn't say it, but she thought so too. More than anything, Zack was selfish. Everything in life was about him and what he wanted. Kendall was somewhat that way too. Kendall sided with her father about Nick and told him what a loser he was to be making furniture when he could be working for their father when he graduated.

The greatest blow of all, especially for Ruby, happened the summer before Nick left for college in London. His great-grandmother Eleanor was in fine form and had died peacefully in her sleep at ninety-one. It was a tremendous loss for all of them. But Eleanor had led a rich life and was a happy woman. She missed Alex once he was gone, but they had shared a lifetime. They buried her in Tahoe, beside Alex. Ruby couldn't believe she was gone. Her grandparents had been such a vital part of her history and had saved her.

Before she had died, Eleanor told Ruby that Kendall reminded her of Ruby's mother, Camille. There was a fire and an anger in her that nothing would quench. She was on the wrong path, and blazing a trail. She wanted to be like her father and was following him blindly, the way Camille had followed Flash to her own destruction. But Eleanor was at peace about her life when she died.

When the kids left for college, Ruby was still married to Zack, though they barely saw or spoke to each other. He carried on his affairs, though less and less discreetly. Kendall blamed her mother for her father's loneliness which drove him into the arms of other women. She didn't see the pain he had caused her mother or the soul-deadening abuse of his constant infidelities. Nick had accidentally seen him with other women on several occasions and hated him for it. It was exactly what Zack had felt about his own father. Kendall was willing to do anything to win her father's approval, including blame her mother for her parents' bad marriage. She no longer remembered the times she had seen her crying during her childhood.

Nick hated the fact that his mother stayed and

didn't have the courage to leave his father. Once both her children were in college, she no longer had the excuse that it was for her children. She was forty-one when Nick left for school in London, and she had been miserable with Zack for the last fifteen years. Eventually she didn't even know she was. She was just numb. Her grandmother had seen it for many years, and reminded her that she needed a life too, not just a father for her children. Once they were gone, what excuse would she use? Her grandmother hadn't lived long enough to see her free of him.

Ruby spent more and more time in Tahoe maintaining her grandmother's gardens, in memory of her and for her own peace of mind. She had no reason to go back to the city, to the house where her grandmother and her own children had grown up. It felt hollow now, with no love in it. She was more at home in the simple cottage in Tahoe. Her grandmother's house in Tahoe stood empty now.

Zack traveled extensively, and had apartments in New York and London, and still had the boat. Ruby disappeared to Tahoe when he came back to San Francisco, so they didn't have to be in the house together. It was an unspoken agreement, and she came back from Tahoe when he left.

They both attended Kendall's graduation from UCLA, and left separately immediately afterward. Zack had flown in from London and Ruby had successfully avoided him for six months before that, although officially they still lived at the same address.

And the rare times they saw each other, the house was large enough that they could avoid each other. They'd had separate bedrooms for years.

Kendall went to work for her father as soon as she graduated, and met a young architect, Ross McLaughlin, when she moved back from L.A. He was tall, dark, and handsome, and he looked surprisingly like Alex, her great-grandfather, although she didn't notice it. By contrast, she was blond and blue eyed like her grandmother Camille, who had died shortly after her mother was born.

Ross was building small beautiful homes in San Francisco. He loved fine craftsmanship and small, elegant spaces, combined with a cozy, warm feeling throughout the house. Kendall gave him a tour of the house she had grown up in and he was overwhelmed by the sheer beauty of it. He told her that his dream was to buy houses and restore them and then sell them. He didn't have the funds to do it yet, but he hoped to one day. She thought his dreams were paltry considering what he was capable of. He didn't have great financial ambitions, he was an artist at heart.

"You sound like my brother when you talk about fine craftsmanship," she said with a slightly patronizing tone. She was a tough girl with a sharp tongue but Ross was intrigued by how smart and ambitious she was.

"What does your brother do?" He was curious about her and wanted to see more of her. But she was often busy with her father and still lived in their family home, although both her parents were away a lot, and she usually had the enormous mansion to herself.

"He makes furniture in England with his girlfriend. He dropped out of the London School of Economics." It was obvious that she didn't approve of him. Their father was an icon and Ross already understood that she worshipped him and everything he stood for, although Zack Katz had a reputation for being ruthless and self-centered, narcissistic, and had a huge ego. He didn't sound like a good guy to Ross.

"Your brother sounds like an interesting guy," Ross said gently.

"He's an underachiever. He could do a lot better. He doesn't get along with my father." Few people did, from what Ross had heard about him, but he didn't say that to Kendall. She had a hard shell that made him want to melt it.

"What does your mother do?" He was curious about them.

"She grows orchids and takes care of her gardens."

"So your family is composed of two underachievers and two stars, you being one of the stars, if I'm assessing that correctly," he teased her and she laughed. She liked him a lot but he didn't fit the profile of the kind of man she wanted to be with. She wanted to meet a man like her father one day. Ross was the exact opposite of her father, and different from the men she knew. He was a talented architect and a warm, intelligent, sensible person. He had self-confidence and good values. He wasn't a show-off, he didn't want to set the world on fire. He wanted a normal life, not to be a legend. He had grown up as an only child in a family where everyone liked each other, and he was close to his parents. Originally from San Francisco, he had gone to Yale, and had then come back to San Francisco, to build his dream houses one day.

"I think that's about right," she said, dismissing her mother and brother as the underachievers. She didn't respect either of them, only her father for everything he had achieved and wanted to be like him. "And my great-grandparents ran a fancy antique store after the family lost all their money in the Crash of '29."

"But they kept the family mansion," he said, digging for clues to who she really was, what she came from, and what was important to her. It was easy to believe that she was very spoiled, given who her father was. And there was a hard shell around her. He wanted to know what was beneath it. Ice or fire. He hoped the latter.

"No, they sold the house," she explained, "and everything they had. My great-grandparents started the antique store with furniture from the house they sold, and my great-grandmother became a decorator after the war, when my great-grandfather was wounded and lost his legs. Before that, when they lost everything, she was a teacher, and he became a bank clerk when he lost the family bank in '29."

"That sounds impressive. Brave people," he said admiringly.

"I guess so," she said, pensive. "My father bought back the family mansion when he married my mother and gave it to her as a wedding gift."

"Wow! Generous man!" Ross was intrigued by her family history. He knew her father could buy many mansions if he chose to, and yachts, and planes.

"*Very* generous!" Kendall confirmed proudly.

"And how do you fit into all that?" Ross asked her, searching her eyes for clues. She was outwardly cool, but he sensed someone warmer inside, or hoped there was. He wasn't sure.

"I want to be like my father and be a genius like him and blow everyone's minds," she said and he smiled at her honesty.

"And live happily ever after in a cottage with the man you love and two adorable children, or maybe three or four?" That was what he wanted one day, Kendall made a face the minute he said it.

"Definitely not." She laughed at him. "No kids, and I don't think 'happily ever after' matters all that much."

"No? How so?" She was becoming more intriguing by the minute.

"My parents don't get along and never have. I think they stayed together for us, or whatever reason. My mother probably likes being married to a legend like my dad but doesn't admit it. And I'm not sure traditional families are all that important. My mother's mother died right after she was born. She was kind of the bad seed of the family, or black sheep or whatever. And my mother's grandparents raised her, and were wonderful to her."

"The ones with the antique shop?"

"Exactly." He was bright and fun to talk to and interesting, and very good looking, and she couldn't understand why he had such meager ambitions. "What about you?"

"Son of an artist and a building contractor. Put them together and you get an architect." They both laughed at that.

"Your father was the contractor and your mother the artist?"

"Nope, which is why I don't believe in traditional roles. My mother is the contractor. She inherited the business from her father, and she runs a tight ship. I use her occasionally for my clients." He smiled at Kendall. "And my father is the artist. Stuart McLaughlin." He was a well-known contemporary artist and she was impressed. "And both families were pissed when they got married. My mother's family thought my dad wouldn't amount to a hill of beans. And my father's fancy East Coast family thought that my mother's family were a bunch of redneck construction workers. And they did live happily ever after and had me. They got it right on the first try, so I'm an only child. And I'm looking for the woman of my dreams and I'm thirty-three. It's a shame your mother's not single. She sounds like just my type with the gardening and the orchids." He laughed. And Kendall very definitely wasn't, with her fierce ambitions and determination to outdo her father. He had picked up on that immediately. She behaved like a shark, and he wondered if there was something meeker under the armor. If not, he wasn't interested.

They were intrigued by each other, dated for six months and had fun together, and then the man of Kendall's precious dreams really did come along. Cullen Roberts worked for her father and was exactly the kind of man she had always wanted to be with. Ross had finally admitted to her that he was falling in love with her, and a month later she dumped him for Mr. Ambitious. Princeton undergraduate, Harvard Business School. He had impressed her father who had hired him in New York and lured him to San Francisco. He was as tough as nails and a computer genius like her father, and Kendall fell head over heels in love with him and they lived together for three years. He had as little interest in marriage as she did, and neither wanted kids. A match made in heaven, with their careers as their first priority. Then she figured out that dating the boss's daughter was part of his scheme for success, when he bragged to his coworkers that he had his future sewn up and how little she meant to him, but it was a small sacrifice to make to get ahead with her father. It got back to her when someone anonymously sent her a string of his text messages for her perusal. She was twenty-six years old and it was her first serious emotional beating. She was still licking her wounds and bitter about it when she ran into Ross again at a party in Marin six months after she and Cullen had broken up.

"How's Mr. Wonderful?" She had told Ross exactly why she was leaving him when she did, that she had met the man of her dreams. She had left Ross flat, and it took him awhile to get over her. He had dated a few women since but no one he cared about particularly. He looked around to see if Cullen was at the party with her, but he didn't see him. He hadn't seen Kendall in almost four years. She was beautiful, but she had been heartless with him and he was leery of her. He didn't have a penchant for mean women and didn't want to get one now.

"Not so wonderful after all," she said honestly.

"Ah. When did you figure that out?"

"About six months ago."

"And you never called?" He seemed good humored about it. "How's your interesting brother who makes the furniture in England? I wanted to meet him."

"Still there, and making money at it hand over fist," she said sheepishly. "There's a market for what he does in England. Old-fashioned craftsmanship. He says he'll never come back here to live. He thinks all people care about here is money, and they have no soul."

"Harsh, but possibly right," Ross said, thinking about it. "I think that's where we parted company. You thought my small dream to do tasteful houses with fine craftsmanship was pathetic and unambitious of me."

She winced when he said it. She vaguely remembered telling him that, but she was younger and tactless then.

"Still working for your father and striving to be like him?"

"Yes." But in the meantime she had seen how he ran over people and used people, and how cruel he could be, although she didn't say so to Ross. Her father had hardened over the years and lost the innocence that her mother had originally loved. A fortune in billions had corrupted him in some ways. He was used to getting his way, and expected nothing less.

"Are you happy working for him?"

"Sometimes." And then she added, "Not really. It's hard to mix that kind of success with the milk of human kindness." It was the gentlest way she could think of to say it. Ross nodded and knew it was true. People like her father scared him. He had had clients like that and hated doing business with them. You always came away with your wings singed and the taste of ashes in your mouth.

"I'm going to start flipping houses one of these

days. I can afford to do it now. I couldn't when I met you. Some dreams take longer than others." He smiled at her. He had a warm easygoing style that was irresistible to most women, even to her. And he was the opposite of Cullen Roberts in every way, and her father.

She opened the subject cautiously. "I might be interested in doing that sometime, as an investment, flipping a house." He nodded and didn't leap at the opportunity. She had been harsh with him before, but she was still a beautiful, intriguing woman. He wondered if Mr. Right had knocked the wind out of her sails a little. He told her it had been nice seeing her, but didn't ask for her number when he left. He wondered if it had changed.

It gnawed at him for days after he ran into her. He liked her, but he didn't want to get burned by her again if another Mr. Right came along from the business world. She had seriously disappointed him the last time. And then he figured what the hell, what did he have to lose except his sanity and his heart, and he called her. The message was the same so it was still her number. He left a brief message and then forgot about her. He had a busy few weeks finishing up two houses for clients.

Her father had left for the boat in the meantime, after telling Kendall how tired and lonely he was. Her mother was almost always in Tahoe now, ever since her grandmother had died seven years before. Kendall felt sorry for him, and decided to surprise him over a long weekend, and she had nothing else to do. He had looked so sad when he left. It was a big trip for her, but she decided to do it. She flew to Nice and got a driver to take her to Antibes where he said he was going. At least he wouldn't be alone. She knew her mother hadn't been to the boat in years. She wouldn't go near it. Her brother, Nick, wouldn't either. She was the only family member who occasionally joined Zack on the boat, when invited, which wasn't often, but she enjoyed it. It was a fabulous two hundred and eighty foot yacht.

She saw the boat immediately when she got to the dock in Old Town, Antibes. It was the biggest boat there. She paid the driver she'd hired at the airport, and carried her small bag on board. The boat was quiet and there was no one around, except a deckhand on the dock to keep strangers from coming aboard. He had greeted Kendall courteously, and had seen her when she spent time on the boat with her father. She walked onto the passerelle and on board, and headed downstairs to her father's cabin. There were no other crew around, and she wondered if they were having dinner in the galley. She headed toward her father's suite, and opened the door to stick her head in, and found herself inches away from a naked woman. Her father had her against the wall and was having sex with her as the woman moaned, and her father stared into Kendall's face with a look of horror as the girl had an orgasm and screamed with her eyes closed. Kendall slammed the door closed and ran to her cabin. Her father pounded on the door five minutes later, and Kendall looked mortified when she opened it.

"I'm so sorry, Dad . . . I had no idea . . ." He thought there was no one on board to interrupt them, so he hadn't locked the door. The crew knew he had a woman with him. They were used to it, since it was a frequent occurrence. The boat was the perfect place to bring women. It always impressed them.

"What the hell are you doing here?" he shouted at her.

"You looked so lonely and upset when you left, and you complained that Mom never comes on the boat anymore. I spent my weekend and my money coming over to see you to cheer you up. How was I supposed to know you had a woman with you?" She was angry and hurt, confused and embarrassed. She had misjudged the situation entirely, and had been misled by her father. It wasn't the first time.

"Do you expect me to check my guest list with you?" He was still shouting at her, and she was fighting back tears. The woman hardly looked like a "guest" to Kendall. She looked like a hooker or something very akin to it.

"Is she staying on the boat?" Kendall asked in a shaking voice.

"Obviously. She's here from Paris for the weekend. She's an old friend," he said gruffly, which only made him seem more ridiculous.

"Are you leaving port tonight?" Kendall asked, still horrified that she had caught her father having sex with a woman in his cabin.

"No."

"Then I'll go back to San Francisco in the morning."

"I'm sorry you made the trip for nothing," he said, but he didn't want her there either. It would spoil the weekend for him.

"I'm sorry I walked in on you," she said meekly.

"I don't make a habit of this, you know," he said awkwardly. But it was obvious even to his daughter that more than likely this wasn't the first time, and she really didn't want to know. And all of a sudden, as he walked away down the hall in his bathrobe, for the first time, she felt sorry for her mother, and wondered if she knew that he was unfaithful to her. If so, it explained a lot about their marriage, and her mother's years of withdrawal, and avoiding her husband. Kendall had known more or less, or guessed, that he was unfaithful, but she had always blamed her mother for it. But seeing him with a girl who looked almost like a hooker cast a whole different light on it. She wondered suddenly if this was the cause, not the result of their unhappy marriage.

She was hungry and went up to the galley a little while later, and helped herself to something to eat. The crew were either out or asleep. She made herself a sandwich, and took it out on deck to eat it, and minutes after she sat down, the girl who'd been having the orgasm came bounding up the stairs. She looked to be about twenty, and was considerably younger than Kendall. She was wearing one of Zack's bathrobes, and looked delighted to run into Kendall, who stared at her father coming up the stairs behind her. This was definitely not her night. She kept running into them, although the boat was certainly not small. Her father rolled his eyes, and sat down at the table as the girl slid over next to Kendall.

"Hi, I'm Brigitte. That looks so good. I'm starving, can I have some? Sex always makes me hungry." She smiled and without a word, Kendall offered her half her sandwich. The girl had a low-class British accent. "The last time I was on the boat, they made us omelettes and caviar at midnight. Is there no one in the galley?" Kendall exchanged a glance with her father, the point was not lost on her. The girl had been on the boat before. "This is my third time here. We went to Portofino last time." Zack looked like he wanted to strangle her. Kendall didn't know whether to laugh or cry. Portofino was one of Kendall's favorite ports too. Meanwhile Brigitte had happily devoured half of Kendall's sandwich. "We always have such a good time when I come here. Where did you come from tonight?"

"California," Kendall said, trying to keep conversation to a minimum so her father didn't have a stroke.

"Zack said he'll take me to California sometime. Maybe to L.A. I want to go to Disneyland."

"Oh, you'll love that," Kendall said, and her father interrupted. Brigitte had done enough damage for one night. Kendall found it interesting that he had promised to take her to California, but to L.A., not San Francisco.

"We should go to bed now," he said sternly to Brigitte, and she giggled and acted like it was a sexual invitation, which it probably was. Brigitte got up and waved at Kendall, as she headed for the stairs and Kendall's father followed her, without looking at his daughter or saying good night.

"Nice to meet you!" she called back over her shoulder, and Kendall waved. She sat at the table for a few minutes, thinking about the whole experience.

Her father's head popped back up a moment later and he looked uncomfortably at his daughter. "You can stay if you want to," he said stiffly, and Kendall shook her head. It would have been agony being on board with them, with all the sexual innuendo. Tonight had been bad enough. She didn't want her mother to hear about it later and think that she had been in collusion with her father and his floozies.

"I'd rather not, but thanks anyway." He disappeared down the stairwell again, and she left a note for the captain to call her a cab at six in the morning, and she set her alarm for five. All she wanted to do now was get back to Nice, and from there she'd get a flight to either Paris or New York, to connect to San

Francisco. It had been a totally wasted trip except that it gave her new insight into her father. She wondered how long it had been like this and if it was partially or fully responsible for the disintegration of her parents' marriage.

The cab showed up on time in the morning, and the captain saw her off. He seemed surprised to see her there, but less so at her rapid departure in the circumstances.

She was at the Nice airport by seven, and caught a flight to Charles de Gaulle which connected to a flight to San Francisco. With the time difference, she would be back in the city by one-thirty in the afternoon, which would be ten-thirty at night for her. It had been an expensive escapade for nothing. After she checked in, she called her brother in the Cotswolds. She hadn't talked to him in months, and wondered if he would pick up when he saw the call was from her. Their conversations were never pleasant, usually about their parents. He answered sounding guarded, and had let it ring, as if he wasn't sure whether to pick it up or not.

"Hi, I'm in Antibes, I thought I'd give you a call."

"Are you on the boat?" Nicholas asked her.

"I was for about five minutes. I think I owe you an apology," she said, "about our mother."

"What about her?"

"I just dropped in on Dad, for an unscheduled visit. He came over for a long weekend, and he was whining about how lonely he was going to be, so I thought I'd surprise him and fly over and keep him company."

Her brother laughed and could guess the end of the story. "And you ran into him with one of his tarts on the boat, I assume."

"How do you know?"

"Because it's happened to me. The first time when I was about sixteen. I've run into him a few times in other places too. Most of the time with girls closer to my age than his. I think he's been doing that for years."

"What do you think came first, the chicken or the egg? Do you think he screws around because Mom shut him out? Or do you think Mom shut him out because he cheats on her?"

"I'm pretty sure he's been playing around for years. I ran into a woman years ago in London who got all dewy eyed and said she had an affair with my father. But when I figured out the time frame, I was about three at the time. I think Mom just got fed up with it. Who wouldn't?"

"Why do you think she stays with him? The money?" Kendall was always more practical than her brother, and harsher.

"Why do you always assume the worst about her? I think she probably stayed for us at first, and then she just got stuck there. I think she's too depressed to leave by now."

"Well, she can't use us as an excuse anymore," Kendall said coldly.

"Maybe after a while you just don't care. I don't know why they bother to stay married. They hardly see each other and they never talk to each other. I wish she'd leave him," he said sadly. "She deserves a better life. She doesn't care about the money."

"Maybe she'd be happier if she did leave. How are you, by the way?" Kendall asked her brother.

"I'm fine." He was expecting the usual diatribe about how he was wasting time making furniture, but he loved what he was doing and was a true artist. One of the royals had recently commissioned one of his pieces, but he didn't bother to tell his sister. She never understood. She was just like his father. It didn't matter to either of them if he loved what he was doing. All that mattered was making billions of dollars and becoming a legend.

"How's Sophie?"

"Also fine." They called her flight then, and she had to leave.

"Call me sometime," she said, sounding friendlier than she had in years.

"Yeah, sure," he said as though hell would freeze over first. She had been too unkind to him too often. She thought about it all the way back to California, and about their mother. Kendall knew she had been hard on both of them. She always defended her father.

She slept part of the way back, had lunch, and watched a movie. They arrived on time, and when she got to her apartment to change, she decided not to go into the office. It was Friday. She got her car out and drove to Tahoe instead. She arrived at eight o'clock. It was already dark, but her mother was coming back from her garden. Her hands were dirty and she looked relaxed. She was startled and jumped when she saw her daughter. Kendall didn't know where to start, so she got right to the point.

"I just saw Dad on the boat, and I wanted to come and see you."

"Why?" Her mother looked instantly suspicious and guarded. Kendall was usually tough on her, and never kind.

Kendall took a deep breath and decided to be honest. They were standing outside the house and it was chilly. "He had someone with him, and it made me realize that I haven't been fair to you. I talked to Nick and he said Dad's been doing that for a long time, maybe forever." Her mother didn't comment. She never complained to her children about their father.

"Do you want to come in for dinner?" her mother asked her.

"I'll have a cup of tea or something. Anyway, I just figured that I've been wrong blaming you for the way things are with Dad. I guess he has a part in this too." After all, they were still married, and she had never seen her mother with a man and was sure there had never been one. Her mother was an honorable woman.

"Your father and I haven't gotten along for a long

time. There are a lot of reasons for it. It doesn't matter anymore. He has his life, I have mine." They walked into the house and Kendall sat down in the kitchen while her mother made tea.

"Did you stay together for us?" Kendall wanted to know now. She wanted to understand her better.

"I thought so. Now I'm not so sure. Maybe in the end it was just laziness and cowardice. I didn't want to get a divorce. I wanted to be like your great-grandparents, married forever. But you have to pick the right person to do that with. Your dad wasn't, for me. He's a genius. You can't expect someone like him to behave like other people, or want the same things." She smiled and set down Kendall's cup of tea, and then sat down across from her. "You don't need to explain it or apologize, or tell me about his other women. I know about them, or most of them. Who was he with? The really young British one from Paris?" Kendall nodded. Ruby always found out, from different people. She couldn't keep count anymore, and hadn't for years. "She's been around for a while."

"I'm sorry, Mom. And I've been harsh with you about it."

"I guess that's what daughters do. They blame their mothers." Nick was much kinder about it and had always tried to protect her. It made Kendall feel even guiltier for how nasty she had been at times, blaming her for everything. "Do you want to spend the night?" Kendall nodded. She wanted a different kind of relationship with her mother than the one she'd had, but she didn't know how to start it.

Ruby made her an omelette and then they both went to bed, and in the morning, Kendall found her in the garden again. It reminded her of her great-grandmother. Her mother was trimming back some bushes, and she looked peaceful as she did.

"You like it up here, don't you, Mom?" Ruby smiled as she nodded.

"Maybe I'll move up here one day."

"Wouldn't you miss the house in the city?"

"Maybe. I don't really need all that. It meant more to Grandma than it did to me. She grew up there, I never did. I grew up over the antique store, and up here in the cottage. It was a nice gesture of your father, to buy it back for us. It really meant the most to her. They went through so much. It must have been a terrible time. By the time I came along, the worst was over." Ruby had always been comfortable when she was young, and the only great wealth she'd ever known was while she was married to Zack, and they didn't live on the grand scale her family had before 1929. It was hard to conceive of that kind of wealth. Or even Zack's. It wasn't very important to her. It meant more to Kendall, who wanted to compete with her father. "Sometimes the simple solutions are better. Maybe I'll be a gardener when I grow up." She smiled at her daughter.

"I think you already are." Ruby leaned over and gave her a hug.

"Come up and visit whenever you want." Kendall nodded and waved when she got in her car and drove away later that morning. It was the first peaceful visit they'd had in a long time, and she realized again how hard she'd been on her mother, and it was painful now to realize she might have been wrong, and in fact probably was.

Kendall found Ross's message when she went back to the city. She listened to it, and realized she had been hard on him too. She had dumped him flat for a man she considered a bigger fish at the time, who turned out to be a bad guy who was just using her. She had a lot of fence mending to do. She called Ross back after she listened to his message.

"Hi, thanks for your message."

"I'm not sure if this is a crazy idea, but do you want to have another shot at dinner with me? No strings attached. No crazy delusions. Maybe we can talk about flipping houses." He wasn't even sure if he would want to partner with her on that. But there was something about her that always drew him to her. In the past, he had thought it meant she was the one for him. Now he just thought she was a very attractive woman, but probably the wrong one. She had proved that once.

"Sure, I'd like to do that," she said easily and he smiled when he heard it.

"Good. Thursday?" He named a restaurant where they'd had dinner before, and when she hung up, she was excited. She had forgotten how much she liked him. Seeing him had brought it all back. And who knew, stranger things had happened. Maybe they could work together. Suddenly she liked the idea. She had nothing to lose.

Chapter 20

It was embarrassing for both of them when Zack came back to the office. Kendall was hoping he wouldn't mention her ill-timed visit to the boat. But he found a time to slip into her office and close the door.

"I'm sorry about what happened on the boat. It came together at the last minute, I thought I was going to be alone, and Brigitte just dropped out of the sky and turned up in Antibes." She knew he was lying again. And even if Brigitte had fallen out of the sky, as he put it, he didn't have to have sex with her, as a married man. That didn't even occur to him. It was the weak part of the story along with all the rest. She could see it was why her brother hated him, because he lied a lot. Maybe all the time.

"You don't owe me any explanations, Dad. What you do is your business. We're all adults. The only one you owe an explanation to is Mom, since you're still married to her. It must be hard for her to go back to the boat, knowing someone else was there. I guess that's why she hasn't been to the boat in years."

"Why? Did she say something?" He looked panicked. "Your mother has a lot of misconceptions about my life. And if she hadn't shut me out the way she does, none of this would have happened." Kendall could see now how easy he made it to blame her mother, and she always had out of loyalty to him.

"Not really. But I'm sure there's more to the story. That's between you two."

"I just don't want you to think it's ever happened before."

"What, having a woman on board for sex? I'm a big girl, Dad. I assume it has. That can't have been the first time." She looked right at him, and she could see desperation in his eyes. Her reaction was one of disgust.

"Actually, it was." He was digging himself deeper and Kendall didn't want to hear it. "I'm sorry you came all that way for nothing."

"Yeah, me too. You said you were going to be alone on the boat, and I believed you. I'll know to check with you next time," she said coolly, wishing he'd leave. Suddenly talking to him was upsetting, and she wondered for how long he'd been lying to her. She felt as though she had sold her soul to the devil and she wanted it back. Her father was a liar, and a cheat. Her role model in life was turning out not to be a good guy. It was unnerving to discover that at twenty-seven, or any age. He was brilliant, and a creative genius, but immoral, and dishonest. She could see now why her brother wanted no part of their father's life, and hadn't for a long time. He had found a life that worked for him, and was sticking with it.

"Well, just so you know that was a one-time thing. It won't happen again."

"Tell that to Mom," she said softly, but he probably had, a million times. Maybe it was why her mother's eyes went dead anytime someone said his name. He had killed her soul. Maybe she had walked in on him too. It made Kendall wonder now.

She met Ross for dinner at the restaurant on Thursday night. It was a funky old Italian restaurant in North Beach. Nothing trendy or chic, just good solid food. He got a quiet booth in the back, and sitting across the table from him was like a déjà vu for both of them.

"So, here we are back here three and a half years later. It's kind of weird, isn't it? You met Mr. Right and disposed of him. Now you're back eating spaghetti with Mr. Wrong, for old times' sake?" He laughed wryly.

"I never said you were Mr. Wrong," she said softly. "I thought you were Mr. Wrong for Me. I wanted different things then."

"I know you did. You wanted to work for your dad and be like him. I can't blame you for that. Who wouldn't want that kind of success?"

"Some people don't. My brother, for instance, and you. My mom. She owns the biggest house in the city, and she'd rather be in a cottage barely bigger than this booth. She said to me the other day 'Sometimes the simple solutions work better.' It's taken me a long time to figure that out. Like three and a half years, with a good swift kick in the ass from Mr. Right. It turns out he considered me a career move, not a human being."

"I'm sorry, Kendall, that's ugly, and it must hurt."

"It did, after three years, but better then than later, or married." She thought of her parents. "A life like my father's pulls a lot of fish into the net. Some of them are rotten. It's kind of the luck of the draw."

"You're a smart woman. You can figure out which ones are the bad ones."

"Not always." She thought about being duped by her father, and going all the way to France to hold his hand, when in fact he was getting laid.

"So, are we going to flip a house together?" he asked her to change the subject to something less personal. He didn't want to go off the deep end over her again.

"It sounds interesting. Tell me what you have in mind."

"There are two I'm considering right now," he

said. "They're both in good locations, both currently a mess, one slightly bigger than the other, both with good bones. One needs a little more architectural work, which is fun for me. I was going to do one of them alone, but it might be nice to have a partner. We can look at them if you like."

"I'd like that." She didn't know why, but the project sounded like fun to her, and he'd be good to work with. He was a solid, reliable, responsible guy, and a talented architect. "How long do you think it would take?"

"Probably a year, maybe less. Some of it depends on permits and how fast we can get them. Do you want to take a look on Saturday? We should move pretty quickly if we want to buy either of them. They're both good fixer-uppers at a decent price. Someone else is going to see that and make an offer soon. I'd like to get there first, so we can keep the profit margins appealing for us." He was businesslike and professional, talented and had good taste. If she wanted to learn how to flip houses, he would be a good partner. At the end of dinner, they made a date for Saturday to meet at the first address. He said he'd set it up with the realtors for both houses starting at noon.

She was busy with work for her father the next day. And on Saturday, she met Ross again. She liked both houses and was excited about the project, and the idea of working with him.

"Do you have a preference?" he asked her, she had a tough time deciding, and so did he. They went out for a glass of wine afterward and discussed it. "I've got some plans I roughed out on both of them, of what I would do without spending a fortune on it. I can show you if you want. I've moved since I last saw you. My house is just around the corner." She was startled by the invitation, but it made sense to see the plans. They walked a block and a half, and he lived in a very good-looking, well-designed house, which was much nicer than his last one. He had come up in the world in three years.

She followed him up the stairs, while he turned off the alarm, and let her in. He walked her to a large studio on the second floor of his house, with a drafting table, and he laid out the plans for both houses. Once she saw them, she had a marked preference for the first one.

"I think you can really make a difference with this design," she said and smiled at him. She was trying to concentrate on the drawings, but he was so damn handsome, and the glass of wine had hit her. She was having trouble keeping her mind on the designs he was showing her, and then she noticed him staring at her. "I'm sorry, I think I'm a little drunk," she said, looking embarrassed.

"Actually, I think I am too," and he put an arm around her and kissed her and she no longer cared about the houses or the blueprints for the remodel.

She didn't care about anything but him. He had been determined not to fall for her again. Afterward, she had no idea how it happened, but she wound up in bed with him, and drunk or not, it was the best sex she could remember and to make things even more complicated, she remembered how much she liked him. He had been back in her life for five minutes and she was falling for him.

After they made love, she lay in his bed for a minute, trying to catch her breath, and she turned to look at him and he looked woebegone.

"This is really bad," he said. "We're trying to talk business, and I can't keep my hands off you. There is something about you that drives me insane." As he said it, he nuzzled her neck, cupped her breast with his hand, and kissed her, and the next thing they knew, they were making love again.

When they came up for air afterward, he lay in bed smiling, and staring up at the ceiling. "What are we going to do about this, Kendall?"

"I have absolutely no idea," she said happily.

"We may have to make it part of the agreement that we have sex two or three times a day," he said.

"Make it four, or I won't do the deal."

"All right, if you insist. And then what? Would there be an increase if we do a second house together? Should we include an option, you know like a rent increase, but a sex increase."

"Great idea. I swear, Ross," she said, rolling over

to look at him, "I only had business in mind when we agreed to meet today."

"Yeah, me too. And look what a mess we made of it." She remembered now how great he was in bed and how much she liked him, and then she fell for that fast-talking idiot who worked for her father, who was a liar and a user, and she had walked out on Ross. "The only thing that worries me about this is that I get hooked on you so easily, and if you break my heart again, it could really screw up the deal." He was half serious, he had been upset about her for months after they broke up.

She looked at him solemnly. "I promise not to break your heart again. Will you give me another chance?"

"Mmm . . . maybe," he said, thinking about it. "Maybe we should just check things out again to be sure." They made love again and forgot about the blueprints and the plans. She spent the night with him, and they ate dinner naked in his kitchen, and then went back to bed. In the morning, they decided to buy the first house together, and made love again. And afterward they called the realtor and said they would make a written offer by that afternoon.

"Do you think we can stay out of bed long enough to do it?" she whispered to him as he hung up. They raced through the forms they had to fill out, and then leapt into bed again, and afterward, they dressed, dropped off the offer, and went to lunch at the Zuni Café on Market Street to celebrate. They had oysters so he could keep up his strength, pasta and salad, and went for a long walk afterward. He didn't tell her he was crazy about her because he didn't want to scare her off, but he was, and she felt the same way about him. It was as though she hadn't been ready before, and now it was all different. She couldn't remember why she had thought being with him was a bad idea, except that he didn't want to be her father when he grew up, and Cullen Roberts did.

Their offer was accepted the next day, and they got to work on the plans immediately. Ross was going to file for the permits. She transferred the money for her part of the deal. Everything went smoothly, and they had fun doing it. He hired his mother's firm as the contractor. Kendall met her and liked her. She was a smart, efficient woman who knew her stuff and made many good suggestions they agreed to follow. So far, she and Ross agreed on all of it, and then they wound up in bed again.

"I'm worried," he admitted to her late that night.

"What about?"

"We're slipping. That was only twice today. We've been in business together for three days and it's already affecting our sex life. You may have to spend the night." She did, and they made love more than once to make up for it. They were running together at full speed, on the house, and personally. And they were both excited about their project, and each other. Every now and then, Kendall felt a wave of panic about how fast it was going and then she decided to ride the wave. He made everything easy for her, and she felt safe with him.

Three months into the project, they had hardly left each other, and the remodel was going well. They could already see improvements in the house and Ross was holding a hard line with the budget. He was good at what he did.

She hadn't told anyone about him, and after four months of working on the project, she knew she was in love with him. At the six-month mark, they were halfway there on the house, and she moved in with him.

"I think maybe I should introduce you to my mother," she said one day over breakfast. She felt less inclined to introduce him to her father after the scene on the boat.

They went to Tahoe that weekend, and Ruby liked him, a lot. He reminded her of Alex, her grandfather. While they were there, Kendall asked her if she would do the garden of the house they were working on, and she was excited to do it. Ruby met them in the city a week later and had wonderful suggestions for the garden. She submitted an estimate and they approved it. She had done another job for a family she had met at Lake Tahoe, and it had given her an idea. She told Kendall that she wanted to open a landscaping business and design gardens for people. Kendall was proud of her, and she was in much better spirits than Kendall had seen her in years. Ruby had made another decision as well, but she hadn't told anyone yet.

The house was finished on time, and they put it on the market. Before it sold, they had another one picked out, which was slightly more challenging than the last one, but exciting.

"Are you game to do it again?" Ross asked her.

"Definitely." They had an offer for the first house three days later, and they accepted it, and made an offer on the second one. They were on a roll, and their relationship just seemed to get stronger and stronger. She and Ross talked seriously about it. Everything was different this time. They were both four and a half years older, she was more mature, and her goals had changed.

Kendall had also made a decision about her father, which was a big one for her. She didn't want to be him, or live in his shadow. She wanted to quit her job, and continue flipping houses with Ross. It was proving to be a lucrative business and she had learned a lot with the first one. Somehow she had changed. She was gentler and mellower and had lost her sharp edge. She was happier than she'd ever been.

She told her father at the office that she was quitting, and predictably, he was furious. He thought her remodeling projects were ridiculous, and assumed that Ross was incompetent and trying to take advantage of her.

"I've already done one with him," she said quietly.

"What do you know about flipping houses? And that's not a career for chrissake. Think of the degree you have, and now you're going to pick plumbing fixtures for a living?"

"I'm happy, Dad. We got our money out of the first one, and made a healthy profit. And we'll do better this time."

"You're wasting your time and your brain," he said nastily. She was disappointed by his reaction, but not surprised. She didn't offer to introduce him to Ross, she didn't want to expose him to her father's bitterness. Zack had a million women, but no one he loved, and no one who loved him. He had wasted the one good woman he had ever met, and somewhere deep down, he knew it.

Kendall gave him two weeks' notice, which was all he needed to replace her. And the day she did, he ran into Ruby just in from Tahoe in the hallway of their house. She had come to town to meet a client and he hadn't expected to see her. She seemed in a good mood when he saw her, and she smiled at him, which was rare.

"I'm glad to see you, I was meaning to call you, Zack."

He looked instantly defensive. "What about?" He was afraid Kendall had told her mother about her visit to Antibes.

"I'm starting a landscaping business. I'm just setting it up. I had to meet with the lawyer today," Ruby told him.

"In Tahoe?"

"I'll take jobs wherever I get them, Tahoe, San Francisco, Marin." She looked happy. "And I'm filing for divorce," she said simply. It was years overdue.

"Aren't you going to discuss that with me?"

"I am. I just told you."

"This house is yours. It was a gift. The boat and plane are mine, and my lawyers will make you a settlement offer. But is this really what you want, Ruby? It seems to work like this." It had for years. They'd been married for twenty-eight years and the marriage had been dead for twenty-six.

"For whom?" she asked, giving him a skeptical look. "I don't know about you, but I've been a member of the walking dead for more than twenty years. You were cheating on me when I had Nick, the day of, in fact, and maybe before that. You cheated on me with that English girl in Saint Tropez three years later. You've had dozens of girls ever since, maybe hundreds for all I know. Is that the life you want? Just a lot of sleazy women who are willing to cheat with you and get what you'll give them? You deserve a nice woman, Zack, one who cares about you." He looked sad and he knew she was right.

"You cared about me."

"You're right, I did. I really loved you, but you beat it out of me, lying to me and cheating on me. I felt like shit for twenty-five years."

"What changed?"

"I don't know. My gardens, landscaping, starting this business, people's faith in me. I don't feel like second or third or tenth best anymore, the wife you cast away for some cheesy piece of ass. It takes a toll. I finally decided I have to do something about it. I decided to get divorced. I feel better now."

"Do you think we could put Humpty Dumpty back together? I loved you too. Maybe we could find that again." He looked momentarily hopeful.

"I don't think so. It's been dead for a long time. Our kids aren't even here anymore. There's no reason to keep this going. You need to be free and so do I."

"So you're firing me?" He looked grim about it.

"No, I'm firing me, as your wife. I'm doing the dirty work for you."

"You know, I won't leave you high and dry."

"I don't need much. Just enough to live on if I have to stop gardening one day. I'm busy now." It was over. Finally. For both of them. She felt like a new person.

"Is there a guy?" he asked her as an afterthought, looking as though he would fight for her, but they both knew he wouldn't. The fight and the life had gone out of their marriage years before.

"No, there isn't," she said simply. "You should move your things out. I'm going back to Tahoe tonight. You can do it now, before I come back. I don't think we should live in the same house anymore." That had been deadening too, feeling rejected by him, ignored, duped, lied to, unloved, and even hated at times. It was so degrading. They had been terrible years. "I think the kids will be relieved that we've finally dealt with it," she said, and he looked shell shocked. First Kendall had quit that afternoon, and now Ruby was divorcing him. It was a clean sweep. And the alternative women he had suddenly seemed so inferior. They were fine as long as he had Ruby as his wife, as some sort of object he could keep on his mantelpiece. The Wife. But she didn't want to be The Wife anymore. It had taken her twenty-six years to free herself of him, after she first discovered he was cheating on her. It had taken much too long, but it was never too late. She was nearly fifty now, with a lot of good years ahead, especially once she and Zack were divorced. Now that she had started the process, she could hardly wait.

He was still standing in the hallway, looking shocked and sad, when she went downstairs with a light step.

The only thing missing for Ruby was that she wished her grandmother could have seen her do it. She knew she would have been proud of her. They had saved her as a child, and now she had finally saved herself as an adult. She would have liked to be married like them for fifty-five years, and she thought she could have done it with the right man. But she had picked the wrong one. Now she was free at last.

As Ruby knew he would, Zack recovered quickly. He bought a flashy penthouse apartment in the newest, tallest building in San Francisco, as soon as she told him she was filing for divorce.

The day after Ruby returned from the city after seeing her lawyer to start her business and file for divorce, she noticed activity at the main house of the Tahoe property, which had been uninhabited for eighty years. The first earl who had bought it had seen it three times in his lifetime, his son not at all. The son had died around the same time Alex did, and Ruby knew the original earl's grandson had inherited it, but he had never come to see the property either, and now someone was moving trunks and boxes into the house. She wondered if it had been sold again. When she asked the overseer, he said that it was in fact the most recent earl who had come to stay for several months to see how he liked it.

"How nice," Ruby said, hoping they'd be pleasant people. "Does he have a family? Children?" If so, she hoped they wouldn't trample her flowerbeds, and she thought maybe she should put up some signs. The overseer said he had moved in alone. She was working in her flowerbeds that afternoon, rescuing some roses, when she heard a voice behind her, and saw a large golden retriever wagging his tail at her, and a stocky English bulldog sitting next to it, and their owner smiling at her.

"What beautiful gardens you have. I've been admiring them all morning as I walked around. And I peeked and saw that you have orchids in the greenhouse." He looked friendly and agreeable, with gray hair, blue eyes, and a neatly trimmed beard, and looked very British. He was very distinguished. "I'm sorry. James Beaulieu." She knew he was the Earl of Chumley, but hadn't known his other name. And then he turned slightly behind him and pointed to his companions, "This is Rupert," the bulldog, "and Fred," the golden retriever. "If I promise not to give away your secrets, will you help me with my garden? I'd like to get it looking more like yours. And I'm sorry for the intrusion. This property has been in my family for eighty years now and no one wants to come here and love it and see to it. I thought it was high time someone did. Have you lived here for long?"

"My great-great-grandfather purchased the land when no one wanted to be here, and my great-grandfather built the houses. My great-grandparents and grandparents came to live here when they lost their house in the city, in the Crash of 1929, and in 1930, they sold the bulk of this property to your family," she explained. "They retained this very small sliver of the property with the cottage and what used to be the servants' house where I live now."

"My grandfather bought it actually." He smiled at her admiringly. He was mesmerized by her red hair, although it had faded slightly but was still very bright. "How intriguing that you're still here after so long."

"And that you still own it." She smiled in return. "I

haven't been here for eighty years, but my family has. Now I live here some of the time. I've just started a landscaping company actually. I've fallen in love with gardening, which was my grandmother's passion, and her mother's."

"Music to my ears. I need all the help I can get." He held out a hand and shook hers. "So happy to meet you. I didn't catch your name."

"I'm sorry, Ruby Allen. The original family name is Deveraux. My grandmother was a Deveraux." She had just requested to change her name back to Allen. It felt liberating to have her own name back.

"Well, I'm very happy to meet my neighbor."

"If you need anything, or any help, let me know. And you're welcome to use the boats in the boathouse. Most of them are yours, but two are mine. They're classics, but they're all in working order."

"If I promise to drive reasonably, would you give me a tour around the lake sometime?" he asked and she smiled at him.

"I'd love it." And with that, he and Rupert and Fred went back to the main house. He looked to be about Ruby's age, and was a very handsome man. Ruby felt like she had a new lease on life.

Ross and Kendall finished the second house slightly faster than the first one. They needed fewer permits and they completed the work in just under nine months. They didn't even have time to stage it. It sold before it went on the market, the day after it was completed, before the stager could give them an estimate. Someone in the neighborhood had been watching the remodel and loved it. They had dropped by, Ross had given them a tour, and they made a very good offer.

"Well done!" Ross and Kendall congratulated each other, and the profit margin was better this time too.

They hadn't found a third one to buy yet, but were going to start looking in the next week or two.

"Now what are we going to do?" Kendall asked him, as they lay on the bed, after accepting the offer.

"Maybe we should take a vacation with all this money we're making. Europe? Japan? China? Paris?"

"That sounds very exotic. Actually, I like that idea. What about Venice? I love Venice."

"I have another idea," he said, as he reached for her hand and rolled slowly off the bed onto one knee. "I actually think that Venice is more of a honeymoon spot, don't you? And we've been doing this house-flipping thing for two years. I think we're a pretty good team. Kendall Katz, will you marry me?" he asked her formally as she stared at him, not sure if he was joking or not.

"Are you serious?"

"Actually, yes, I am. I think we should get married before we start another house. We cleaned up this time. Let's take a nice long honeymoon in Europe. Paris, Rome, Venice, what do you say, Miss Katz? What will it be?" He leaned over and kissed her, and when he stopped, she smiled at him. She loved him more than she had ever thought possible, and her feelings for him grew every day.

"That would be a yes, Mr. McLaughlin. Definitely a yes," and this time, she kissed him.

Chapter 21

The house was filled with flowers. It looked almost exactly as it had for Eleanor and Alex's wedding, minus the army of footmen, although there were almost as many caterers serving champagne from silver platters. And the guests were wearing black tie, instead of white tie and tails. There were only two hundred guests instead of four times as many.

Zack was waiting nervously in his old study, and Ruby was helping Kendall dress, and carefully step into the eighty-two-year-old gown. It had needed just a touch of restoration, where a few of the pearls had come loose. Kendall was the third bride to wear it. She was taller than her mother, but only a little, and Kendall was wearing the same veil, and her great-great-grandmother's tiara. Ruby handed her her bouquet, which was entirely made of orchids and lily of the valley, as Eleanor's and Ruby's had been.

Ruby had grown them herself in the hothouse she'd built in Tahoe. She was wearing a simple deep purple gown, which set off her red hair, and she had a tan from working in the sun all the time. She stepped back with a smile and Kendall left the room to meet her father. His hands shook when he saw her. She looked so much like her mother, a blond version this time.

Zack walked down the grand staircase with his daughter, and she smiled at him. He knew his sins hadn't been forgiven him, but he had been accepted as he was, and he was still her father. It was the best he could hope for, and he was proud of giving Ruby back her family home. She spent occasional nights there when she came to the city, and had improved the gardens immeasurably, adding her own touch to what was already there. It was the perfect place for their daughter's wedding, and maybe her daughter's children's one day too. The wedding gown Kendall wore looked as though it had been made for her. Ross caught his breath when he saw her, waiting with the minister for her to reach him on her father's arm.

"Oh my God, you look so beautiful," he whispered when she stood next to him. "You're the most exquisite woman I've ever seen."

"It's the dress," she whispered back, proud to be wearing it, as her mother and great-grandmother had.

"It's the woman in it," he said softly. She had just

turned twenty-nine, and Ross was thirty-five. It seemed the perfect age to marry in these modern times. They were ready. They both were. Kendall had found herself and knew who she was and wanted to grow old with.

And then they turned to the minister, to get down to business, as Zack took his seat next to Ruby. She patted his hand, and he smiled at her. He hadn't brought the woman he was living with now and was glad he hadn't. It was right that he was here with Ruby. And Nick sat on her other side and smiled at his mother, with Sophie beside him.

After the ceremony, everyone drank champagne and the band started playing. Zack asked Ruby to dance with him, after Ross and Kendall had their first dance. Ruby felt so familiar in his arms that it made Zack want to cry as he held her, thinking about what a fool he had been.

"I don't suppose you'd want to try again?" he asked softly. Their divorce had been final for six months. She'd been ridiculously reasonable about it, and wouldn't take most of the enormous settlement he'd offered, just enough to live on comfortably for the rest of her days once she stopped gardening, if that ever happened, and maintain the Deveraux mansion, which would belong to Kendall and Nicholas one day. And Ruby wouldn't stop working for a long time. She was only fifty-two, and with her freedom and her work, she felt fully alive again, and excited about the future.

"No, I wouldn't want to try again," she answered his question, "but I'll always be your friend, Zack. That's how we started, and how I want it to be. We have wonderful children, and we should always be friends." They hadn't even been friends for years now. He nodded, with a lump in his throat when he heard her answer. He knew he would never find another woman like her. He had totally missed the boat for their entire marriage. "Besides, you can't marry your gardener, it's not dignified. You need someone a lot jazzier than that." He laughed, and when the dance ended, she went to talk to her son, Nick, and Sophie.

Ruby smiled thinking of how it had all turned out. A cabinetmaker, a gardener, and a house flipper. Hardly lofty aspirations, but they had each found exactly the path they wanted. And as she had said to Kendall, sometimes the simplest solutions were the best ones. All three of them were happy. Zack was the computer genius, the stuff of which legends were made. She had discovered that it was much harder to love a legend than an ordinary person.

She watched Kendall dancing with Ross. She had taken off the veil and the tiara, and the gown looked exquisite on her. Ruby wished that Eleanor and Alex could have seen it, the grandparents who had saved her. But she was sure that they were watching from somewhere. Their wedding had been eighty-two years before. And the wedding dress Kendall was wearing was just as beautiful as the day Eleanor had put it on. The history they all shared was remarkable and precious, like the house Zack had given back to them. It had been his greatest gift to her.

Ruby was smiling, thinking about it, as James Beaulieu walked up to her, looking very dashing in a perfectly tailored dark blue suit. He was impeccable with his silver hair and immaculately trimmed beard. She had brought him to the wedding with her. He was the mystery guest no one had expected, nor had she. He had arrived in her life at just the right time. Both of them divorced, and looking forward to new adventures, living together on the property their families had owned for nearly a century, and the Deveraux for even longer.

As James led her onto the dance floor, Ruby said something to him in a whisper and he laughed as they circled the floor so elegantly that people stopped to watch them. They looked perfect together and totally at ease with each other.

The Deveraux mansion and the Jeanne Lanvin wedding dress Kendall wore were alive again, as history lived on, never to be forgotten.

About the Author

DANIELLE STEEL has been hailed as one of the world's bestselling authors, with almost a billion copies of her novels sold. Her many international bestsellers include *The Affair, Neighbors, All That Glitters, Royal, Daddy's Girls, The Wedding Dress, The Numbers Game, Moral Compass, Spy, Child's Play,* and other highly acclaimed novels. She is also the author of *His Bright Light,* the story of her son Nick Traina's life and death; *A Gift of Hope,* a memoir of her work with the homeless; *Expect a Miracle,* a book of her favorite quotations for inspiration and comfort; a book of her favorite quotations for inspiration and comfort; *Pure Joy,* about the dogs she and her family have loved; and the children's books, *Pretty Minnie in Paris* and *Pretty Minnie in Hollywood.*

daniellesteel.com
Facebook.com/DanielleSteelOfficial
Twitter: @daniellesteel
Instagram: @officialdaniellesteel

Look for *Finding Ashley,*
coming soon in hardcover

In this blockbuster novel
from Danielle Steel, two estranged sisters
get the chance to connect again and
right the wrongs of the past.

Chapter 1

The sun beamed down on Melissa Henderson's shining dark hair, pinned up on her head in a loose knot, as sweat ran down her face, and the muscles in her long, lithe arms were taut with effort as she worked. She was lost in concentration, sanding a door of the house in the Berkshire mountains in Massachusetts that had been her salvation. She had bought it four years before. It had been weather-beaten, shabby, and in serious need of repair when she found it. No one had lived there for over forty years, and the house creaked so badly when she walked through it, she thought the floorboards might give way. She'd only been in the house for twenty minutes when she turned to the realtor and the rep from the bank who were showing it to her, and said in a low, sure voice, "I'll take it." She knew she was home the minute she walked into the once beautiful, hundred-year-old Victorian home. It had ten acres around it, with orchards, enormous old trees, and a stream running through the property in the foothills of the Berkshires. The deal closed in sixty days, and she'd been hard at work ever since. It had almost become an obsession as she brought the house back to life, and came alive herself. It was her great love and the focus of every day.

She'd learned carpentry, and made plenty of mistakes in the beginning, taken a basic plumbing class, hired a local contractor to replace the roof, and used workmen and artisans when she had to. But whenever possible, Melissa did the work herself. Manual labor had saved her after the worst four years of her life.

As soon as the house was officially hers, she'd put her New York apartment on the market, which her ex-husband, Carson Henderson, said was foolish until she knew if she liked living in Massachusetts. But Melissa was hardheaded and determined. She never backed down on her decisions, and rarely admitted her mistakes. She knew this hadn't been one. She had wanted to buy a house and give up New York for good, which was exactly what she did, and had never regretted it for a minute. Everything about her life there suited her, and was what she needed now. She loved this house with a passion, and since moving there, her whole life had changed dramatically.

The four years before she'd bought it were the

darkest days of her life. Melissa sat on the porch and thought about it sometimes. It was hard to imagine now what she and Carson had been through when their eight-year-old son, Robbie, had been diagnosed with an inoperable malignant brain tumor, a glioblastoma. They had tried everything, and taken him to see specialists all over the country and one in England. The prognosis was always the same, one to two years. He lived for two years after the diagnosis, and they made them the best years they could for him. He died at ten in his mother's arms. Melissa had been relentless trying to find a cure for him, and someone who would operate, but they were battling the inevitable from the beginning. Melissa had refused to accept Robbie's death sentence until it happened. And then her whole world caved in. He was her only child, and suddenly she was no longer a mother.

The two years after his death were still a blur, she was half numb and half crazy. She had stopped writing a year after he got sick, and she never went back to work as a writer after that. Once a bestselling author, with five smash hits to her credit, she hadn't written a word in seven years, and swore she never would again. Previously a driving force in her life, she had no desire to write now. All she cared about was her house and she wanted to make it the most beautiful Victorian home in the world. It had replaced everything else in her world, even people. It was the outlet for her to soothe all her sorrows, and vent the unbearable rage and grief she had felt. The

368

Danielle Steel

agony was a little gentler now. Working on the house was the only way she could ease the pain she was in, using her hands, shifting heavy beams, rebuilding the fireplaces, helping the men to carry the equipment, and doing most of the carpentry herself.

The house gleamed now, and was exquisite. The grounds were lush and perfectly maintained, the historic home restored until it shone. It was something to be proud of, and a symbol of her survival. Everything about it was a tribute to Robbie, who would have been sixteen now, and had died six years before.

Her marriage to Carson died with her son. For two years they had fought to keep him alive, and lost. After Robbie died, she no longer cared about anyone except the little boy who was gone. It still took her breath away at times, but less often now. She had learned to live with it, like chronic pain or a weak heart. Carson had been paralyzed with grief as well. They were both drowning, too lost in their own miseries to help each other. The second year after Robbie died was worse than the first. As the numbness wore off, they were even more acutely aware of their pain. And then she discovered that Carson was involved with another woman, a client of the literary agency where he worked. She didn't blame him for the affair. She wouldn't have had the energy to spend on another man, but she readily acknowledged that she had shut Carson out for two years by then, and it was too late to reverse it. She made no attempt to win him back, or save the marriage. It was already dead, and she felt dead inside herself.

Carson had been her literary agent for her five successful books. She'd found him after she'd written the first one, and took the manuscript to him at the recommendation of a friend. She was thirty-one then. He was bowled over by her talent, and the purity and strength of her writing, and signed her on immediately as a client. She had worked for a magazine after college, and had been writing freelance articles for several years before she wrote her first book. She attributed her success to the brilliant first book deal Carson made for her. After several glasses of champagne, they wound up in bed to celebrate, and a year later they were married. Robbie was born ten months after their wedding, and life had been blissful until Robbie got sick. It was a respectable run, they'd had eleven happy years since they met.

Carson was a respected and powerful agent, but he modestly claimed no credit for Melissa's dazzling success. He said she was the most talented writer he'd ever worked with. When she stopped writing to take care of Robbie, neither of them thought it would be the end of her career. Afterward, she said simply that she had no words left, and no desire to write. The profound visceral need to write that she'd had for all of her youth and adult life had simply left her. "Robbie took it with him," was all she said. No amount of urging by Carson, or her publishers, convinced her to start again. She abandoned her marriage, her career, New York, and everyone she knew there. She wanted a clean slate. She spent her energy and passion on the house after that. There was no man in her life, and she didn't want one. She was forty-three when Robbie died, forty-five when she and Carson finally separated, and forty-nine as she stood in the summer sunshine, sanding the door with all her strength, using old-fashioned fine-grained sandpaper.

The quiet affair that Carson had engaged in with a mystery writer in the final months of their marriage turned into a solid relationship after Melissa left. Jane was a few years older than Melissa and had two daughters whom Carson had become close to. They fulfilled some of his need for fatherhood after Robbie died. He and Jane married after his divorce. Melissa wanted no contact with him, but she wished him well and sent him an email every year on the anniversary of Robbie's death. With their son gone, suddenly they had nothing in common anymore, and had too many heartbreaking memories of the hard battle they had fought for his life, and lost. It was a failure that tainted everything between them. To escape it, Melissa had isolated herself and preferred it that way. She had run away.

She had done the same with her younger sister, Harriet, Hattie, and hadn't seen her in six years since Robbie's funeral. She had nothing to say to her either, and no energy left for their battles. As far as Melissa was concerned, her sister had suddenly gone off the deep end eighteen years before, for no apparent reason. Despite a budding and promising career as an actress, Hattie had joined a religious order at twenty-five. Melissa insisted it was some kind of psychotic break. But if so, she had never recovered, and seemed content in the life she'd chosen, which Melissa could never accept. Melissa had a profound aversion to nuns, and considered Hattie's decision not only an abandonment, but a personal betrayal, after everything they'd been through together growing up.

Their mother had died when Hattie was eleven and Melissa was seventeen. She had been a cold, rigid, deeply religious woman from a Spartan, austere background, and had always been hard on her oldest daughter. Melissa had fallen short of her expectations and disappointed her, and once her mother died, there was nowhere for Melissa to go with her past resentments of how her mother treated her and no way to resolve them. She began writing seriously to vent her feelings in the only way she knew how. It made for brilliant books, which her readers devoured. But the memories of her mother remained painful. It was too late to forgive her, so she never had. In her own way, without realizing it, Melissa was like her mother at times now, with her harsh opinions, criticism of others, and black and white view of life after Robbie's death. Hattie was gentler and more like their father, who hid from life with the bottle. He had been a kind man, but not a strong one, and had let his domineering wife run the show, and ride roughshod over him. She made the decisions about their daughters, which Melissa had been furious about. She wanted her father to temper her mother's verdicts, but he never had. He'd abdicated his role and relinquished all power to his wife. Melissa resented him for it, while Hattie easily forgave him everything. But she had never suffered at their mother's hands as Melissa had. She had taken the brunt of her mother's harsh decisions, while Hattie was treated as the baby.

Hattie was eleven when their mother died, and Melissa became her stand-in mother. For fourteen years they couldn't have been closer. Their father died a year after their mother, and Melissa was all Hattie had to parent her and it had been enough. Melissa was always there for her, to protect and encourage her. And then suddenly at twenty-five, Hattie had thrown it all away, and on what seemed like a mad impulse, had decided to become a nun, which Melissa told her was her way of avoiding life, like their father, and was the coward's way out. All Hattie wanted was to hide in the convent, protected and removed from the world. She said acting was too hard.

She had had dreams of becoming an actress, and studied drama at the Tisch School at NYU, and gave it all up after her first trip to Hollywood and a single screen test. Melissa saw it as pure cowardice, but Hattie didn't listen to what her sister had to say. She claimed that the religious vocation she had discovered was stronger than her previous desire to be an actress.

Once their parents died, there were no other adult influences in their lives, other than Melissa and a trustee at the bank who barely knew them. Both their parents were only children, and history had repeated itself. Their respective parents had died young too. Melissa and Hattie's mother had been left nearly penniless, and had to drop out of Vassar College and get a job as a secretary. She'd been bitter ever since.

Their father had been left with a sizable inheritance, which dwindled over the years, after long bouts of unemployment, working at various banks, and mismanaging his money. It was the cause of endless fights between Melissa and Hattie's parents, and their mother was terrified of being poor again. Their father was ill equipped to take care of himself once he was orphaned as a young man and began drinking heavily, which cost him many jobs. They often lived on what was left of his inheritance, with no other income. Despite that, there was enough of his money left when both their parents died for Hattie and Melissa to pay for their education and live in a small apartment, after they sold their parents' Park Avenue co-op. Their father had had the foresight to pay for a large insurance policy which would carry both girls for a long time securely, not in luxury, but in comfortable circumstances, as long as they worked at solid jobs after they'd graduated from college.

At eighteen, when their father died, Melissa shouldered their responsibilities and handled them well, better than their parents had. She was bright, determined, and capable. She saw to it that they both attended good colleges, and made sure Hattie kept her grades up. She was serious beyond her years, less stern than their mother would have been, and far more responsible than their alcoholic father. She moved them to a decent, less expensive neighborhood in New York on the West Side, and stuck to a rigorous budget so what they had inherited would last as long as possible. And took good care of Hattie. Everything seemed to be going well, and then Hattie had run away to the convent. It shattered Melissa's world yet again. After caring for her sister for fourteen years, she suddenly found herself alone, and began writing more seriously then to fill the void and try to process why Hattie had abandoned her dreams.

Melissa vented her anger at their mother in her first very dark book, which was an instant success. She could better understand her mother's bitterness at finding herself a pauper when her parents died than she could fathom Hattie's flight from life. It made no sense to her. She'd had such a bright future ahead.

Losing Hattie to the convent came as a severe blow. Melissa wrote incessantly after that to exorcise her demons, with excellent results, once she met

Carson, he became her agent, and sold her books for real money. But she had never forgiven Hattie for retreating to the convent, nor could Melissa understand what Hattie had done, or why. Hattie had real talent, and Melissa had encouraged her. Hattie had had a few small parts on daytime TV, and a walk-on in a Broadway show. She got a chance to audition for a movie then, and went to L.A. for a screen test. Faced with a real opportunity, she had panicked, come back from L.A. in less than a week and told Melissa about her impulsive plan to join a religious order. She said it had been a lifelong desire she had hidden from her sister, knowing how Melissa hated nuns. Eighteen years later she had never forgiven Hattie and the two sisters were still estranged. Melissa had barely spoken to Hattie at Robbie's funeral. She didn't want to hear what her sister had to say, the platitudes that Robbie was in a better place and his suffering was over. They hadn't seen each other since.

Melissa wrote to her once a year, as she did to Carson, mostly out of a sense of duty in her sister's case. And Hattie dropped her a note from time to time, determined to stay in touch with the sister she still loved and always had. She was convinced that one day Melissa would come around and accept the decision she'd made, but there was no sign of it yet. Melissa preferred to be alone now. She didn't want anyone's sympathy, which rubbed salt in the wounds left by her losses. All she wanted was her house and the satisfaction it provided her. She didn't need people around, and certainly not her cowardly sister who had run away from the world, or her ex-husband who had cheated on her and was married to someone else. And she didn't need an agent anymore, since she had stopped writing. She didn't "need" or want anyone.

The convent had sent Hattie to nursing school when she joined the order. She was a registered nurse now at a hospital in the Bronx. Melissa went to her graduation when she got her R.N., but had refused to attend the ceremony when Hattie became a novice, and later took her final vows. Melissa didn't want to be there. It was too painful to see Hattie in the habit she wore.

After her vows, Hattie had spent two years working at an orphanage in Kenya, and had loved it. Her life had taken a completely different turn from Melissa's, and she was content. Melissa said she was happy too, married, with a child and a successful writing career, but her sharp edges hadn't softened with time. They had gotten harsher. And once Robbie died, the walls around her were insurmountable.

After she bought the house in the Berkshires, the men who worked for her considered her an honest and fair employer. She paid them well and worked as hard as they did on the projects at hand. But she wasn't friendly or talkative. Melissa said very little when they worked side by side, and they were impressed by how strong and capable she was. She didn't balk at any task, no matter how difficult, and accepted every challenge. She was a courageous woman, but not a warm one.

The men she hired often commented to one another about how taciturn she was. She was a woman of few words. Norm Swenson, the contractor she used, always defended her. He liked her, and sensed that there was a reason for how hard she was on herself and others. Now and then he saw a spark in her eye and guessed that there was more to her than she let anyone see now.

"There's usually a reason for people like her," he said to her critics, in his quiet New England way. He liked her, and enjoyed his occasional conversations with her, when she allowed that to happen. They talked about the house, or the history of the area, nothing personal. He felt certain there was a good person in there somewhere, despite her cold demeanor and sharp tongue. He always wondered what had caused it. One of his workmen called her a porcupine. It was an apt description. Her quills were sharp. The locals left her alone, which is what she wanted. None of them knew about Robbie. They had no reason to, and it was a part of her life, and a time, she didn't wish to share with anyone. No one in the Berkshires knew anything about her history or personal life.

The fact that Melissa had written under her maiden name of Stevens made her anonymous life in the Berkshires possible. She had kept Carson's last name when they divorced, in part because it had been Robbie's name too and was a link to him, and in part because the name Melissa Henderson rang no familiar bells for anyone. But "Melissa Stevens" would have woken everyone up to the fact that there was a famous author in the neighborhood. This way, as "Henderson," no one knew.

To their old friends in New York, who hadn't seen Melissa in years, Carson always said that some people just never recovered from the death of a child, and Melissa was apparently one of them. It seemed a shame to everyone and many people said they missed her. Carson had his own struggles after Robbie's death, but he had strengthened close personal ties, which had supported him. Melissa had severed hers and set herself adrift. Carson's marriage to Jane suited his quiet nature better than his marriage to Melissa. There was a dark, angry side of her that ran deep, from the scars left by her parents. She had been happy with him but didn't have her sister's innocent, sunny nature. And Jane, Carson's current wife, was a solid, stable woman. She didn't have Melissa's brilliant mind, enormous talent, or tortured soul, which was easier for him.

Carson had talked to Hattie about it a few times in the early days after Robbie's death. Hattie had thought it would soften her sister, but it had the opposite effect, and hardened her.

Carson had always liked his sister-in-law, but lost touch with her when she went to Africa. He still had warm feelings for her. He had also sensed that Hattie didn't want Melissa to think that she was disloyal, staying in touch with him once he had remarried, so Hattie no longer contacted him. She had written once to congratulate him when he remarried, and said that she was happy for him, and would keep him and his new family in her prayers. He never heard from Hattie again after that. All ties with Melissa were severed except for her yearly emails.

Melissa's literary career had taken off around the time that Hattie entered the convent, so Hattie hadn't been present much during their marriage, but she had come to the hospital regularly when Robbie was sick, and had offered to stay with him so Melissa could get some rest. No matter how angry Melissa was at her for becoming a nun, Hattie's feelings for her older sister had never wavered, and she was there until the end of Robbie's life.

Melissa had never invited her to Massachusetts once she left New York, and Hattie had never seen the house that Melissa loved so much. It had replaced people in her life, and the writing she had loved and been so good at. To Melissa, the house was enough, it was all she needed and wanted now. She didn't want anyone in her life, and no contact with the people who knew her when she was married, and were aware of the fact that she had a son who died. She didn't want to be the object of anyone's pity.

When Melissa finished sanding the door, she lifted it and carried it back into the house. She had grown stronger from all the work she'd done. She examined it closely when she set it back on its hinges, and studied the intricate molding she'd been sanding. She was satisfied with her work. She had removed all the old coats of paint, and had decided to varnish it instead. The original carvings and moldings were delicate and beautiful. You could see them better now. All she cared about was improving the house.

After her morning's labors, she made herself a cup of coffee and stood drinking it, looking out past the lawn and the trees, and the gardens she had created, to the orchards in the distance. They harvested the apples and sold them at a local farmers market. She had the time and the money to do what she wanted and what she enjoyed. After five astoundingly successful bestselling books, she had enough money saved to live as she chose. She led a simple, uncomplicated life, and had more than enough in the bank. Two of her books had been sold as movies.

For a while, she'd been one of the country's most successful writers, and then she disappeared from public life, to the dismay of her publishers. Carson hated to see her waste her talent. But now, working on her house and property interested her more.

She hadn't been back to New York since she bought the house, and said she had no reason to. She had let friends fall by the wayside after Robbie's death, and purposely avoided them. She didn't want to hear about their children, or see them, most of whom were teenagers now, as Robbie would have been. At forty-nine, she knew there would be no more children in her life. Robbie had been the center of her universe, just as Carson had been, but that was all over now.

Once in a while, she contemplated how odd it was never to experience human touch anymore. There were none of the adoring hugs as Robbie wrapped his arms around her neck and nearly choked her in his exuberance, or the gentle, sensual passion she and Carson had shared. She wasn't close enough to anyone now to have them hug her, or embrace them in return. Now and then someone working for her would touch her shoulder or her arm, or her contractor, Norm, who was a friendly guy, put a hand on her back. It always startled her. It wasn't a familiar sensation anymore, nor a welcome one. She didn't want to remember what that felt like. Physical contact with other humans was no longer part of her life, even though it had been important to her before. In their early years, Carson considered her a warm person. And Robbie would respond to her saying "I want to give you a hug" by leaping into her arms, and nearly knocking her down to hug her. He had been a sturdy, happy boy, until he became too weak to walk or even raise his head, and she would sit beside him holding his hand until he fell asleep. In the end, he slept most of the time, as she watched him, making sure he was still breathing, and savoring every instant he was alive.

"You can't cut yourself off from everyone!" Carson had warned her after Robbie died, but she had. She had survived the worst that life could dole out to her, losing a child. She wasn't the same person anymore, but she was still standing and functioning. She used to love to laugh. Hattie had been livelier and more mischievous as a child, but Melissa had a good sense of humor. There had been no sign of it since Robbie got sick. The immensity of the loss had changed her.

She rose early every morning and watched the sun come up, and then got busy with her day, doing whatever work was at hand, and she often went to bed soon after dark. She read at times, and liked to sit by the fire relaxing and lost in thought, but the memories snuck up on her then. She didn't like giving herself time to think and drift back to the past, and avoided it. She was living in the present, and her present was the house she had restored, mostly by the work of her own hands. She was proud of the results and what she had achieved. The house was living proof of how far she had come since she had bought it, and a symbol of her survival. No one in the area knew how hard she had fought to cling to life and not give up when she'd lost the person she loved most. Working on the house had brought part of her back to life, and kept her busy, happy, and fulfilled for four years. It was her therapy and had become one of the handsomest homes in the Berkshire mountains, with exquisite handcrafted workmanship. In its own way, it was a work of art. To Melissa, the house was alive, a living being to be cherished and embellished, and had become her reason for staying alive.

She let herself think of her sister, Hattie, sometimes, with her fiery red hair and huge green eyes, like a pixie when she was a child. Her copper hair was hidden under her nun's veil now. She had been a tomboy, and then blossomed into a beautiful young woman with a natural, striking beauty men were drawn to. Boys pursued her even when she was a teenager. Melissa, with dark hair and blue eyes, had a cooler beauty and seemed less approachable. When Melissa went to Columbia, she was more concerned with taking care of her sister than meeting men. She never dated until her junior year.

When Melissa graduated from college and got a job, Hattie was sixteen and a beautiful, voluptuous young woman by then. All the boys at the school she went to in New York were crazy about her, which made it all seem even more absurd when Hattie decided to become a nun. She had always been the boy-magnet of the two of them and loved to flirt. Melissa was more reserved. Hattie was fun-loving, gregarious, and at ease with everyone. The idea of her being sequestered from the world seemed a criminal waste to Melissa. She was sure her sister would fly back out of the convent in six months, it was all a whim, but she hadn't. She had stayed for eighteen years, faithful to a vocation Melissa couldn't understand, and had never accepted, although she knew their mother would have loved it.

They had shared an apartment until Hattie joined the order. Melissa met Carson around that time, before she published her first book, right after she wrote it. He sold it, and a year later they were married and she gave up their old apartment. She hated being there once Hattie was gone. It was silent and lonely, but she didn't feel that way about her house in Massachusetts now. She was never lonely there, and had made peace with the solitude she'd chosen. It was a relief to be alone when she and Carson had separated in New York. They'd lived in Tribeca, and their marriage felt so dead to her by then that it was painful being with him, and she was grateful for her freedom when he left.

She'd started looking for a house immediately, and had found the right one quickly. It was a merciful release when she left New York and started fresh. She didn't have to look at Robbie's empty room anymore. It was the end of the happiest time in her life, when Robbie was alive, which was nothing but a memory by the time she moved to Massachusetts.

When Melissa went upstairs that night, after sanding the door all day, she glanced at a photograph of Hattie in a frame on the desk in the small den off her bedroom. The photo was of Hattie dressed for her senior prom at her high school in New York. She was wearing a pale blue dress, with her bright red hair pulled back and swept up in a mass of curls. She looked sexy and gorgeous and was beaming in the picture. Melissa perfectly remembered the moment when she took the snapshot. She had helped her sister pick the dress. There were no photographs anywhere in the house of her dressed as a nun, only a few from their childhood and youth, which was how Melissa still thought of her. Her sister's habit was a costume that made no sense to her.

Melissa smiled briefly at the photograph of Hattie as she sat down at her desk and signed some checks, and then she went to bed to read for a while, before falling asleep. She always slept with the light on, to keep the memories at bay. She had gotten good at it over the years, and had learned to live with the loss. It was part of her now, like everything else that had happened to her, her marriage to Carson and the divorce, the career that was an unexpected, startling success that she walked away from, the people she no longer saw, the sister who betrayed her by becoming a nun and was a stranger now, the father who had died of alcoholism, and the mother who changed Melissa's life forever and then died with none of their issues resolved, especially the most serious ones. As Melissa slipped into her comfortable bed, she had so much to forget. The ghosts of the past would haunt her if she let them, but she had become an expert at avoiding them. She looked around the bedroom and smiled. All that mattered to her was in the present. The past was buried and almost forgotten, a dim memory now. She was at peace in the silent house. She reminded herself that the past was gone, and she was happy now. She almost believed it, as she got under the covers and fell asleep, exhausted from the hard work she'd done all day. She had learned that pushing herself to her limits physically was the only way to escape the ghosts that still waited for her in the silent room at night.